IN THE BLOOD

Anna Fodorova

ARACHNE PRESS

First published in UK 2022 by Arachne Press Limited
100 Grierson Road, London, SE23 1NX
www.arachnepress.com
© Anna Fodorova 2022
ISBNs
Print: 978-1-913665-60-9
eBook: 978-1-913665-61-6
The moral rights of the author have been asserted.
All rights reserved. This book is sold subject to the condition that it shall not, by way of trade or otherwise, be lent, resold, hired out or otherwise circulated without the publisher's prior written consent in any form or binding or cover other than that in which it is published and without similar condition including this condition being imposed on the subsequent purchaser.
Except for short passages for review purposes no part of this publication may be reproduced, stored in a retrieval system or transmitted in any form or by any means, electronic, mechanical, photocopying, recording or otherwise, without prior written permission of Arachne Press.
Although the key historical events of this book are real and the plot contains autobiographical elements, any resemblance of characters to real people, living or dead, is unintentional.
Thanks to Muireann Grealy for her proofreading.
Cover design: Phil Barnett 2022.
The publication of this book is supported using public funding by the National Lottery through Arts Council England.
Printed in the UK on wood free paper by TJBooks, Padstow.

To my family,
to those I am lucky to know and love
and in memory of those I have never met.

ACKNOWLEDGEMENTS:

I want to thank all the members of my two writing groups (there are too many to name) for their time and encouragement over the years. And special thanks to my publisher Cherry Potts for her sharp insight, her attention to detail and her patience.

IN THE BLOOD

1

On waking, Agata's cheek feels cold. She peels herself away from Richard's back, and before he draws her into his large warm body, she quickly flips the pillow over so that he won't notice the damp evidence of her tear ducts working overtime. From what uncharted part of her have those tears sprung? Do they actually belong to her or to someone else? Someone from far back, before her memory can reach, someone she doesn't know. When she scrunches her eyes, Agata can make out the contour of a cheek, the shadow of a smile.

*

The morning traffic crawls along, slower than usual, and Agata hopes that breakfast with Lily will compensate Mama for being left behind. This after Mama kicked her legs in the air can-can fashion to demonstrate that she has already changed from her home-knitted slippers into her outdoor shoes. Because Mama knows no greater pleasure than driving around London on errands with her daughter.

'But Mama!' Agata moaned. 'I'm only going to the dentist, and I'm already late.'

*

Looking for a space in the hospital car park adds another ten minutes. They are already waiting for her. Agata steps out of her jeans, the nurse stretches a fresh length of paper over the bed, straps Agata's feet in clamps and turns the ceiling light off. In the glare of the computer screen the radiologist adjusts a condom over a plastic instrument, then tips it with a generous dollop of lubricant jelly. 'Easy does it.'

The instant the icy gadget slips inside her the room fills with an amplified hum. While the radiologist moves his hand this way and that, they are both quiet: he is concentrating on her internal bumps and cavities and Agata, hardly daring to breathe, on mortifying any response her flesh may be conned into by his expert probing.

'Now this might just look like a blur, but I assure you, anything nasty would look very different.' The radiologist flicks a smile to the nurse who, whenever Agata shifts, veils her discreetly with a blanket. And every time she performs this little dance, Agata sniffs her sweet coconut scent. 'Here, see that area I'm highlighting green?' The radiologist invites the nurse to peep at the screen and Agata, craning her neck, catches what looks like a hazy weather map.

'That's the right ovary… ehum! Looks clear. Left ovary… left ovary…?' The radiologist's hand shuffles back and forth and Agata grips the side of the bed. What has he seen there? Is it possible that his probe detected Richard's recent presence inside her?

'Have you had anything to eat this morning?'

'A cup of tea, I only drank half.'

'Left ovary hidden.'

She knew it! Why hadn't she refused that toast Mama popped in her hand? Now she'll have to worry if anything 'nasty' has invaded her left ovary. Thank God they removed Mama's in time, her right breast too. Now Agata reaps the benefits of her mother's misfortunes. Being in a high risk category guarantees her a yearly ovarian scan: every August, to be precise. Richard books the car in the garage every July; so first the car, then the ovaries. Easy to remember, and no need to trouble Mama with either.

While she is pulling her jeans on the radiologist opens a form. 'Today is…?' He checks the tag on the nurse's breast. 'Baduwa?'

'Twenty-first August.'

Exactly to this day, twenty years ago, Russian tanks rolled under our Prague balcony, Mama reminded Agata only this morning. *Imagine! Military invasion in central Europe! 'Now we'll never see our daughter again, she'll stay in England,' your father said – no, he sobbed. Soft. That's what Pavel was, but here – here they are not interested in what happened to us in 1968, here the radio is interested in some actress from some Corporation Street and her stupid breasts!*

'So Mrs Upton, besides your mother, any other relative with breast cancer in the family?' Agata shrugs. Every time she comes, there is a new radiologist and a new form to fill. 'No one else on your mother's side then?' No idea, she says. 'On your father's side?' The radiologist's freshly scrubbed hand hovers above the page. To get the whole thing over she informs him that her father is dead. And so, besides her mother, her daughter and husband, she has no other relatives. 'None?' None. The radiologist hesitates, then crosses out several boxes.

'Any death from cancer on your mother's side… father's… siblings? Cousins… aunts?' Agata keeps shrugging and he ploughs on scribbling UNKNOWN. Frowning as if she lost her forbears by her own negligence. This side, that side… How many times will she have to go through this? And how many relatives is one supposed to have? In any case, what business is it of this young man with bitten nails and pimples around his ears, to know how her relatives died?

'Are you sexually active?' Now that he is familiar with her innermost parts the radiologist wants to know. She nods and he ticks off the relevant box with almost a sigh of relief, a flourish. Their first definite *Yes*. He then instructs Baduwa to tighten a rubber band around Agata's arm.

The blood test signals the end of the procedure.

Straight into the freezer, soon we will be able to tell what's coming your way, it's only a question of time, last year's radiologist said.

Watching her blood slowly climb the glass, thick and dark with bubbles of orange froth, Agata promises herself a cake and a hot chocolate in the cafeteria downstairs. Baduwa corks the vial with a rubber plug, gives it a playful shake and as she passes it to the radiologist she giggles, they must be new to each other. Next: the radiologist's fingers are grabbing the empty air, the vial hitting the floor and Agata's blood spilling over the gleaming lino. She watches some dribble down Baduwa's naked legs, as if it were hers.

*

She skips the cake, heads straight for the car park. Mama's stomach must be rumbling, it's almost lunchtime. Less traffic now. Rachmaninov's concerto, one of the few pieces Agata can identify, is playing on the radio. Each note resonates in her strangely empty interior. She follows a diversion sign and takes a right turn. Now the black arrows on a yellow ground order her to bear left. Now to the right, then left again. Just as well she didn't tell Mama about the scan; the less she knows the better. Mama probably employs the same tactic with her; they are two spiders knitting a web of, not so much lies as omissions. Holes. As though there was something to tiptoe around. Left, and then right, the arrows guide her. Only there are no secrets, just a habit. A habit of protecting one another. Take that cough Agata heard last night. What if Mama caught a chill at the barbecue, what if...? Must get her a thicker blanket tonight and switch on the heating, Agata reminds herself.

'Right! It said right!' Agata yells. 'The arrow pointed to the right!' She hears herself protest as a towering wall of red swings in from the left and something slams into the side of the car. Then, as abruptly as it burst into view, the red is gone again and the car is careering forward, Agata hanging onto the wheel, jamming the brakes to slow down the metal gate hurtling towards her, her entrails, as if loosened by the radiologist's probe, threatening to burst through her back.

When she opens her eyes, the one thing she notices is the radio dangling from the dashboard, still crackling Rachmaninov. Lucky she refused to give the radiologist more blood, she might need every drop of it now.

*

Richard is the first person she runs into at home. He is en route to the studio, in his tatty corduroy waistcoat – the sign he trained them to read as not to be disturbed. She fell in love with Richard because of his colours. Or more accurately – their intriguing absence. When she first saw him in a packed underground train, he was wielding a tube of rolled up papers, a strand of flaxen hair falling over his forehead. Beneath his pale eyelashes his eyes, drops of water at the point of freezing, took her in. They both got off at Charing Cross and, without much being said, headed for St. James's Park where, in the tangle of the bushes, Richard let go of his designs. At the time, Agata's erotic experience was limited to a few groping raids in the school cloakroom, and the totality of her English to just a few words, but at the grand age of eighteen she couldn't wait to get rid of what had become an encumbrance; and that it should be with a stranger whom she was never likely to meet again seemed a bonus. What she didn't expect in that prickly patch of metropolitan nature was to feel rapturously, breathlessly happy. Richard's hair smelled of windswept northern steppes, of low skies, of a tribe reassuringly disparate to hers. Yet it was her genes that got the upper hand when a few years down the line a tiny creature with enormous black eyes and a brush of dark hair popped out of her: Lily, their daughter. Lilian, Lily, Lilinka.

'Sorry I'm late. Please don't get alarmed,' she warns him before he notices her rumpled state. 'I was driving, and they played Rachmaninov.' She takes care to impart her information in manageable doses. 'Concerto No. 2, I think.'

'Rachmaninov is kitsch,' Richard says, tenderly fingering a microchip he is on his way to install in his computer motherboard. 'Ask Dora.'

'Rachmaninov was on the car radio,' she clarifies. 'But the car was involved in a little accident.' Richard freezes in mid-step. 'Don't worry, I'm ok,' she quickly assures him, but he has already leapt to the front door, thrown it open and cast his gaze up and down the street.

*

In the tube earlier, she rehearsed a limited version of the event. Why mention that the windscreen looks as if someone shattered it with a hammer into a thousand splinters and then painstakingly glued them back together? Or that she distinctly remembers seeing something like this before: mannequins flung across a car seat, straw poking out of their wounds, dead stare in their glass eyes, bent metal on the wooden plinth, but where…? In a gallery? Faces peered at her. Hands pulled her out. *Public not allowed to touch the exhibit,* she wanted to warn them. Then the police arrived and notified her that as she had driven into the main road without slowing down and collided with a double decker bus, she might face prosecution for careless driving.

'Gatushka? Thank God you're back,' Mama calls from the landing; to exercise her English, the minute her mother lands at Heathrow she stops speaking Czech, even to Agata. 'Come, come, we need your help.' In a quick whisper Agata asks Richard to keep quiet about her misadventure, then follows Mama to the kitchen where she finds a grim-faced Lily struggling to smudge Nutella over one of the circular wafers Mama brought from Prague.

'Mum!' Lily greets her with a whine. 'I need to make a cake for tomorrow's school fair, but Babi doesn't know how to bake.' Lily calls her grandmother Babi – a shortening for *Babička* – granny in Czech. 'Babi, what is this called again?'

'Waffel chocolade torte, darling. You glue Carlsbad wafers together with chocolate, no need to bake.'

'But Babi, that's not a cake!'

'Hey Lily, what about a Victoria sponge?' Agata infuses her voice with good cheer, and Lily's face lights up. 'We have everything we need. Flour, butter, eggs,' Agata chants, fooling them with her culinary know-how. 'All bobs and bits, you're in luck Lilian.'

'Bits and bobs, you foreigner!' Lily laughs.

It works; how little it takes to deceive those who are supposed to know you best. Agata clambers onto the stool with the ease of a grasshopper and although the kitchen cabinets spin and sway as if she were on a choppy sea, she starts hauling from an upper shelf bags of flour and sugar. What wouldn't a mother do to make her daughter happy? Whipping the mixture she meets the bottomless holes of Mama's eyes sending her the old, knowing look: *Yes, Lily is lucky, thank God for that*. Ignoring the pain at the root of her neck Agata pours everything into the baking tin, sticks it in the oven, sets the timer, even tidies up the counter. Then excuses herself.

She closes the bedroom door and collapses on the bed. When her jaw begins to tremble, she lets it. Must be a reaction to the shock. Perhaps she should have agreed to go to the hospital, shouldn't have told the paramedics that she has just come out of one, but she felt no pain and there was no blood. It was only when they took her to retrieve her handbag from the car and Agata saw that the seat next to hers, the passenger's seat where Mama would have sat, had half disappeared under the car's squashed metal cheek, that her legs gave way under her.

'Babi, why don't you know how to bake?' She hears the voices from the floor below.

'My mother never had time to teach me. She worked in a shop,' Mama replies. 'We had a girl who cooked for us... Jarmila. In English I don't think you have such name.'

'And your sisters, Babi?'

'Two sisters, darling. Laura and my little sister Annette... We spoke Czech and German. That's right darling, bilingual. Yes, we had fun. Unfortunately Annette died... And Laura too, they both did, darling.' Agata listens to her mother tossing Lily the crumbs of her history. A history that as a child she knew not to ask too much about.

'You've never shown me their pictures, Babi.'

'Oh really? Have I not? Well, I'll show you next time you come to Prague…' Mama coos. 'Me? No, I wasn't there; I was in France. From there I went by ship to Buenos Aires… Yes, that's in Argentina, Lilinka. Clever girl.'

A passing train rattles the window, undulates the air. Agata's legs feel dead and the wall opposite, together with the chest of drawers, keeps charging towards her with dizzying speed. Then something blurred slides in the periphery of her vision.

'You ok, Agu?' Richard ruffles her hair. 'Where's the car then?'

She finds his hand. 'I'm sorry Ricky, but it was a write-off, I'm afraid.'

'Jesus! What happened? Are you alright?' When Agata puts her finger to her mouth Richard stares at her in disbelief. 'You crash the car, and we must keep it quiet?'

Then she loses track of time and next thing she knows, Mama is bending over her, a mug in each hand. 'It's only Nescafé, I can't use your complicated machines. Why are you in bed, Gatushka?'

Agata would prefer a shot of something stronger, but how is Mama to know? She drains the tepid liquid in one go, searches for something to say. 'Why don't you talk to Lily properly, Mama? Just tell her the truth. Tell her why there are no photos of your sisters. Or of anyone.'

Ach yo.' Mama slumps heavily besides her. 'What you want me to do? Tear my hair out? Load it all on that poor child? Besides, I'm sure you already told Lily all there's to know. A fabulous daughter you have, Gatushka. A great girl.' She pats Agata's cheek as she has always done, with verve. 'See how lucky you are?'

'Not sure.'

'Not sure about what?'

'About telling Lily all there is to know.'

Mama plucks off a few shrivelled leaves from the plant on the bedside table, busies herself searching for somewhere to deposit them. 'Well, maybe we can discuss this another time.'

'What other time?'

'When we're more relaxed.'

'I feel totally relaxed,' says Agata, the pain now radiating from under her shoulder blade – what if something vital has broken in her? She clenches her teeth and sits up. 'Anyway, how am I supposed to tell her, if you never talk about that stuff?' Instead of an answer, Mama silently scrutinises the vein pulsating on Agata's neck. 'What are you looking at me like that for?' Agata barks at her. Then seeing her mother pull back startled, she catches her arm. 'I'm sorry Mama. All I meant was that you could help me break the taboo.'

'Taboo?' The word alone makes Mama shudder. She stuffs the dead leaves into the empty mug and stands up. 'What nonsense you talk, Gatushka, there are no taboos. At least I don't know of any.'

And then, as if on cue, the phone rings somewhere in the house and they both listen to Lily chatting to a friend, to her shrieks of laughter. Greedily they soak in her happiness.

2

'Bobbie Greengrass,' the counsellor introduces herself.

It was Dr Rupinda's idea that Agata should see this woman, all she wanted to hear from him was that she hasn't broken any ribs. Dr Rupinda rotated her head, raised her chin, pushed it down.

'A mild whiplash,' he said. 'Let's get you a collar.' Wear a collar while Mama is in town?

'My mother mustn't know about the accident,' Agata explained. In fact she has already invented a plausible explanation – an irreparable fault – for the car's unprecedented disappearance. After a moment of reflection, Dr Rupinda suggested a compromise: wear the collar only in bed at night. Which was when Agata confided in him that in bed at night her eyes water a lot.

'You mean you cry in your sleep?' Dr Rupinda said it – not she.

Bobbie Greengrass hands Agata a questionnaire and gestures towards the pea-green armchair. Agata scans the questions: *No interest in life; Feeling nervous; Anxious* and so forth. The choice is from 0 to 8. Zero means never, eight means all the time. She circles mostly four, assuming that anything below would make her sound trouble free and anything above too unhinged. Further questions: *Poor appetite?* Also, *I'd be better off dead?* Here the options are: *Not at all* or *Sometimes* or *Always*. In keeping with her strategy Agata mostly chooses *Sometimes*. While she scribbles, the counsellor, a middle-aged woman with thick hair and nondescript clothes regards her from her chair. Sitting to one side, she has beside her a little purse and a bunch of keys with a rabbit foot attached to the ring. As if luck has a part to play in this game of questions and answers.

'Thank you.' Bobbie Greengrass skims the completed form. 'Self-employed, I see. Would you mind telling me what you do for a living, Agatha?'

Agata says that she is an animator. She works from home. She animates drawings for children's TV and for advertising, that sort of a thing.

'Ah! So you're an artist.' The counsellor seems to find this of interest. 'Perhaps you tell me in your own words what brings you here, Agatha?'

'Actually, it's Agata. No *h*.'

Bobbie Greengrass apologises and cocks her head to let Agata know that she is listening. And Agata feels a rush of hope; finally here is someone trained to help someone like her. She tells Bobbie Greengrass about her night-time tears and that she doesn't know what they mean; and that her husband

Richard, whom she met when she came to work in London as an au pair, finds her nocturnal grief disturbing, even though Agata doesn't make any noise.

'Richard was my first man,' she explains. 'Well, he still is. So I'll never know what I've missed,' she smiles at the counsellor. 'Sometimes,' Agata adds, 'I catch myself looking at us three – Richard, our daughter Lily and myself – the way you study your fellow passengers before boarding a plane. In case you spot something that would make them likely air-crash candidates.'

'Anything violent happened in your childhood, Agata?' Bobbie Greengrass asks, her face darkly serious.

'No, no, I had an ok childhood,' Agata assures her. 'Well, not entirely, but show me a child who's always happy. What I couldn't figure out was that besides my mother, my father and myself, everyone else was dead.' For a moment Bobbie Greengrass looks perturbed. 'What I mean is that there was no one left,' Agata clarifies. 'And not a single snapshot or an object or anything, as if they never owned a thing, as if they disappeared before the invention of the camera.'

Bobbie Greengrass keeps nodding, her brown hair with wiry silver streaks – one side shorter than the other as though she lopped it herself with household scissors – grazing her thin shoulders. 'Thank you, Agata for sharing this with me,' she says, scribbling something in her notepad. 'However, I need to explain, if it hasn't been made clear, that I provide Cognitive Behaviour Therapy, or CBT for short. In the NHS, this is a new treatment. An effective therapy that, rather than exploring the past, focuses on the present.' She stops to check if Agata is taking it all in. 'I can only offer you eight sessions I'm afraid, with a possible addition of another two. Would this be all right with you, Agata?'

Despite her fixed smile, Bobbie Greengrass seems not fully at ease. If Agata were in a position to pay, she'd have asked Dr Rupinda to refer her to someone else. Someone who has more time to give and nods less, but with Richard only ever on one exhibition design job at a time, and not paid, sometimes, for months, and with the studios sending cartoons to be animated in China for peanuts instead of paying the likes of Agata, they are often strapped for cash.

'What did she say?' After the first appointment Richard was eager to know. When Agata told him that the counsellor has sketched a worry tree for her, he looked nonplussed.

*

This is her third session. 'Today we need to talk about how to create a worry-free zone, even if just a brief one,' Bobbie Greengrass suggests. 'Can you think of an activity that would lend itself to this? Something easy, like... like waiting for the kettle to boil.'

Worry-free zone? Waiting for the kettle? What Agata needs urgently is to tell the counsellor how, on the rare occasions her mother mentioned a name like Annette or Hugo or Laura, something prevented her from going on. A sound at the back of her throat. 'You can't imagine how terrified I used to be that she was choking,' she tells Bobbie Greengrass. 'Laura was one of my mother's sisters, the older one. It also happens to be my second name, I'm Agata Laura,' Agata hears her voice rising, thinning out… The counsellor sighs and hands her a tissue. 'And Hugo was that sister's little son, I think they moved to another town, but since I never met any of them, I can never be sure who was who and so… and so…' Agata scrunches the tissue, squeezes it into her palm. So why, she longs to ask Bobbie Greengrass with her rabbit claw and her trout grey eyes, *why am I missing them?*

In the window behind them, the sky is turning scarlet. How many sunsets can you catch in a lifetime? For little Hugo, probably only a few.

'And your first name? Was it also given to you after a deceased relative?'

'Exterminated, not deceased.' Agata puts her right; after all it's her therapy.

'Exterminated.' Bobbie Greengrass duly corrects herself.

'You must understand, we were a tiny family, exposed on all sides, nothing to hold on to, no buffer of others connected by blood. Just an absence. So anything could knock us out, any little chip a larger family would heal over would shatter us fatally.' Agata soldiers on, phlegm dripping down her throat. Poor, poor Agata, making a spectacle of herself. If Mama could see the state of her, if she knew.

Checking the clock, Bobbie Greengrass's left eyebrow twitches. An involuntary mini-disturbance that Agata noticed before and that endears Bobbie Greengrass to her. The counsellor's gaze drifts past Agata's head, its inward look signalling that something behind that pale forehead is taking shape. Bobbie Greengrass draws a breath and, gravely pausing between each word, says, 'Yes. I can see. This must have been very…' Agata hangs on her lips. She knows what she longs for Bobbie Greengrass to say: she wants her to say that this cannot be; that this must be some kind of a misunderstanding; that no one could be so alone in the world. 'It must have been deeply… deeply unsettling,' Bobbie Greengrass concludes. Sensing Agata's disappointment she quickly adds, 'for a child.'

Agata stumbles down the corridor, the flecked carpet swimming under her feet, her cheeks damp. The receptionist, who had looked a little under the weather on Agata's way in now smiles at her, all dimples and shine. Same story outside. A patch of pansies, an hour ago a mere salad of leaves, have also benefited from the passage of time; their smug little features erupting in colours, ogling the sun. Then a shadow falls over them, an arm slips under Agata's and a voice whispers in her ear: 'Cured?'

*

When the session is over, Agata usually walks around to gather herself. Except today Mama is here, pinching Agata's waist, as if making sure that she is real, chuckling at her surprise. 'I'm inviting you to an exhibition. *Ancient faces: Mummy portraits from Roman Egypt.*' She produces a newspaper clipping with a picture of a young woman. A slim face with an aquiline nose meets Agata's gaze: prominent brows, pearl earrings, a halo of rich curls depicted in a surprisingly lifelike manner. 'See her expression? As if she was here only yesterday. And her hair! A bit like yours, isn't it, Gatushka?'

In a show of goodwill, Agata studies the woman's features. What did she die of all those millennia back? Was she as young as she appears? One thing is apparent: in ancient Egypt they didn't have hair products to tame frizz.

'Amazing, don't you think? After more than two thousand years we can still see their portraits, even their beds and chairs. While our people...' Mama pins her gaze on Agata, waiting for her response. Colonising her thoughts. Locking her in a cage with her.

'Sorry, I'm not in the mood.'

'Not in the mood?' Mama repeats, as if doubting she has caught the right words. Not in the mood? What sort of a daughter would use such words to her elderly mother who has come to take her to a fascinating show?

'You and Dora and your secrets, it's pathological,' Richard said, when Agata asked him not to mention her sessions. If Richard had kept his mouth shut, Mama would have gone off to the museum by herself. And Agata wouldn't be standing here shaking with an insane urge to smash that cage, that lonely prison of theirs, the two remaining exhibits from the not so ancient past.

To make it up to her, she drags Mama, now monosyllabic, to the place she knows Mama adores: Kensington Garden café, where the breeze ripples the water teeming with birds, and elderly ladies, in chiffon scarves which match their hair, sip tea. They take their tray to a table occupied by just such a specimen. Before sitting down, after a polite pantomime assuring each other of their good intent, Mama positions her chair to face the entrance. 'An old habit of mine,' she informs the lady, 'should the secret police burst in.'

'Indeed,' the lady murmurs her gentle agreement.

An hour later, leaving the park with arms intertwined, Mama confides in Agata how much she has come to love this city: the courtesy of its people, the dramatic skies, the swish of the pigeons, the ever-present wind, the sea so near.

'When the sea is near, why would one want to travel somewhere exotic?' The exotic travel is purely hypothetical, since any time Mama wants to come, she has to apply for an exit permit, and provide a document of formal invitation signed by Agata in front of a commissioner of oaths, certifying she has enough funds to cover all her mother's expenses including, in the unfortunate case of her sudden demise, the cost of a coffin to transport her back to Prague. Mama adores the sea and hopes to see it again, even if only for a few hours.

'You mustn't forget, Gatushka, that back home we have no sea.' And Agata, ashamed of having neglected even such a humble wish, promises to right this wrong as soon as possible; mother and daughter, they are like a positive and a negative, slipping in and out of alignment.

Chatting, they stroll down Exhibition Road. As they pass the Goethe Institute, Agata notices a banner above the door: *Tonight's Lecture: The Impact of the Holocaust on the Second Generation.*

'Second generation?' Mama seems intrigued. 'Who do they mean?'

'Perhaps someone like me,' Agata ventures.

'You?' Her mother looks puzzled. 'But nothing happened to your generation, Gatushka, you were born after it was all over.'

Agata goes to enquire if there are still tickets left. There are. Should they go in?

Mama only wags her finger. '*Tzz…tzz…* I already know more than enough about the subject, thank-you-very-much. You go in, Gatushka, find a good seat. And don't worry, I know how to get back. If you're late, I will put Lily to bed.' And she marches off, the way she always does, without turning.

3

The hall is packed, mostly by people of Mama's generation. Mostly women. They make an odd gathering: lined faces caked with makeup, hair dyed bright, gnarled bodies in garish clothes, as if to say: Look at us! We have no precedent how to age, we've been robbed of the chance to see those before us growing old graciously, so what the hell!

The main speaker, a psychoanalyst, sits on the podium in a cherry red jacket. She is in her late seventies, as are most of the audience. Agata has never heard of this woman, but the moment she opens her mouth, Agata knows she is talking to her. Transfixed, she soaks in every word: *Disavowal. Shared silence. Delayed mourning...*

During the question time an elderly lady in a tailored suit raises her hand. 'I have a question,' she announces. 'I have been asking it for nearly fifty years, I've read all the literature, even went to Germany to find an answer.'

'What is the question?' Someone calls. Several people laugh.

'Why did they do it?' The woman demands quietly. The audience shifts. 'Why?'

'Unfortunately there's always someone lowering the quality of the discussion,' whispers the young, smoothly shaven man with round glasses sitting next to Agata. 'There are plenty of books on the subject,' he calls out. The audience joins him:

'Next question!'

'I've looked.' The woman stands her ground. She has read all the books she could find and not a single one explained this hatred to her. Not one.

At the very back an old man gets up. 'I'm an Auschwitz survivor.' The audience turns to him. 'My granddaughter is twelve.' The man's Adam's apple slides nervously up and down. 'What should I tell her to prevent her anguish?'

Agata's neighbour purses his lips. 'Please!' he groans, this time only for her ears. 'Isn't this supposed to be about the effect on the second generation?' His English is impeccable in the manner post-war Germans learned it in their newly-built schools. 'My doctoral dissertation is about the inter-generational transfer of trauma,' he explains. 'But the second generation seems to be under-represented here tonight.'

'How do we protect our grandchildren?' The old man's Adam's apple threatens to rip his skin, sharp as the rolling Rs of his adopted tongue.

'Talk to them,' the psychoanalyst suggests. 'That's the only way.' Then someone shouts, 'What's the point of being Jewish anyway?' and someone else, perhaps to lighten the atmosphere, shares a joke about a Jewish refugee who lost everything except his accent, which brings up a few chuckles but mostly a wave of protest. And to her surprise, Agata feels at home among these ancient faces. They remind her of her childhood, of hearing her parents and their friends arguing politics around their kitchen table long into the night. Later she learned that each of them had returned from wartime exile or from the camps, uncles and aunts to dead children, siblings of ghosts. She takes out her notepad, a small book with hard red edges she bought on Bobbie Greengrass's advice to record her thoughts. To turn a radar on them, to observe but not to judge.

'Are you also an academic?' her neighbour asks. She shakes her head. 'You must be the second generation then, correct?' She nods and instantly feels exposed. 'Super. Why don't you tell them what it's like? Here! Excuse me!' The young man waves his arm and before Agata can protest, a microphone is thrust into her hand and everyone turns in her direction.

'I... I was born in Prague.' She rises slowly, frantically trying to come up with what to say next. The audience hums with approval, she even hears someone call, 'So was I', and someone else 'Ach, the golden Praha'. Everything swirls around her; the blood rushes to her temples and she wonders if she will faint. She has never stood in front of a crowd, never felt so many eyes on her. 'So that makes me a Czech. At least that's what I thought,' she goes on. 'But when I was about ten, a boy at school shouted in my ear *You shitty Jew*. You see, my parents forgot to tell me that's what we were.' Quite a few laughs, not derisive, more in sympathy. She takes them as a prompt. 'I can't remember why he said it, although I knew it was an insult, but why pick on me? I went home and asked my parents. Even before I finished, I felt their fear. It sat with us in the room. My parents, they never told me about the Menorah or Passover, nothing like that, but in that moment, I understood that I now belonged in that heap of scary matchstick people I saw once in a book. I was horrified. Please, let me not be it, I begged my parents. Please!' she tells the sea of ancient faces, the first time she has ever spoken of this to anyone. The hall is now filled with uneasy silence. Only her neighbour, his glasses glinting with excitement, gives her a little salute.

*

How she came to be in this cosy Kensington drinking hole with a young man half her age Agata can't now recall – but here she is, lounging on a papal red velvet settee on her second glass of white wine. Klaus Tuttenhoffer of thinning hair, smooth cheeks and brownish moccasins is on his fourth. It turns out he doesn't come from Germany, but from an Austrian village on the banks of the Danube where the slopes ripple with vineyards and every house has a vaulted wine cellar. Klaus seems to expect her to have a great insight into the mentality of the second generation and Agata, feeling obliged, offers him a few personal anecdotes from her early years: for instance how her parents tried to boost her confidence with examples of Jewish excellence, Einstein and Chagall and Freud and Marx and Ilya Ehrenburg, but Agata doesn't care about these people she'd never met. What mattered to Agata was that in Czech a chair was called *žid-le* and a Jew was called *žid*. Which meant that any time someone said, 'Take this *žid-le*,' instead of sitting down, she panicked.

'That's it, Agata! That's what trauma does.' Klaus sounds thrilled as though she has given him a present. 'You're talking about trauma, the deep trauma you inherited from your parents.'

To Agata this sounds unnecessarily melodramatic. She asks if Klaus has invited her out so he can use her in his research. 'I'm hoping,' he says with such earnestness that Agata has to laugh. She has already warned Klaus that she is no good at drinking and he has informed her that back home they drank Riesling like it was water. With every gulp she finds her new friend more amusing; his teeth are tiny and uneven as if he never managed to grow an adult set, and are as endearing as his early baldness.

It doesn't take long before Klaus offers a trauma of his own. His dates back to the night when he, maybe five at the time, witnessed his grandpa, his Opa, breathe his last under a thick eiderdown. His Mutti, his mother, closed Opa's eyes, then fastened a kerchief around her head, grabbed a pickaxe and hurried out to grandpa's vegetable garden where, in the cold twilight, Klaus saw her digging everything out: every carrot, every onion, every leek, every *Rote Beete*, every *Weisskraut*, every *Rotkraut*, every imaginable *kraut*, till there was nothing left but raw black soil that she turned over twice. '*Komisch*, isn't it?' Klaus chortles, squinting through his specs and Agata, unsure where all this is going, laughs and clinks glasses with him.

From the window Klaus watched his Mutti chuck everything on a pile, douse it with petrol and light a match. The flames burst out like fireworks, there was a sound of popping and a thick smoke, although young Klaus knew better than to shout *hurra!* Already he understood that this had nothing to do with the vegetables. This act of destruction had to do with something else. Something much larger than the biggest turnip.

*

Light under Mama's door — she has been waiting up for her, she always does. Agata knocks quietly.

'Gatushka! Come in, come in, I'm still up.' Mama sits in bed, an open newspaper in front of her. Agata bends to kiss her hair – the bob Mama has kept all her life – and settles at the other end of the bed to hide her alcoholic breath.

'Hello there,' she says, hugging the two small humps under the duvet. Her mother wriggles her toes in her hands. They always do that. *You know what's worst about prison? That your feet are always icy cold,* Mama once told her.

'I see you made some new *second-generation* friends,' Mama says, glancing at her watch before looking back at her paper. 'Now listen to this, Gatushka: *Thousands of striking shipyard workers carried pro-Solidarity banners during a pilgrimage to Poland's holiest shrine.* Those Poles. Such bigots, but still, they protest. Same in Hungary and Germany. Even in Russia. Only we keep silent.' She lays her paper down. 'But guess what? Mr Ricardo offered to show me the designs for his exhibition. You never told me it was about froggies.'

'It is an educational exhibition about Reptiles, Amphibians and Inter...' Agata struggles to straighten her words: 'In*ver*tebrates.' But she is pleased that Richard and Mama talked, they probably get on much better when she isn't around.

'Yes, Miss.' Mama arches her brows and Agata wonders if Richard has mentioned that the biologist in charge of the exhibition is a hopeless drunk, which means that Richard has to make all the decisions by himself, but then, Richard soaks in knowledge like sand absorbs rain.

'So how was your evening? Educational?'

Cautious not to alarm her, Agata tries to describe what she heard: how the children of parents whose families were killed in the war, identify with their murdered relatives. Or how they feel obliged to be replacements for those unknown dead for their parents. Or how...

'You poor thing!' Mama interrupts her, irony having always been her forte. 'All this analysing... Perhaps it's fashionable now. I suppose the times have changed.'

'But Mama, wasn't Freud around during your time?' she pulls out of her bag the abstract of the talk. 'Here, have a look at it and see what you make of it.'

Mama pushes her hand back. 'Sorry, I'm too old for this.'

'The psychoanalyst must've been about your age,' Agata points out. She helped Agata realise that she isn't alone, that others too have grown up in such families. There was an American girl she mentioned, born in New York, the same year as Agata, who would sneak out to eat garbage from the trash cans at night.

'Garbage?' This intrigues Mama. 'You want to eat garbage from the dustbins?'

'No, I don't, but that girl did, although she didn't have a clue why, she wasn't poor or anything. Then, during her analysis it came out that her aunt died in a concentration camp. No one ever told her, but that girl needed to do this.'

'That's ridiculous!' Mama guffaws. 'That girl was obviously *meshugge*.' She pats Agata's hand, her own light as parchment. 'You do dramatise, don't you, Gatushka? Even Lily agrees with me. She taught me a new expression: OTT.' When Mama laughs her eyes twitch back and forth, urging others to join in. 'Tonight you'd be pleased with me – I talked to Lilinka about my family. I told her how my father pricked himself with a sewing needle and how the tip of it broke off and got lodged in his wrist. He claimed he could feel it traveling around his veins. Hurry up, he would call us girls: it's here in my leg, come and touch it. He believed that one day it would reach his heart and kill him. Hmm… He should've been so fortunate.' In her buttoned up pyjamas, hair neatly combed – every night one hundred strokes to get the brain-blood flowing – Mama looks like a child ready for a goodnight kiss. 'I also told Lily how my mother worked for her rich brother-in-law, her sister's husband. They had two children – Franz and Ruth, my cousins. One day I came to their jewellery shop and saw that brat Ruth ordering my mother to go and fetch something from the window, it was snowing heavily outside. So I whacked her and told her to go get it herself.' Agata chuckles, this being one of a handful of stories Mama has ever volunteered. 'Lily thought it served her right. I bumped into him soon after the war, we had nothing to say to each other. *Ach yo,*' Mama sighs, 'we've been getting along here so well while you were out, Gatushka.'

'Into whom? You bumped into whom after the war?' Agata assumes that Mama has moved on to someone else.

Her mother brushes an invisible something from the cover. 'Into that Franz, who else?'

'Mama?! Your cousin Franz, he didn't die in a camp?'

'Oh no, not him and his sister, their parents sent them to England, hung with gold.'

'So they… you mean they may be living here in England?'

'Hey, calm down. You've gone all red.' Mama picks up her newspaper again, thumbs through the pages as if to remember where she was before Agata interrupted her. 'Frankly, I don't care where they live. Or if they're alive or dead.'

'But they are our relatives,' Agata reminds her. 'Our family.'

Mama folds the paper and arranges it next to the glass of water she never touches yet meticulously changes every night. 'Let's go to sleep. It's late.'

Relatives. We have relatives, the words bounce around Agata's head. What mad, totally unexpected news! Relatives, who may be living in England, perhaps even right here in London; whose children may turn out to look like her, or even Lily. She jumps up, shoots across the dark landing, grabs an armful of phone directories and lugs them back. *Quick, quick!* Somewhere among all those names are her cousins, uncles, aunts, people she could get to know and love in that natural, effortless manner reserved for family, who would love her back. 'Franz, Ruth... Ruth who? What's their name?'

'You crazy? It's middle of the night! Some stupid relatives, why should you look for them?'

'For God's sake Mama, just tell me their names!'

'Didn't you hear?' Mama speaks in an angry whisper. 'She was rude to my mother. Their parents only looked after their own. The old Frankel, their father, he never offered to save my sisters, not even the youngest one.' Her voice falters. 'Nor the other one with her child. None of my family got a chance.'

'But they are your family!'

'No!' Mama's face is now ashen. 'No. My family are all dead.' She reaches for the bedside light and turns it off.

'Frankel? Frankl? How do you spell it? Please tell me.'

The dark ball of Mama's head rolls across the pillow. 'I'm sorry, I won't. So stop all that.'

'Mama, please. Please! Don't you understand what it would mean for me to find them?'

'I'm warning you, Agata. Stop!' Mama wraps her duvet tightly around her – she would make the tiniest of mummies – and turns to the wall. 'If you carry on like this, then I'll have to leave. So please, drop this silly idea right now. Or at least until...'

'Until...?'

'Until...' A sharp round of words: 'Till – I – am – dead.'

Agata drops to her knees. 'But I don't want you dead,' she howls. Keeping still, Mama gives her a taste of the day she will fail to respond to her knock on the door. 'Mama, please!' Agata's face is now buried in the duvet, the wet stain spreading under her nose. 'Please!' She sobs, groping for her mother's hand.

'Just look at you,' Mama finally capitulates. 'You're an adult now, Gatushka, a mother, not a child. *Ach yo.*' Her sigh rises all the way from her heart. Reaching into her pocket she passes Agata her handkerchief. 'I don't know what you talk about to that woman of yours. All that talking, and for what?'

4

The low table between them, the armchairs, the desk, the clock on the wall – an identical set up to their usual room, only today everything is as in a mirror – back to front. From this angle Bobbie Greengrass looks unfamiliar.

'You asked for an emergency meeting, Agata.'

Agata has hurried all the way here, she has so much to tell Bobbie Greengrass, so much to talk about. 'We have relatives.' She lets the bomb drop.

Bobbie Greengrass rests her hands calmly in her lap, waiting.

'They – are – alive,' Agata spells out to give her time to digest this amazing news. 'Or, you know, if not they, maybe their relatives are. I mean my relatives.'

'Oh, but didn't you... didn't you say you talked to someone who... Who lived in a different...' Bobbie Greengrass flounders, then has another go. 'Sorry, but which part does your family...?'

'Which part? We come from Prague, the capital. It's in the middle of Europe. I'm sorry, but who was I supposed to talk to?'

'Last time, didn't you say...?'

Heat shoots up Agata's spine and before she can stop herself, she is out of her chair. 'You're mixing me up with someone else, aren't you?' She yells, watching a blob of her saliva land on Bobbie Greengrass's ridiculous hair.

The counsellor also stands, as if in self-defence.

'It's me, Agata! Remember? Me, who was told that my relatives, every single one, were whooshed up in smoke! Don't you ever take notes?' Her anger catches Agata by surprise, catches them both. Now she finds that her legs are wobbly. She wants to do worse, she wants to jolt the counsellor's shoulders, to rattle her bones. Standing so close to her, she glimpses fear in Bobbie Greengrass's eyes; her rage is gone and all that remains is shame. She gathers the purse and the rabbit foot that have fallen on the floor, pops them back on the counsellor's seat, and on the way back to her chair snatches a bunch of paper tissues from the box, passes Bobbie Greengrass some. The counsellor attempts to wipe her forehead, but her hand trembles so much that even such a simple undertaking becomes something of a task. Once they are both seated again, Bobbie Greengrass leans forward, perhaps to reach the emergency button Agata imagines hidden under the desk, then changes her mind midway and sinks back.

*

There is a silver apparition parked in front of their house. As Agata gets closer a window rolls down and Richard grins at her from inside. 'Only two and a half grand. I always wanted to own an old Merc. Guess I have you to thank.' He motions to the back. 'Came with a message.' On the rear window a sticker reads: *Caution! This driver doesn't give a shit!* Seeing Agata grimace, Richard laughs. 'I bet Dora will be chuffed!'

And indeed, after several turns about it, Mama declares the vehicle rather elegant, if a tad oversized. Lily, too, is visibly impressed. Once she has inspected each mirror with its self-activating light, each leather padded compartment, the surround speakers and the sliding seats, she dashes back to phone her friends with the news.

*

Richard started to call Agata's mother Dora soon after they met. *Dora this, Dora that.* It sounded more intimate than Doris, and Agata was pleased. And also appalled, as if Richard has usurped something to which only she has a right. Jealous, was she? Who wouldn't be with such a formidable mother? Richard's own mother was a dour woman who ruled her husband Cedric in their modest two up two down in Poulton. Both had died some years back. Richard's first memories were of the nauseous odour of ammonia his mum used to scrub the stove and of a scary baby-size doll in a red satin dress and a black cap his parents bought on their only holiday abroad, a permanent fixture on their matrimonial bed. Richard was a big boy and always hungry. Resenting his appetite, his mother frequently hid food from him, condemning him to secret night raids of the fridge. Back in his room Richard gobbled up what he stole. When he was six, out of the blue another boy arrived: baby Roy, who true to his name, instantly became the household's king. Richard escaped to London as soon as he could, aged seventeen.

*

Agata climbs into the passenger seat and watches Richard checking all the buttons and switches, his long legs knocking against the dashboard. She watches him brush his palm over the polished wood and remembers how the two of them used to drive around, Richard coaxing the wheel nonchalantly with one hand, the other resting on her thigh. It stirred in her such longing, such an ache, that she wished to die with him right there, amidst the roaring traffic, but that was before they had Lily. She catches his wrist, circles it with her fingers. Next time, she promises herself, running her fingertips along his forearm as if tuning an instrument, next time I'll apologise properly to Bobbie Greengrass. What does she expect of that polite, mild-mannered woman on hearing one of her clients has relatives – delirium, ecstasy? Richard's arms are covered with silky blond hair, so is his chest and even his buttocks, but only

Agata knows that. He pretends not to notice, although when she reaches the soft inside of his elbow, he clamps her hand and murmurs, 'Whoa.' Richard keeps a tight control over his physique, as tight as Mama keeps over her mind. With both of them Agata's role is to keep trying to break down their guard. Why this should be so, she doesn't know, it's just how things have panned out.

The car interior reeks of leather and cigarettes, and of something musty: old dogs' farts, perhaps. The previous owner, Richard was told, used the car exclusively to drive her pets to the dog parlour. Agata isn't fond of showy cars, but this one is different; its plush upholstery seems to forecast a turning point in their lives. Already she can picture the three of them setting off in their spacious Merc for a Sunday roast with the relatives she will, no doubt, soon find. Afterwards they will pack everyone in, the three of them, the Frankels and the kids they're bound to have, maybe even a family dog. Fooling about, chatting over each other, the dog licking their face, they'll drive together for an afternoon stroll in the park. Yes, perhaps Richard's choice is a lucky sign.

5

D. Frankel, Homestead Ave… 01 764 2391, O. Frankel, Adelaide Rd… 01 821 8543… The phone directory propped on her knees, Agata sits on the toilet, the bathroom her temporary office. While she copies the numbers into her new journal, she pulls the chain now and then as an alibi for her extended sojourn. The house is still, Lily and Mama are already in bed, Richard in his studio.

Dr P. L. Frankel, 01 462 3829 … M. Frankel… another M. Frankel… Alas, not a single Frankel preceded with 'F' for Franz or R for Ruth; but then, he might not live in London, she might have married and have a different name, plus who is to say that Agata has even got the spelling right?

When she stands up, it takes a moment to recognise herself in the mirror: folds in her skin, bloodshot eyes, she looks more related to one of the reptiles in Richard's show than to any Frankels. Still, if Franz or Ruth have children, they would be a similar age. Fluorescent strip lights may not be flattering but they are functional. So are the gleaming tiles climbing all the way to the ceiling. Easy to wipe, cheap. Tiles make it possible to fix the shower right up high, Richard explained; what could be more pleasant than a hot stream beating on your body and not having to worry about wetting the walls? Yet, every time she stands under the shower, Agata can't help but think how they showered her relatives, then wiped the tiles clean for the next lot. Not Richard's relatives, so at least Lily has a family, not that they ever see them. Agata would love to exchange an occasional phone call or a postcard with Kim, Roy's wife, except Richard isn't one to keep in touch. See them only when you need to, that's how families work, but how would she know? And who said that there were tiles? Showers there were, common knowledge that; she heard camp survivors describe how the gas seeped from the ducts and how everyone screamed and shat and clambered over each other to snatch one more gulp of life. And how, once the door was open the corpses tumbled out all bunched up. Tell this to Richard, as he lovingly places one tile above the next.

While collecting her things, the phone book slips out of her hands and flops straight into the sink, which someone had left half full of soapy water. *Look what you've made me do! Look what you've reduced me to: searching for our family in the loo!* Agata curses her mother, silently assessing the damage: some of the D and F pages appear a little soaked, no more than that. She wonders if Mama, whose bedroom is right underneath could hear her. After all, Mama claims to hear everyone's 'business' as soon as, or at times even prior to, it hitting the bog. 'Sometimes there's heavy splash, sometimes a drip,' Mama would report in the morning. 'Someone went around two, and then around four someone else wasn't feeling well, I could tell it was that restaurant food; a bit too good, *zu gut* as my granny used to say.'

Clutching the directory, Agata quietly opens the door and as her eyes become accustomed to the darkness, she discerns a shape slowly creeping up the stairs, pausing between each step.

'Problems?' Mama whispers, her features creased with concern. 'Come to my room, Gatushka, I'll give you some charcoal tablets, they're best for cleaning the guts. I'm having some myself.'

Next day, during one of Mama's regular afternoon lie-downs – nothing major, twenty minutes maximum – Agata drives to nearby shops where she remembers seeing a phone box. Close, but distant enough should her mother, refreshed by her nap, set out for a stroll. Ignoring the huge pimples of chewing gum stuck all over the dirty glass, she takes out her list of Frankels and after a moment of indecision taps in the first number. 'My name is Agata... I apologise for disturbing you,' she says as soon she hears a click. 'I'm looking for a person who has the same surname as yours.'

'What surname?' Young man's voice. Pleasant. Their son?

'Frankel. The name is Frankel.'

'Mine's Harding.'

'But in the phone book, it said...'

'Look, if there's some outstanding bills it has nothing to do with me, I'm a new tenant.'

She reassures Harding there is nothing to fear, and moves to the next Frankel, O. Frankel in Adelaide Road.

'Hello?' A woman's voice. Elderly. Husky, must be a smoker. 'Hellooouuh?' A drinker.

'Terribly sorry to disturb you, but do you happen to have a connection with someone called Frankel who originally comes from –'

'Oooh, do I happen? You may say that again, I certainly do.'

'The person I'm looking for comes from Prague.'

'Just a moment dear, it's him who comes from that side of the world, I'm only married to the man.' Agata's heart lurches, she sucks in her breath. So quickly, so effortlessly?

'Your husband, is he then...?'

'Oh Oskar knows it all, he'll tell you all about it. O-skar? O-skaar...!'

'Oskar Frankel.' Deep voice. Warm. Does she detect an accent?

'I'm looking for a relative who…'

'How *mar*vellous of you,' the voice plays with each syllable as if it were a ripe fruit. There definitely is an accent.

'My relative comes from Prague. He has the same surname as yours and he came here—'

'I come from Budapest, dear.'

'Budapest? Well, that's practically next door.' Years ago, Agata went on a school trip to Budapest and now recalls parts of it looking remarkably like Prague. 'Wouldn't it be possible that perhaps someone in your family…?'

'They all started in Riga, I'm afraid.'

'Oh I see,' she exhales. 'Sorry to have taken your time.'

'Not at all, the regret is on my side.' Oscar Frankel wishes her good luck.

A man in a large coat appears from a corner shop, lights a cigarette and heads for the phone box. Agata turns her back to him and dials the next number: P. Frankel. No one picks up. P. L. Frankel doesn't pick up either, but S. Frankel does. As soon as Agata hears a voice she enquires straight away if he comes from Prague.

'No, I no come. I call Fabion, one of boys. *Pronto.*' 'Fabion here… Who? Lady, I sing mistaken *numero.*'

And on and on until, suffocating in that coffin-like box stinking of urine, all the numbers become a blur and Agata can't bear to hear herself asking the same futile question again and again. Mercifully, just then the man outside crushes the cigarette under his boot, raps on the glass and points to his watch.

*

They are back in their regular room, sizing each other up. First Agata apologises for her behaviour the last time. 'Yes, you were rather, well what shall we say…' Bobbie Greengrass readjusts her skirt and Agata notices the thinness of her legs, exaggerated by her clunky shoes. 'This time I'd like to talk about negative and benign thoughts,' she says. 'But before we start, I want to hear how you've been, Agata.' What Agata notices most today is the concern in Bobbie Greengrass's voice. In fact, despite her chopped off hair and home-knitted cardigan, today the counsellor seems quite attractive, pale and dark.

Agata recounts her phone-booth saga: how humiliating it was having to steal out of the house and then hear herself parroting the same words, as she tried twenty different numbers, all in vain. And so, in an attack of hopelessness, she bought herself a raspberry jam roly-poly in the corner shop and gobbled the disgusting thing there and then, straight from the wrapper.

'Like sucking on a toxic breast,' Bobbie Greengrass suggests.

Is this a joke? Agata wants to laugh. Yet, she's intrigued at such an unusual response. Maybe this woman does understand what's going on between Agata and her mother.

'Yes, that's exactly how it felt. The thing is, I'm already losing hope of ever finding anyone.'

'An automatic thought,' remarks Bobbie Greengrass. 'And as we know, such thoughts affect our mood. So changing this negative thinking pattern would be a powerful tool for change, Agata.' Bobbie Greengrass has already mentioned that one way to go about this is to record those thoughts, to catch them the moment they pop up. Has Agata started her journal?

Agata pictures her notebook with the list of Frankel phone numbers and not much else and glumly stares at the central heating pipe that no one has bothered to box in – if Richard could see such shoddy workmanship he would flip. No, Richard does nothing by half.

'In my home,' Agata says, 'in my home nothing negative was ever allowed. Not unhappiness, not even a lousy mood. I honestly believed that if my parents caught me looking miserable it would kill them.'

'Another automatic thought,' comments Bobbie Greengrass.

'Perhaps. And yet, as much as I've tried, I never managed to make my parents happy. Never managed to help my mother to do something about that sound in her throat. I think I inherited that sound.' Agata pauses to steady her voice. 'It's in here, waiting…' Holding her breath, she presses her collarbone. 'My fear is that if I ever let it out it will rip me and everything apart.'

An audible exhalation comes from Bobbie Greengrass, her fingers groping for the rabbit foot. 'I do appreciate you telling me this, Agata, but…'

'I often wonder if Lily, my daughter, feels the same,' Agata cuts her short. 'Is she also afraid? But I don't dare to ask.' She is now peering at Bobbie Greengrass through a haze. 'I worry that I do with Lily the same my parents did with me. Keep silent. I can't remember what I thought when they told me that my mother's mother, her daughters and everyone else died in the war. I think I told myself they were hit by shrapnel on a battlefield.'

'You mean your grandmother and your aunts, Agata.' Gently the counsellor corrects her.

'Yes. My grandmother… my aunts… You see, I have never said those words. Ever.'

Tears are now dripping down Agata's cheeks. Bobbie Greengrass pushes the box of tissues towards her, discreetly checks the clock and spirits a handkerchief out of her sleeve. The high-pitched sound she produces while clearing her nose reminds Agata of how, as children, they used to blow through blades of grass held stretched tightly between their thumbs. Only the counsellor's sounds more mournful.

6

Every Saturday morning Richard performs a ritual. The procedure never varies: he cuts five even lengths of greaseproof paper, takes ten slices of bread and butters each lovingly. The Monday sandwich he spreads with peanut butter, into the Tuesday one he forks tinned tuna and a spoonful of mayonnaise, the Wednesday one he garnishes with slices of cheddar and pickles, into the Thursday one he folds a layer of ham and adds a lick of mustard and the one for Friday he slathers with a generous layer of Nutella and a chopped banana. He wraps them into individual parcels, each in a slightly different fashion as if creating a work of art. Then he shoves them into the freezer to be taken out on the morning of the right day in time to be defrosted by lunchtime, when, disturbed by no one, Richard tucks into them in front of the computer screen.

On this particular Saturday, Agata and Mama are driving to the sea, just the two of them. Mama prefers it this way. Conveniently, Lily has a party to attend and Richard his exhibition deadline. Just as they are pulling on their coats, a brown envelope drops through the door. The postmark says The Royal Free Hospital. Instantly, the words *Tuumor! Tuumor!* begin to ring in Agata's mind. She tears off the flap:

Dear Mrs Upton, your medical file came to my attention ... from your maiden name I wonder if you have an Ashkenazi Jewish background... interested in genetic research ... grateful if you could get in touch ... update your family tree... Prof. A. Chalabot Senior Lecturer in...

While she reads, the phone rings. Mama picks it up and handing it to Agata, whispers, 'You won't be long, will you?' and Agata automatically hands her the hospital letter in exchange.

'Good morning, Klaus Tuttenhoffer speaking.' At first Agata is at a loss as to who this might be. And even when she remembers she can't recall giving Klaus her number. What she does recall clearly is the figure of his mother blitzing vegetables in the moonlight. 'So, Agata, when are we meeting?' Klaus sounds as if the two of them were long-time chums.

She makes her excuses and while they talk, Agata watches Mama briefly skim the letter, then pace the floor: there and back, there and back, like she paced the solitary cell her party comrades locked her in during the Stalinist trials. To preserve her sanity Mama used to concentrate on music in her head. There and back, there and back, she paced to the tunes by Schubert or Mozart until the guard pushed in a bowl of filthy water they called soup and shouted: *Lunch!* And Mama, genuinely surprised how quickly the morning had passed, asked: 'Already?' At this place in the story Mama always chuckles. 'They never got over it, those *bachaři*.' Agata was only five then, and to protect her, her father told her that Mama was busy; too busy to come home, to pick up the phone, to send a little present. So Agata assumed that either her mother was dead, or she had left because Agata did something that made Mama angry with her; she didn't know which was worse.

The moment Agata gets off the phone, Mama waves the letter at her. 'They want to research you because you're Jewish? Unbelievable! They've never heard of Mengele? I hope you'll say no.'

*

She has never driven such a massive car. All the same, she quickly gets used to its smooth gliding motion, its leather luxury. They are off to have a nice time with Mama, and the yet unprocessed Frankels in her notebook, together with all the other Frankls and Frankles in the phone directory will have to wait. While steering, Agata drafts a letter in her head: *Dear Prof. A. Chalabot, I'm very happy to take part in your research. Regarding my family tree I'm afraid I only have limited information, as aside from my mother all* – here she triumphantly replaces *all* by *most* – *of my relatives died in the war.* Already, she feels sympathy towards this unknown scholar. She imagines him in a white coat in the lab late at night, thawing her blood, checking it under the microscope. Searching for clues to locate her in the web of her kin.

It is still light when they arrive. They are lucky, the B&B they stayed in before has a vacancy sign. 'You will hardly recognise the place,' the landlady warns them as they follow her up the newly carpeted stairs. 'Nowadays everyone expects an en suite bathroom. And how delightful to take a short break with one's mother, so rare these days. Living so far apart you must have a lot of family gossip to catch up on.'

As soon as she leaves, they spray the room with Mama's eau de cologne – 4711, never another – to neutralise the aroma of frazzled bacon, toss a coin to decide who will sleep where, sample the new bathroom cubicle, big enough for one person to either stand under the shower or sit on the loo, and every time they find themselves out of breath with the hilarity of it all, Mama repeats 'unbe*lie*vable', and cracks up.

Energised by their renewed camaraderie, they drive out of town. They park in a lay-by and wander along the road until they spot a narrow path.

'Let's go this way,' Agata suggests.

'This leads down to the caravan park,' Mama reminds her. 'To get to our beach we have to follow the road.'

'But this is a short cut, remember?' They can walk through the caravans and get to the beach this way. Mama eyes the dense undergrowth.

'As you wish,' she finally concedes, but, seeing her edging cautiously into the darkness, Agata regrets her decision; she didn't expect her mother to give in so fast, only last summer she wouldn't have.

'Mama?' She touches her shoulder. 'Please hold my arm.'

'I prefer walking on my own,' Mama says, but then, after a few more steps she stumbles.

'Oh for Christ's sake, why are you so bloody proud?' Agata squeezes next to her.

Instead of leaning on her, Mama grips her elbow and begins dragging them forward, making them flounder over the uneven ground like a pair of drunks.

Below them, the caravan park lights swing into view; sounds reach them through the clear air. Soon they are passing groups clustered around portable homes, men tilting beer cans, women chatting to each other, their miniature versions paddling about on their toy bikes in colourful pyjamas. They call good evening and hello to them – the two lonely shipwrecks navigating through their good cheer. Except that, for Agata, the world has changed: now anything could mark someone out as a potential candidate for kinship; an angle of a forehead; a manner of holding oneself. The shadow of a smile…

The dusk envelops them again until, gradually, the hum of the sea fills their ears, and they emerge on a beach. The swell rolls and crashes ahead, the sky is a vastness above. They sit on the cool wet sand. 'Hmm…' Mama inhales deeply. 'This air… the sound of the waves… Ach I'm so happy to see this again, so happy. It reminds me of the ocean in Argentina. Have I ever told you that the day the Nazis marched into Prague I phoned my mother? I was in Lyon. *Dorinka, my love,* she said, *no need to come back.* I knew what she meant. Last time I heard her voice. A teacher from the Lyon conservatoire helped me to get a visa and bought me a boat ticket to Buenos Aires. I was eighteen then, a girl from Prague.' Mama strokes Agata's hand. 'Nice of you to bring me here, Gatushka. Thank you.'

Agata observes her from the corner of her eye; the dusk smooths her mother's skin, she could easily pass for someone much younger.

'Look up there,' Mama points to the sky. 'There is something moving there. A moving light.'

'Where?' Agata throws her head back. 'Sorry, but I see nothing moving.'

'It's because you've moved. You have to keep still to see things moving, Annetka.'

Annetka. Without noticing, and not for the first time, Mama addressed Agata as if she were her dead sister. In the past, Agata would have demanded a correction, but now she just whispers, 'You're only imagining it, Doris.'

Surprised, Mama glances up; Agata never calls her by her name, it isn't their habit. In any case, she is Agata's mother. Not Doris, who used to listen to her little sister Annette breathing at night. To whom Doris used to say when they sunbathed by the river, *let's wait for the next blue patch*. Then they lay there and talked until the blue changed into black and stars faded in. The sister Doris didn't manage to save.

'Now please, look properly.' Mama tugs at Agata's hair to adjust her head. 'I swear it's moving, perhaps it's a satellite. Or who knows, maybe they're beings from somewhere else.'

They gaze at the dome above, strain their ears to its distant buzz.

'At my age you're grateful for every moment.' Resting her head on Agata's shoulder Mama begins to hum: '*Pom-pom... pom-pom... pom-pom...*'

'Schumann?' Agata chances a guess.

'Schubert.' Mama pecks her cheek. 'You're getting better, Gatushka.'

'I've been thinking, but please don't get upset.' Agata waits a beat before speaking again, her voice casual. 'What if I manage to find those relatives?'

'I told you, Gatushka,' Mama too remains composed. 'I'm not interested.'

'That's perfectly fine,' Agata says. Perfectly reasonable that Mama isn't interested, and she might be right, and they might be awful, but couldn't Mama imagine, just imagine for an instant, that these relatives have a box of photographs and she and Mama would sit together, and Mama would say: 'Here, that's me when I was young and here is my mother, your grandmother, and these are my sisters, your aunts.'

Agata feels Mama stiffen. 'I would never, ever look at such pictures,' she says. 'And I never want to talk about this again.'

'Why not? Why can't you at least consider it?'

'The answer is no! I will never sit with you and say *this is my little sister and this is your granny...*' Mama parodies Agata's 'fairy tale' voice. 'How cruel can you be? Just as I was beginning to feel we're close again you spoil everything.' She stands up. 'I want to go back. I'm tired. And disappointed.'

'Disappointed? What about?' Agata's hastily built resolve to stay calm collapses around her. 'You should be pleased that I want to talk about all this – that I care.'

Unsure which way to go, Mama staggers around, then decides to head for the steep bank behind them.

'Why don't you answer me? You treat me as if I'm not your daughter!' Agata yells after her. She charges forward and grabs her arm.

'What rubbish you talk!' Shaking her off, Mama begins scrambling up the slope. 'Never heard anything so idiotic in my life!'

Agata follows, imploring her mother to stop, pleads with her that this isn't safe, that they should go back the way they came. Mama determinedly clambers ahead, grasping the dry shrubs, digging her feet into the soft ground, sending down showers of pebbles. And all Agata can do is to keep close behind, in case she slips.

'You're besotted with families! You're obsessed!' Mama's voice reaches her through the night air. 'Besides, you have a family. Your husband's family, I've noticed how you run after them.' She is now a good few metres above and although Agata can hear her laboured breath, she has to strain her eyes to make her out in the dark. 'You have your husband; you have your child, but I only have you!'

What if her heart were to give up? But Agata can't resist yelling back, 'Why should we compete over who has less? You probably do have a blood family!'

Something heavy tumbles past her into the night. As Agata turns she nearly falls over but all she sees is a cloud of dust. When she looks back, there is no one in front of her.

*

A bright morning, a glimmering expanse of water. From the lower part of the window Agata's bed is flooded by the sharp sun. If she squints, she almost sees it burning a hole in the white gloss of the frame, almost hears the paint crackle. She raises her legs, colourless against the deep blue monolith of the sea, so near that it looks as though she could topple right into it. When Mama emerges from the bathroom there is a dark bruise near her temple. 'Does it hurt?' Agata asks.

'No, but it was a shock,' says Mama. A dreadful shock. She couldn't sleep, she had to take pills, her heart was pounding.

'You should have let me to take you to see a doctor. Are you in pain?'

'It's not the fall I'm talking about, it's the shock before.'

'What shock?'

'Ok, not a shock then. Call it an upset. Why do you always have to catch me out? The word shock is of no significance.'

'Yes, it is, it is!' Agata sticks to her argument. 'It suggests that I've done something shocking to you.'

'What nonsense you talk,' Mama sighs, dabbing on some lipstick. 'I'm going to get the papers. I need to know what's happening in the world.'

Agata listens to her exchanging greetings with the landlady downstairs. She thinks of the game Mama once taught her. It goes like this: I have a daughter – that is a good thing. I have a profession; I get paid money for what I do. Good! I have a husband and yesterday, as we were leaving, he bent in the car and said, 'Drive carefully Agu and have a great time, you two.' And I love the sound of his voice, love its blurriness that makes it sound as if he is speaking from behind a veil and I'm the only one to hear him. Yes, yes, definitely a good thing. I have a mother; she is still alive and we're on a short holiday.

She hurries towards the high street. People stroll around in short sleeves and sandals; the weather is warm enough to have a picnic on the beach. She keeps smiling and receives a few smiles in return, as if it were known what a remarkably lucky person she is. When she spots Mama walking in her direction, the Guardian rolled up under the arm, she waves. Yet, Mama's gaze glides vacantly over her. At first, Agata thinks she hasn't recognised her, but when they come face to face, she sees that Mama is absorbed in her sorrow, the measure of which, its enormity, Agata can never know, not truly. She says, 'Mama please, smile.' She says, 'I came to meet you. It's a good thing, you see?'

Except Mama can't, won't smile. And Agata suddenly fears that her mother would sooner give up on her than risk her resolve, so vital it is to her. They march side by side, Mama armed with her paper, eyes firmly on the tarmac.

'What's new in the world, then?' Agata asks.

'West German chancellor Kohl visited Russia. And Gorbachev called the idea of a united Germany,' she glances briefly in the paper, 'a defunct illusion.'

Agata steps aside to avoid a beetle then comes to a halt. So does Mama.

'Hey Mama, this is silly.' Agata flings her arms around her, but her mother turns her face away. So Agata lifts one of her arms and drapes it around her waist; then the other one; joins them behind her back.

'I've been so happy.' Mama's voice is as heavy and lifeless as her arms. 'So happy: my visit here, it's been so pleasant this time and now…' She lets her arms drop. 'Maybe it's my nerves. They're not as good. Please promise me you'll give up this silly idea of yours. You know what I'm talking about.'

'OK then,' Agata murmurs. 'I promise.'

7

The first number Agata dials – R. Frankel in Pandora Road – isn't in. Nor is S. Frankel from Groveway. The other S. Frankel has an answering machine. She phones twice to listen to the message to see if it triggers a response in her, whether blood has a voice, but the shrill female reciting 'Sorry we're not available,' only annoys her. Since there are no T. Frankels or U. Frankels she proceeds to V. Frankel, Kennington Road. She happens to know Kennington Road rather well. No answer. She closes her eyes; in the absence of W. Frankels, V. Frankel's is the last number on her list, and she lets the phone ring for a long time. Around her the house is quiet, Richard is tucking into his Tuesday sandwich in the studio, and Mama is out for a walk. The rest of their stay by the sea passed peacefully, without further dramas. Agata is about to put the phone down when someone answers.

'Franz Frankel here,' she hears an old man's voice. 'Who was calling please?' German accent.

'Are you…? Is this…?' She must have misheard. 'Did you say Franz Frankel?'

'Franz Frankel, correct. I was in the kitchen. I don't receive many calls.'

'But your name – is it really Franz? The number I dialled was listed as V. Frankel.'

'Ach yah! Let us explain.' The voice guffaws. 'Volker is my first name and Franz my second. I was given three names: Volker – Franz – Heiner, but *das ist* not important.'

'Yes, it is! It is very important to me! Do you by any chance…?' The receiver dances madly against Agata's ear and trying to steady it she glimpses in the window Mama striding back towards the house. 'Do you by any chance come from…' She takes a deep breath before she dares to ask.

'Ach Prague! *Praha of a hundred towers*. Yah yah.'

'You do?' Agata whispers, feeling pressure building up at the back of her head; as if about to burst it open. 'My name is Agata, and my mother's name is Doris, Doris Weiss.'

Across the road Mama has stopped under a massive tree, so massive that it dwarfs her. She pulls her hand from her right coat pocket and slips it into the left; transferring pebbles from one pocket to the other is Mama's method of keeping count of her rounds. There must be still more to complete because she moves on again.

'Doris?' The voice inquires cautiously just as Mama disappears behind the corner. 'Cousin Doris?'

'Yes!' Agata shouts. 'Yes, Cousin Doris! Do you remember her?'

'Cousin Dorittle! *Also so etwas*... Unbelievable!'

'Unbelievable?' That's exactly what Mama, I mean Doris, always says.'

'Dorittle,' she hears the old man sucking in his breath. 'Please excuse me, I have tears.'

'Yes, tears!' She laughs through hers. 'I also have tears.' And then she hears the front door, feet running up the steps, Lily's voice chatting to someone. 'Just a moment, Lily? Lily come here please.' Lily appears, shadowed by two friends. Agata holds the phone to her. 'Here, say hello to your uncle.'

'Uncle Roy?'

'No, not Uncle Roy, this is Babi's cousin. He is here in London, I found him!' Her voice wavers uncontrollably.

Embarrassed, Lily pulls a face at her friends who slouch by the door in their messy school uniforms, drops an indifferent 'hello' in the phone, then mouths to Agata, 'Can-you-hurry-up? Tamara-and-Melody-came-to-do-animation.'

'That was my daughter.' Agata proudly informs Franz Frankel.

'Beautiful voice,' he says. 'All girls in our family loved singing.'

'I know they did!' she gushes. Of course she knows. And more than that! In fact, she reminds Franz Frankel that when her mother Doris was a young girl, Franz's own mother bought her tickets for the whole opera season. And that this was what started Mama's passion for classical music.

'Ach, classical opera. Yah, yah,' muses her freshly-found relative.

*

Before they had Lily, Agata worked in an animation studio. She started there as an in-betweener, someone who draws movements in between the animators' drawings. Later, she became an animator in her own right and when Lily was born, she invested in a computer to work from home. Sometimes Lily would spot one of Agata's creations on the TV, advertising this or that. Look, she would proudly point them out to her friends: *my mum's mouse; her goofy bird; her funny little man.*

Now Tamara, Melody and Lily are hunched over the kitchen table, necks tense with effort, brows squeezed. 'To make a walking cycle you need to draw at least eight figures.' Agata shows them how. She loves teaching Lily's friends. Yet today she can't concentrate. 'You have to align each drawing on top of the other and change the position of their legs, like this.' To demonstrate the different stages of a step she balances on one foot. The girls giggle. 'It helps to imagine who your character is and where they're heading,' she says. 'It gives them a sense of urgency. Next time we will draw a background to pull behind them in the other direction, it'll make them look like they're walking forward.'

She lets the girls struggle with their drawings and goes to record a phone message for Bobbie Greengrass.

'Something urgent has come up,' she says, 'so I will have to miss tomorrow's session. I've done my homework,' she assures the answering machine, 'and I'm looking forward to discussing it with you next week.' The other night she spent an hour in a room by herself, tuning into the outside world, just as Bobbie Greengrass advised. At first, she heard nothing, just a thin, hardly audible whine which made her think of birch trees trembling in the fog, their skin hanging in tatters. Then she noticed a peculiar rustling noise emanating from one of the lamps. And then, scratching her head, she became aware of the booming sound of her nails on her scalp. A shriek in the garden brought a terrifying image of an infant being strangled, although she knew it was foxes; she has seen them before, on their lawn staring at her with their yellow eyes, their bottoms glued together. She logged all her findings on Bobbie Greengrass's flowchart: the date, the focus of her practice, its duration and so on. Still, what all this is supposed to do for her remains a mystery.

Next day she leaves home as if heading for therapy. She gets out of the tube at the Oval and from there doesn't have far to walk. Her legs alternate like scissors, swift and precise, the Kennington road whizzes behind her in the opposite direction. There is urgency in her steps; she has so much to give, so much to spare; love will flow out of her to embrace them. There is bound to be a *them*, she is certain. You find one and he'll lead you to the others, the people of your tribe.

A Victorian apartment block. Red brick. Agata presses the bell next to the name V. F. Frankel. No reply. She rings again. A crackle in the intercom. She introduces herself.

'Aga-tea? Little Aga-tea?' The warm familiarity takes her by surprise.

'Yes,' she whispers, her nerves tingling. 'Yes, it's me,' she repeats so close to the speaker that she tastes its sourness on her tongue.

'*Komm in, komm in!*'

The door buzzes and she pushes it open. She is expected. Greeted with exactly the same soft 'o' in which her mother pronounces 'come'. Once she presents Mama with her cousin, she is bound to change her mind. Narrow stone stairs. Each door she passes gives off a different aroma, just like in their block in Prague. It's all very well having your own house and garden to cultivate your privacy, but if you grew up in a flat you always yearn for that intimacy of strangers, for the scents that used to seep through the ventilation ducts, similar to yours yet so delicately distinct. He called her *little Aga-tea*, just like that. As she climbs, steps bounce off her feet: *coming to visit my uncle*, her ears hum. She will call him uncle right from the start, simpler that way. Uncle on her mother's side. The sweetness of it!

Top floor, four doors, one bearing a small nameplate: Frankel. That's how he proclaims his name – plainly, openly, like people do back in Prague, no need for anonymity, for English aloofness. Despite everything Mama said about him, Agata is ready to love this uncle of hers.

The door opens before she touches the bell and a smallish upright man peers at her with bird blue eyes. According to Mama, her own mother was the only one in the family to have blue eyes, the odd one out. Well, kiss another family myth goodbye. 'Franz?' It pops out of her as a squeak.

'Yes, *komm in, komm in* please.' Two knotty hands reach for hers, his eyes two floating silvery leaves. '*Komm* Doris, *komm mein kind*.'

'It's Agata actually, Doris is my mother's name.'

'*Ach Aga-tea. Kleine Aga-tea.*' Franz's claws pull her in and as she sways in the haze of his hot breath, something loosens in her and a sob forces its way out. More sobs erupt. '*Ach ish been zo glücklish* you're here, so happy. *Ach du lieber Mensch.*' Franz Frankel kneads her hands, glistening rivers running down his florid cheeks. Is it German or Yiddish her uncle is speaking? Agata knows that Mama attended a German gymnasium, but she never mentioned anyone speaking Yiddish.

Holding hands, they stagger through a dark hall into a room jumbled with furniture. With grace and elegance that must have taken years of practice Franz Frankel navigates them around empty beer bottles and gently deposits her in an armchair by a lit fire. Instantly, Agata begins to cough. Franz seems to be feeding the flames with odd bits and pieces from a heap on the floor: old newspapers, an assortment of hairbrushes, a small address book, old bags of cotton wool... He picks up a pair of beige ladies' gloves and dangles them in front of her. 'You take what you want. Yes? No?' But before she manages to decide if to accept his gift, he hurls the gloves into the fire. They ignite instantly, the black smoke making Agata's eyes smart.

'Whose gloves are they? Why are you burning them?'

'My wife's. What you don't take I burn.' He rolls up his sleeves, chuckling to himself, light dances over his arms, still taut and firm.

'Where is your wife then?'

'*Tot.*' Peering at her with his watery gaze Franz lolls his head from side to side. 'Twelve years, yah yah... Tea. You like tea? But please don't komm in the kitchen, I'm not used to visitors.'

She thanks him and goes to open the window.

'Yah, yah, you look out. From here you can see all that matters: tip of St. Paul's, top of Big Ben, tap of Post Office Tower, tap, tap...' Poor old dear, if only she had known. If only she had found him earlier.

He reappears balancing a tray with a single cup, which he deposits on the floor. Then he sits down in the armchair, his back ramrod straight. There it is – the same self-control as Mama, perhaps he too exercises twice a day. Agata moves her chair closer to him. So what does he remember about her mother, Doris, his cousin?

'I remember her well, lovely girl. *Hübsch*. Pity she died zo young.' His eyelids flutter.

'But you're mistaken!' Agata exclaims. 'My mother didn't die; she is very much alive!'

'Doris still alive? *Um Gottes Willen*.'

She tells Franz that her mother lives in Prague where she is a well-known musicologist, a music historian, in fact something of a celebrity in her field.

'Ach Dorittle is *eine Musikerin!*' Franz Frankel slaps his knee. 'I remember she made beautiful embroidery.'

The thought of Mama embroidering makes Agata laugh. 'No, my mother sang when she was young, that was her sister.'

'Ach yah, die *schöne* Rita.' Agata says she believes her name was Laura. 'Laura, forgive me. *Die schöne* Laura who married young.' He hands her the cup. 'Please drink.'

The tea tastes musty, she sips it anyway. 'Laura had a little boy called Hugo,' she reminds him. 'And of course there was also Annette.'

'Hugerle, he was a funny fellow.' Her uncle murmurs, closing his eyes.

She glances around the unkempt room. 'Since your wife died, you've lived here by yourself?'

'Yah, yah,' he nods. 'And always zo much to do – personal hygiene, taking Morris round the block every week…' Morris? Who is Morris? 'Man from Streatham comes to oil him before winter, but I don't need him now. I don't need a car; I need a lift.' She asks if Franz has any children. '*Kinder? Nein.*' He digs with his foot through the pile on the floor to unearth an old album bound in threadbare green silk. 'If you didn't come, I burn the photos too.'

'Is this the family album?' Agata whispers, bending to touch its golden edge, breathes in the mouldy smell. She turns the first page and hungrily scans the busty women in elaborate dresses, the moustached men.

'Mutti, Vati, Onkel Herman, Tante Emilia, Wolf…' Franz Frankel points out each faded face. None of these names sound familiar, but then her mother hardly ever mentioned anyone. 'Oncles, aunts, cousins, zo many…' He stretches his fingers on both hands. 'All *tot*. In summer we walked in moonshine. We sang, we watched the sunrise. Ach we were happy. *Ichweisnicht was mir esbedeuten dasich so traurichbin…*' Entranced, Agata listens to Franz's cracked voice weaving in and out of the tune her mother has often sung, with the similar nonchalance he had slalomed around the bottles. He has a charm, the old boy, crooning *Lorelei*. They turn the pages together: there is adolescent Franz in leather shorts, surrounded by smiling girls with pigtails tied around their heads. Franz as a young man on a Prague street, she knows exactly the spot. A group on old-fashioned wooden skies – is Doris among them? No, Doris skied with a different crowd. More skiers, more Prague, a youth in a uniform. Peaked cap. Agata stops.

'Who is that?'

'Ach yah, then I was drafted, and everything finished. *Fertig*.'

'Drafted? To where?'

'Where?' He snorts, but she has already guessed. '*Wehrmacht*, of course. I was fifteen when they put me in uniform. For two years I was prisoner of war. By British, *Gott sei Dank*.'

Steadying herself against the overheated mantelpiece Agata stands. Franz Frankel also rises. 'Mr Frankel.'

'Franz, please.'

'Franz, I'm sorry but I must have made a mistake.'

His eyes stare at her, as innocent as a summer's day. 'Mistake?'

'We're not related.'

'I don't understand, you said you were Cousin Doris's *tochter*.'

'There must have been another Doris.' He glares at her; his bottom lip starts to quiver. Agata picks her way back to the door. He treads after her, the album to his chest, bottles crashing around his feet. 'You said you were from Prague. From Frankel family from Praha.'

'It must've been another family. Perhaps Frankel was a common name there.' She has reached the door.

'You come to see me again Aga-tea?' The old man's eyes hang on her, unbearably, uncompromisingly blue. She steps out into the stone landing. 'Take it.' He holds the album to her, and she sees a dark stain creeping down his trouser leg, forming a puddle by his foot.

'But we're not related. You're German, don't you understand?' she yells at him. 'While we...'

'But we are both Frankels, we both love Praha. Please. *Bitte*,' he pleads with her, the album jumping in his hands. 'Please.'

*

The night turns her over like a badly digested meal, the houses two endless rows of rotten teeth. Slow movement is complicated, labour intensive, especially if you are weighed down by pages thick with old snapshots; sadness is even trickier. How does one animate the dull pain of disappointment? It would take more than eight drawings to drag along a downbeat character, a beginner couldn't handle it. Although who said it was going to be smooth sailing? If it were that easy to find your family why would people cross continents, search the internet? The Red Cross would have to dismantle a whole section. So the old boy isn't related to her, so what? It was an experience, not a calamity. The world is full of surprises. In her street Agata glimpses a man in a lit window taking off his shirt, revealing a waxy-pale mound, his belly. Wasn't this worth catching? Further on, in another window a woman stares in front of her, eyes bulging, mouth agape as if in a silent scream. Confronted with such agony Agata gasps. Should she interfere, try to help? But the woman drops her grimace and, smiling dreamily, begins to beat her face with her fingertips. To confuse cosmetic routine with an emergency, German with Yiddish, what is the matter with her?

No one in the next window, although in the one after, a man is gazing up from his chair: sturdy shoulders, fair receding hair, the collar of his t-shirt showing above his green corduroy waistcoat worn out in places, although from this distance you wouldn't know. To gain a better view Agata steps back. In the window above a handsome old woman with a smooth grey bob is watching a girl prancing about. The girl has dark reddish hair, yet Agata knows for a fact she would prefer it blonde: thin, gawky limbs, enormous eyes, even more prominent than the old lady's. When the girl was little, strangers used to peek in her pram: *Doesn't she have beautiful eyes? Unusually big.* The rest of her has caught up now; almost. The girl runs her palms suggestively over her childish hips: a demure seductress from a TV commercial. The old lady claps. The man in the room below is now aiming a long metal ruler at the ceiling, but before he manages to tap it, above him the girl climbs on the old woman's lap and lets herself be rocked like a baby. The light from the lamp makes her ears glow. Grandmother and granddaughter. As if he could see them the man smiles and mumbles something to himself, his rage spent. Agata lets the tears drip freely; she never expected to have so much.

'Aha, here you are, Gatushka!' Mama greets her, Lily still on her lap. 'Your husband cooked for us squid with garlic and ginger, we saved you a portion. I said to him he is a true artist.'

'Dad didn't like that, did he? He left in a huff.'

'Haf? Darling, your daddy is not a dog,' Mama pats Lily's head. 'Guess what? Lily wrote a nice essay. And I suggested she puts in a twist, haven't I, Lilinka? I think she takes after me. A natural.' Mama winks at Agata.

'Babi! Everyone knows about twists; they are in every movie!'

Mama's own life hasn't been short on unpredictable twists: first during the war, then during the Stalinist era. And then, some years back, she stumbled into fame with her biography of an obscure Slovak/Jewish composer called

Imre Lilosh. Lilosh, who came from the furthermost eastern part of the country, took the rhythms of Hungarian, Gypsy and Yiddish and fused them into a unique music form. He worked in isolation, but from what Agata understands, his invention was almost as revolutionary as Schoenberg's atonality. Imre Lilosh died in obscurity in Maidanek, his notations lay hidden in someone's loft. Until, through a twist of fate, they fell into Mama's hands and to everyone's surprise her biography of him became an instant success. Lilosh's music topped classical charts, not only at home but also in Germany and Austria.

Some days later, in the middle of the night, when Richard is asleep stretched on his back, in what he calls *Pharaoh position*, and Agata lies tied in knots, face pressed into the wet pillow, the phone rings. Praying that it isn't old Frankel, she stretches over Richard.

'Gatush? Is it too late?' Her childhood friend Evie is calling from Munich. 'It's finally happened!' An explosion of laughter. 'I've fallen in love. His name is Uli, you're the first to know. He's ... Oh he's coming back from the bathroom,' her friend whispers, and hangs up.

So Evie is in love again. To Agata it has only happened once, perhaps she lacks the courage. Despite her numerous loves, Evie has produced only one child. The same as Julia, Agata's old friend in Prague. Three friends, one daughter each: Lily, Sarah and Ilona. If they didn't live in different countries, their girls would be friends.

Movements downstairs tell her that Mama is in the kitchen making herself some tea. How desolate it must be to live alone. At least her mother is able to come to stay with them. While that poor old Frankel... Agata slides her arm under Richard's neck, feels its damp warmth. The noise downstairs becomes a suppressed cough; a nose discreetly blown. Not in the toilet paper which, to her mother's regret, Agata's London family have adopted as their habit, but in a proper handkerchief Mama keeps in her pyjama pocket. Is Mama not well?

Silence in Mama's room. No one in the kitchen or the dining room. Despite his strict orders to stay out, Agata pokes her head in Richard's studio. That's where his ideas reside and mustn't be disturbed. The only one allowed to share his space is Xena, an albino frog with a pale stomach and long thin legs that paddle in the water tank next to his computer. Agata doesn't particularly mind Richard's territorial demands, but Mama, whose job is to examine the lives of musical giants, holds a different view; her son-in-law is an exhibition designer, not the genius of the century.

There was a time when Richard's clothes used to be splattered with paint and Agata could sniff resin on his skin. He would pick up Lily, rub his stubble against her cheek until she shrieked with laughter, then walk her fingers over his exhibitions' mock-ups, as if he made them just for her amusement. These days Richard slips on his waistcoat, sits by the desk and nudges a grey plastic mouse around a rubber mat; he works out every detail from every possible angle on his computer, then sends it to the printers who print everything on gelatinous sheets that have to be handled in gloves to avoid the danger of human touch. These days Richard's hands stink of plastic.

Quietly moving around the darkened space, Agata inspects the oversized moulded spider, the crocodile X-rays suspended from the ceiling, the free standing model of a lizard's skeleton. It is as if she has stumbled into another era, the only humanoid around. Richard rescued Xena from the biologist who nearly killed her by spilling whisky into her habitat. According to Richard, because of Xena's species' rare ability to respond to stimuli – for instance if she were injected with a drop of a pregnant woman's blood, she'd instantly spawn thousands – the biologist tried to make her into an alcoholic, like himself. Xena's bulging eyes follow Agata around, her grin magnified through the thick glass, the gurgling of the water-pump the only sound.

And then, as Agata is about to turn back, another spectre shuffles into the gloom. Clad in a baby-blue dressing gown, it is clasping in its outstretched arms a square object covered by frayed green silk.

'What is this? Please tell me, Gatushka.'

Agata refused to take the album. Repeatedly, categorically, but when Volker – Franz – Heiner Frankel dropped it on the landing, slammed the door shut and turned the key, she picked it up, there was no other way. Once she got home, she hid it behind the wooden shoe rack by the front door. She planned to transfer it somewhere safer but never got round to it.

'It's an album, Mama.'

'Thank you, Gatushka. At least there is something we can agree on. Now, can you kindly explain to me what is this doing in your house?'

'This?' Playing for time, Agata adopts a thoughtful expression. 'This belongs to an old guy I met by chance,' she says, casually. 'He happens to have the same surname as your cousin.'

'Is that so?' The weight of the album makes Mama's arms shake just as it shook old Frankel's, her face flapping in the shadows, a greying cloth forgotten on a washing line. 'I couldn't sleep, you see? Sometimes I wake up in panic that I won't make it till the morning. When you're my age you'll know what I mean.' Mama's eyes are now gazing at her with such sadness that Agata only hopes they don't keep the same expression when Mama is alone. 'At home I get up and make fenykl tea, but you don't keep fenykl tea. So I decided I'd make myself useful. I noticed yesterday that Lily's shoes were dirty. I said to myself I'd clean them, just this once, so she can see the difference.'

'Mama, I only took it because he has no one else to give it to.' Gently and with great care, Agata attempts to prise the album from her mother's grip. The more she tries the more Mama digs her fingers into its green silk cover. 'No one to give it to? What a pity. Making friends with the Nazis, is this your new thing? Your famous concern for blood?'

'I felt sorry for him. He wanted to burn it.'

Now Mama's eyes nail her. 'These Sudeten Germans who greeted Hitler as their saviour, I remember them well.' She opens the album and rips a photo out, grips it between her teeth and with her free hand tears it in half. 'Let me remind you, in case you've forgotten that everyone I ever had, everyone I ever loved, *burned.*' Scraps of family groupings, infants on naked bellies, men in lederhosen under mountain peaks (how could Agata have been so blind?) begin to litter the floor. Writhing about, Mama tries to crush them with her feet, but her knitted slippers only manage to slide the pictures around. As her mother struggles to maintain balance, Agata recalls what she once heard: when an old person falls and breaks a hip, it usually marks the beginning of… the beginning…

*

They have a new baby, a sister to Lily. Agata lies in bed, the baby next to her, its long sharp teeth protruding. She wonders if this is normal. All of a sudden, the baby spits out two molars, making a sound. It speaks little words! Agata runs around shouting. Of course it does! Everyone is amazed that she hasn't noticed earlier; the little girl's eyes look like Xena's. She says that she was born to people who didn't want her, so she came to them. Choked with joy Agata presses her face to her soft skin. The girl says she loves dancing and Agata watches her strip into a ballet skirt, the sun making droplets of water shine on her thin albino legs. Look at Gatushka, Mama laughs, just look, it was the same with the ants on the windowsill, first she fed them and then forgot about them, the same with everything she does. The peal of Mama's laughter will not go away. Someone is shaking her.

'Agata?' Richard's face is looming over her, no time to check the pillow. 'Have you been in my studio?' She shakes her head and shuts her eyes again. Last night, after Mama had gone back to bed, she picked up the album and the torn snapshots and after considering chucking it all in the bin, stuffed everything in a plastic bag which she hid away at the farthest end of the cellar where no one ever goes. Irrational as it seemed, it occurred to her that perhaps one day someone might keep something for her.

'Well, if it wasn't you, it must've been Dora. She must've got scared then, and cleared the territory.'

Clearing the territory sounds ominous. Agata shoots out of the bed and sprints to Mama's room. And indeed, her bed is stripped bare, with the covers folded neatly on top of the naked duvet. Agata pulls open the cupboard where Mama stores her things. Empty. Even the cup with the slogan *I love London* has gone, so has the toothbrush Mama always leaves behind until her next visit. The room looks like the left-overs from a house clearance, only the grey rubber mat Agata bought so that Mama won't slip in the bathtub lies rolled up on the shelf like a discarded skin.

'I told you, didn't I, I told you hundreds of times that I don't want anyone sniffing around my studio.' Richard waves a long pale stick in front of her. 'See? The salamander's left femur is fucked up!'

'You think my mother did that? I have no one but her and look what you've done with your stupid rules!' Agata gestures around the desolate room. Last night, in the middle of her fury, Mama slipped and steadied herself by grabbing one of Richard's model's limbs. And now the piece of plastic in Richard's hand is showing a dent, but who cares? What's pounding Agata's head is far worse: her mother has vanished. Just like she vanished in the middle of the night when the police came for her all those years back. Another night Agata slept through.

8

She leaves a new telephone message for Bobbie Greengrass: 'I'm sorry, but I have to miss another session.'

Unexpectedly, Richard doesn't protest, he even offers to drive them to Victoria coach station. Yet to Agata, each flicker of his eyelids proves that Richard heard Mama dragging her suitcase down the stairs, heard her carefully closing the front door so that it wouldn't click, and had perhaps been glad of it. Agata doesn't mention any of this and when they speak it is mainly for Lily's benefit. Luckily, there are only two days left until Lily's half term.

The day of Mama's disappearance Agata searched the neighbourhood. She peered in the local cafés Mama liked to frequent, traipsing as far Brixton. Ever since Mama was caught up in the riots there, she regarded herself as the Borough's honorary citizen. On that legendary day Agata waited for her while watching cars burning on the TV. Lily was still a baby and Richard had a meeting somewhere in North London. When Mama finally turned up, her clothes smelled of fire and her bob was in disarray, but her eyes shone. She was reliving her young days in pre-war Prague, days of anti-fascist demonstrations, of arms linked with comrades facing the police on horseback. In Brixton, Mama's favourite place was the market. Strolling around, chatting to random passers-by, that's where she seemed in her element. Once, to Agata's consternation, after enquiring how to fashion such a complicated head-wrap, an African lady removed her starched fabric and arranged it atop of Mama's head. With the stallholders Mama acted the same, demanding a name of a pockmarked fruit or a hairy root, asking for detailed culinary advice. And every time she found herself at the receiving end of some well-worn quip, *à la*, 'What time you expecting me for dinner, darlin'?' she would beam proudly at Agata.

The likelihood of bumping into Mama lugging her suitcase around the market was of course very slim. She has Czech friends, Žeňka and Igor Kadorsky, who live somewhere out of London and to whom Agata drove her once or twice, but she doesn't have their phone number. The idea of launching another round of phone enquiries – there are quite a few Kadorskys in the phone book – fills her with dread. Throughout the day she kept monitoring Mama's number in Prague. By the early afternoon she wondered if she should call the police. Then around five the phone rang and before she managed to race to it Richard, who was having his afternoon coffee, picked it up. 'Someone for you,' he passed her the receiver – 'a man.' The formal tone and the hint of a foreign accent confirmed her fear. Is it about my mother? She wanted to ask, but only managed an unintelligible groan. The voice at the other end dropped a notch.

'Agata? An incorrect time to call?' Klaus Tuttenhoffer, her new young friend calling to propose another night on the town. Finally, around eight in the evening, Žeňka Kadorsky phoned to say that her mother had spent a nice day with them – they had a roast chicken and Marks and Spencer apple pie for lunch, and then she and Igor put her on the train to Prague.

*

They are early; the coach station is swarming with people and a murmur of languages. Richard has driven off with a stony face. Lily waved until their Merc disappeared from view and although Richard must have seen her in the mirror, he didn't raise his hand. With time to kill they join the community of travellers aimlessly circling the streets; they too eye the red brick mansions with their heavy curtains and tasteful antiques dusted twice weekly by foreign maids. When Agata worked in a studio in Earls Court she remembers seeing them waiting in a post office queue to send money back home, or in the evening she'd see a group of them by the bus stop, probably on the way to one of their dingy bedsits for a sleepover. Agata imagined them gossiping and laughing until their words staggered into dreams. How she used to envy them. But now, almost with relief, she feels her own house, her garden, her whole life in this foreign city slipping away, returning her to some half-forgotten memory of flight, of exile.

The journey to Prague lasts twenty-four hours. The coach rocks them about, mainly au-pair girls returning home; each plugged through earphones into her own Walkman, music sending tremors down the spine. It is night and the world outside is barely visible, the cars slither by, silver after-images trailing in their wake. Drifting through the aisle, their joined breaths seem to propel the coach forward; steamy clothes, limp thighs, lolling heads, their reflections in the window repeatedly bleached out by the headlights of passing trucks.

'Mum?' Lily stirs beside her. 'My legs have gone dead. Why didn't we fly?'

'Getting seats at such short notice isn't cheap, you know.' Agata rubs the bumps imprinted by her sweater on Lily's cheek. 'Hey. Wouldn't your friends think it pretty cool to up and go just like that, without planning and stuff?'

Lily glances around worriedly. 'Mum. Please don't speak like that!'

To change the subject, Agata speculates whether her friend Julia will like the perfume she is bringing her and if Ilona will like the mohair cardigan. Her daughter is quick to reprimand her again. Such big presents, she says, one should buy only for one's family. When Agata protests that, rather than friends, she and Julia are more like sisters, Lily rolls her eyes. 'Mum please. Sisterhood. It's so seventies. You'd never buy anything so expensive for an English friend.'

How can Agata explain to her that what she feels for Julia is special because they have known each other since childhood? And that this special love automatically extends to Julia's daughter Ilona. The same goes for her Munich friend Evie and her daughter Sarah. 'You love Ilona and Sarah, don't you, Lilinka?'

'I hate them both,' says her daughter. 'And I hate going to Prague. Babi always wants to show me something boring, the TV is crap, Ilona can't speak real English, and her mum is weird and doesn't even have a husband.'

'Well, she used to have one – Miloš, Ilona's father, but Julia is a very unusual person and men often find it hard to appreciate someone like her. It's to do with their autistic tendencies.'

'Autistic tendencies?' Lily's pupils dilate and Agata already regrets her pronouncement. 'Does Daddy have them?'

'No, of course not. All I meant was that during evolution women have developed something extra in their brains, but not men.'

'How do you know?'

'From the radio.'

'Ha! The radio?' Lily seems triumphant. Well, isn't Agata a proper walking copy of Babi, always parroting what's on the radio or in the papers? That's what Daddy says, although Lily had already figured it out herself.

Time to change the subject again. 'What do you think Babi will say when we turn up out of the blue?'

'She'll have a heart attack, and it'll be your fault,' says Lily before sleep overtakes her.

*

At the border, armed guards solemnly scrutinise their passports as if hoping to find a message hidden between the pages. Two passengers are taken to separate rooms for further questioning, the rest are ordered to wait for them in the chilly air outside, and the toilets are locked. Then, finally, they are allowed back into the fuggy coach. It never ceases to amaze Agata that the moment you cross the borders the clean smooth West German road becomes at once a messy, muddy track. Even the passing forests appear more sinister.

Except for a small crowd huddling by one of the aisles, the Prague coach station looks deserted. Icy October wind blows around the litter, the benches are missing planks, and the battered red and white railings are camouflaged by dirt. The moment they disembark the au-pair girls are whisked away in the waiting cars. It is much cooler here than in London and Lily and Agata are already shivering in their flimsy jackets. In the past they have always been collected by Mama and driven home by taxi. Now they have to lug their bags towards the tram stop. There, on hearing where they want to go, someone advises them first take tram number 3, then change to number 9. 'Mind you,' the man says, 'because of yesterday's national holiday things are still in one big *bordel*.'

As the tram trundles along the familiar streets Lily's eyelids grow heavy again. Somewhere near Wenceslas Square the conductor announces that they are being redirected to a different route but will rejoin the old one further on. At first, the noise from outside rumbles like approaching rain, but now Agata notices people running from the direction of the square with handkerchiefs pressed to their noses, on some faces she even glimpses what looks like blood. A police van tears forward with jets of water spurting from its windows but as it passes Agata realises that it is a shower of shattered glass. A curtain of mist follows and a blast of voices shouting, *Gestapo! Gestapo!* Then the tramway turns the corner and Lily opens her eyes.

'Mum, what's happening?'

'Nothing darling,' Agata pats her head. 'Go back to sleep.' Something in her voice makes Lily glance out, but all she sees are people waiting at a tram stop. It happened so fast that if it weren't for the other passengers' alarmed faces Agata could convince herself she imagined the whole thing.

Lily takes the lift, while Agata prefers to walk. Passing each door she sniffs the familiar smells of her childhood and on the third floor, by the Svobodas' flat, her heart quickens, as it has always done, so near home but still in danger of bumping into Mr Svoboda with his scary face. Only by now all the Svobodas are dead. She runs up the stairs to the last floor. There, in the safe vicinity of Mama's door she waits for Lily to emerge from the lift. And only then she presses the bell.

The door is opened by a blonde woman in a smart wine-coloured dress who addresses them not in Czech, but in German. 'Excuse me,' Agata stammers in English, 'but this is my mother's apartment.' The woman opens her mouth in surprise, then quickly covers it with her hand, her nails painted seashell pink. 'Where is my mother?' Agata demands.

'Mum?' Lily nods towards an opulent wreath of white gardenias resting on a chair, filling the air with a sorrowful scent. Feeling her belly tighten Agata grips her daughter's hand; she mustn't panic, whatever is coming she'll have to manage. And she will. For both of them.

*

There was another time, a time that Agata will never forget: a few years after she married Richard. Mama was finally allowed to travel from Prague to England, but there was a snag: she had to leave Agata's ill father in the care of a kindly friend.

The weather was good, so Agata offered to take Mama to the seaside for a few days. Lyme Regis. At midnight the phone rang in the hall downstairs. Mama sat up; they were both already in their beds. After a few minutes the B&B landlady knocked on their door complaining that she wished people wouldn't phone from overseas so late. Agata went to take the call. When she came back, her mother was exactly in the same position where Agata left her.

It's your father, isn't it? she said.

Yes, said Agata. *Daddy died at eight o'clock this evening.*

I knew it, Mama said, *as soon as I heard the phone, I knew.* She stretched her arms and they held each other. Then they lay awake through the night, each in her own cold bed, each alone with her grief. The million-years-old fossils they had collected for Father that day on the beach, their imprints fresh as if they lived only recently, lay on the top of the wardrobe.

In the morning, while they were packing their bags, Mama said, *Gatushka, you should have a child.*

*

Holding her finger to her lips, the blonde beckons them to tiptoe in. Everything looks in its place: Mama's shoehorn propped against the shoebox, the kitchen exuding the sour odour of Nescafé, the paint on the wardrobe peeling in the same spot it has done for years, although to get to the sitting room they have to step over thick cables snaking along the hallway. At first, Agata can't make sense of the jumble of people there, everyone talking in German. Only when they draw apart, she sees that in their midst, surrounded by lights on tripods, propped up in an armchair like a queen, sits Mama.

They are asked to repeat their embraces, Lily's squeals of joy and Mama's cries of surprise for the benefit of the camera. For Lily – the very first taste of fame. Is this going to be on TV? In the UK? Really? She can't wait to notify her friends. Mama, of course, is an old hand at this. The BBC correspondent came here from Bonn to cover yesterday's official commemoration of the 70th anniversary of Czechoslovakia as an independent state. The news about today's unofficial rally and its brutal repression which Agata had seen from the tram hasn't yet reached him; his crew are here to record Mama's views about the pre-war cultural mix of Czechs, Slovaks, Germans and Jews.

'That's true,' Mama agrees, 'after all, we were a democratic country, but it's also true that we have never taken our nation's existence for granted; how else would you explain that our anthem starts with a question: *Where is my home?*'

They have picked two backdrops for Mama's interviews: her cluttered bookshelves and the tombstones in the ancient Jewish cemetery. Mama loves her books, but the idea of the cemetery leaves her cold. No family of hers lie there thank-you-very-much, nor in any other graveyard for that matter. Eventually she relents and everyone, along with Agata and Lily, is put in cars, minus the wreath.

'Don't you TV people know that Jews place only pebbles on their tombs?'

'Oh, our apologies, madam; why not make a bouquet of it and stick it in a vase? Gardenias last forever.'

*

After Mama's cemetery performance the Bonn crew departs, and Mama offers to take Agata and Lily anywhere they wish. 'Oh it's unbelievable to have my girls here!'

Since they are already in the old Jewish quarter, Agata suggests that they show Lily the Pinkas Synagogue with the inscription of the names of Holocaust victims.

'Sounds fun,' Lily sighs.

'Not worth the effort,' Mama agrees, 'the place is always overrun by tourists.'

'You hear that?' Agata nudges her daughter. 'Everyone wants to see it, but not everyone can find their names there, like us.' That does the trick. They join the queue for the tickets, then shuffle in.

Several rooms open in front of them. The walls are covered from floor to ceiling with hand-painted names in alphabetical order: the surnames in red, the first names, the dates of birth and death in black. The effect is overwhelming. In an instant the 77,297 victims quoted in the handout become 77,297 names, each belonging to a real person. Somewhere among them are those who belong to them.

'Weiss, Weiss…' chanting her grandmother's maiden name, Lily jogs from room to room. Mama and Agata hurry after her. Passing the wall with the names starting with F, Agata spots Frankels, two densely packed lines of them, but there are also Frankles and Fraenkles and quite a few Franks. Perhaps she should write down all those names in her journal, but then, she is looking for people who are alive, not those who are dead.

'Babi! I found them! Here they are! Our family is right down here, near the floor!' Lily calls from another room. 'Weiss Samuel, Elly, Otto, Karel, Eliska, Rosa, another Samuel… Babi? How many Samuels were there?'

Heads turn, at first disparaging, then smiling at Lily's eagerness.

'Darling!' Mama hurries after her. 'These are the members of all the families with the same surname, not just mine.'

'So how many were yours, then?' Lily's finger follows the names, letting everyone see that she is no ordinary visitor here.

'Shhh!' An elderly custodian heads in their direction, a silver Star of David pinned to her blouse, her mahogany wig shaking with disapproval. *'Bitte! Bitte nix* touch!'

From her squatting position by the wall Lily lifts her head. When the woman is just a few feet away she scurries off quickly and hides behind the tourists; one or two secretly chuckle at her attempt to play hide and seek in these bleak chambers.

Agata knows she should call her back. Should forbid her to run, to speak loudly, to laugh. Next to her, Mama also keeps Lily in her gaze; their skinny little girl with rich thick hair and large dark eyes that could single her out should she one day, God forbid, need to blend in a crowd.

'Come on, you two!' Mama begins to steer them towards the exit. 'Let me treat you to lunch. I know a nice restaurant not far from here where they serve great dumplings.'

What an effort it must be for her to lend her voice that cheery ring, Agata thinks. She makes a quick dash back for the last glance at the Weisses: Laura, Karel, Otto... To her surprise she can't see her mother's younger sister's name. She goes through all the names again, then catches up with Mama. 'Where is Annette? I couldn't find her.' Not there, her mother replies without turning. 'Not there?'

'You must understand, there were so many dead, they were bound to miss some.'

Agata can't believe what Mama has just said. Surely, they shouldn't have made such a mistake. It's outrageous. Mama's laid-back attitude to such an appalling omission shocks her. Her mother stubbornly moves forward, repeating that they have all had a long day, that Lily must be hungry, and that yes, she has already complained, and has been promised they'll look into it.

'Well I'm sorry, Mama, that's not good enough. We should speak to someone about it right now!'

'Yep,' echoes Lily, noticing that the custodian is staring in their direction, the silver star glistening on her breast. 'Let's ask the sheriff.'

'Lily? What a way to speak!' Mama whispers, gripping her granddaughter's arm.

'Mama, please.' Agata yanks her free. 'It's not Lily you should be angry with, it's not her fault.' She feels her mother's eyes on her. *Can't you see how you're hurting me?* they demand. *Here, of all the places.* From a distance, the custodian follows their little wrangle with a disapproving glare. *It's all right for you,* Agata addresses her silently. *You know what's it all about. While all I know is that our dead don't add up.* The least they could do is to write Annette's name somewhere else. She looks around for an empty spot – an inch or two would do them, that's all they need – but in vain.

On their way out they stop in the museum shop to find that the only postcards on sale are of inscriptions starting with letter B going on to E and M to P.

'Babi!' Lily whines. 'Why can B and M people buy postcards with their names on them and not us with W? It just isn't fair!'

'Such is life, darling,' Mama sighs.

Agata says nothing, she too feels cheated.

9

Piano music, murals, vast parquet floors – the hall is teaming with swirling adolescents, the boys in formal suits, the girls in taffeta. They find Julia sitting under a gilded mirror. 'Sorry for being late,' Agata bends to kiss her friend. 'Richard rang to check if we're all right, he heard on the news about the demo and the police. Seems things are finally beginning to move here.'

'Easy for you in the West to talk,' Julia scowls before kissing her back and Agata is pleased to sniff the perfume she gave her.

As soon as Lily takes off her coat, a dance assistant appears followed by a reluctant youth in an ill-fitting black suit and white gloves. The assistant pushes him towards Lily. *Miss, may I ask for a dance?* The youth addresses her in Czech. Lily goes deep crimson. Unsure what to do, she looks at Agata who nods on her behalf. The assistant arranges the young couple into position and pushes them towards the dance floor. The piano accelerates into an energetic waltz.

'Is this Strauss?' Agata asks, making herself comfortable next to Julia.

'Come on Agata, it's Lehar, of course. Haven't you picked up anything from your mum?'

Looking awkward in a borrowed pink gown, Lily spins past them in the stiff embrace of her young partner. Julia's Ilona follows in the arms of a boy a head shorter than her, his white glove glued to her back. Towering over him, Ilona has a dreamy smile on her face. How grown up she has become since Agata saw her last. How old is she now? Fourteen?

Julia says she hopes Agata doesn't mind that Ilona won't wear the little cardigan she bought for her. Has Agata forgotten that Ilona is allergic to mohair? Agata does mind, but decides to keep it to herself.

'Did I tell you that Ilona has to drop her piano lessons?' Julia whispers. 'She was already grade eight, but her fingers started to make trouble. It must be the ivory. And her ballet, Ilona has to give that up too. Because of water on her knees.'

Agata finds Ilona's blooming cheeks, she is now swinging her hips, head bopping to the rhythm, her partner clapping: cha-cha-cha. As is Lily's youth, while Lily, standing a little apart, looks on embarrassed.

'What water?' Agata asks, secretly glad that her daughter's time of dallying with young men hasn't come yet.

'What water?' Julia imitates her. 'You're just like Miloš and my mother. You all think I'm making it up, don't you?' As she speaks the sides of her nose sharpen in a manner Agata hasn't noticed before, it makes her uneasy.

*

That evening Mama is having a meeting with her publishers, so while Agata and Lily wait for her they raid one of her bottomless drawers in search of photos from Agata's ballroom days. Not an easy task since over the years Mama has been shoving her snapshots in without a slightest regard for chronology. 'You were a right little vampire,' Lily comments when she finally unearths an old print of Agata in a nylon dress and a beehive, eyes blackened by kohl, lips obliterated by white lipstick. 'And who is that?' She holds to Agata a picture of a scrawny-looking young girl with several teeth missing.

'That's my first day at school,' says Agata.

Lily examines the thin arms strapped into a school bag, the crumpled shirt, the knee-high socks already at half-mast. 'Didn't Babi take you to school?'

'No darling, Babi was in prison then.'

'Oh you poor little girlie, look how skinny you were without your Mama.' Lily snuggles up to Agata. 'Tell me again, why was Babi in jail?'

How is she to describe to Lily her mother's odyssey, the party purges, the communist trials? Regardless of which words Agata picks, it would never make sense to Lily. Just as well, she tells herself, just as well. 'My daddy, your grandpa Pavel, he looked after me very well,' she says. 'But when Babi finally came back, guess what? None of my dresses had any buttons. Your grandfather was a surgeon, and he didn't know how sew on buttons. It's funny, don't you think?'

Agata never told Lily about the unheated cell with a toilet in which Mama had to wash as well as defecate. Or that she came back with rotting toenails. At night in her bed, Agata used to secretly listen to her parents talking about *them*. *Them*, the comrades who had never taken Mama out for a walk, not even once, who shouted *Hands out!* when she slipped them under the thin blanket in her sleep. *Them* who hadn't allowed Mama a single parcel, a single visit. *I hate them, I hate them, I fucking hate them*, Agata used to mutter into the pillow hot with her powerless tears.

'Mum! You're not looking!' Lily is now holding another photo. 'Is this Babi getting married to grandpa?' Agata glances at the black and white shot of her dad, grandpa Pavel, whom Lily never met, smiling at his bride in a polka dot dress, his hair in soft waves around his forehead. He holds a bouquet, while his new wife is signing a book held by an official, her features shaded by the rim of a hat. Nearby stands a group of guests grinning at the newly-weds. Everything how it should be. Except that in the only photo of her parents' wedding that Agata has seen previously, Mama was wearing a two-piece suit with a large floral print, and no hat. And her father's hair was slicked back.

They install Lily on the sitting room sofa and Agata sleeps in Mama's bedroom, in her old bed. A low table crowded with a profusion of plants flanks her now obsolete cot. From there, through a forest of leaves, she follows Mama's exercise routine. Having witnessed it over the years, Agata is curious about the newest additions and, of late, omissions of some of the more energetic moves.

'Nice seeing you in your bed,' Mama says, spreading her arms, shaking her wrists.

'Nice to be back,' says Agata.

Pushing the air loudly in and out of her nose, Mama begins to swing her head from side to side. 'Now watch.' While keeping her pace she makes her eyes meet in a squint. 'Chinese yoga. I read about it in a book.' Next, she forces each eye to roll to its outer edge. 'Repeat ten times. It's tricky but unbelievable how it improves your vision. You might find it useful with your computer. Which reminds me,' Mama chuckles. 'Someone told me that the police confiscated Havel's word processor. A brilliant idea for one of his plays, don't you think?'

To see her in such form gives Agata courage. 'Before you and Dad got married,' she says casually, 'had he been married to someone else?'

Temporary stillness. Then a slow-motion wiping of the forehead; a symbolic tossing away of daily worries. 'Why do you ask?'

'Lily found the wedding photo. Only she didn't realise that it wasn't you in the picture.'

There follows rapid beating of under-chin with the back of the hand.

'So who was she then, his first wife?'

'She...' Mama does her rhythmical music hall-walk on the spot – good for the toes. 'She was...' She gradually works up speed, swinging her arms higher and higher, as if hoping to take off. 'She was a – young – woman – your father – met.' Up and down, up and down, till she is out of breath.

'Oh, come on, Mama. Tell me more.'

Breathing hard, nostrils pale from the effort, Mama comes to a standstill. Then, vertebra by vertebra, she gradually folds down until her grey hair brushes the floor, her torso quivering like an athlete's after a marathon. As Agata watches her, a thought pops in her head: what if somewhere in the world there is a man or a woman made out of the same bone and blood as her, at least partly, alive at this very moment? 'They had a child, didn't they, Dad and his first wife?'

Mama slips on her dressing gown and heads for the bathroom. 'No, there were no children.'

'Are you sure?' Reluctant to give up her fantasy, Agata trails after her.

'Don't you think your father would have told me?' Mama runs water into the sink. Once it is full, she slips a face cloth on her right hand, rubs some soap on and starts washing her left arm, her left shoulder, left breast.

'Do you know what happened to the other wife?'

Mama switches the face cloth to her left hand to repeat the procedure on the other side. The side on which, instead of a breast, a long thin scar crosses her ribs. Mama has always presented this loss as a gain: hadn't the Amazons chopped off a breast to better draw their bows? Mama rubs herself dry with the towel's narrow edge, reserving the wide side for her private parts and the middle for the bottom and feet; as instructed three quarters of a century ago by Mama's own mother. As Mama, in turn, instructed her own daughter, although Agata draws secret satisfaction from drying herself every which way, while Lily hasn't even noticed that towels have different sides.

Mama pulls on her pyjama top. 'Anyway, she died young.'

'Why did she die?'

'Why do people die?' Balancing on her right foot Mama lifts her left one and sticks it in the sink. 'Why do you ask such stupid questions?' Watching her swap her feet rather than simply climb in the warm bathtub Agata wonders again if the function of this laborious ritual is to perform a daily memorial. If through her gestures Mama is remembering her own mother who had to clean herself in the icy Theresienstadt washrooms. And then later in Auschwitz... Later doesn't bear thinking about.

Back in the bedroom with the lights off, they chat about this and that. Outside, everything has become suffused with the approaching night and in the open windowpane the emerging moon is twinned with the reflection of the dying sun. When Agata casually asks if Mama ever met Dad's first wife, pretending she hasn't understood, Mama replies, 'Please, Gatushka, touch the soil in one of the pots.' Fairly dry, Agata reports. 'Oh,' Mama sighs. 'With you two around I forgot to water the plants, I hope they'll forgive me.' The issue of the house flora resolved, Agata returns to her topic: what was the first wife's name? After a short pause during which she could have sworn Mama went through a list of likely names, she says, 'Steffi.'

'That Steffi, she could have easily passed for you in that photo,' Agata ventures.

'And you,' Mama laughs, 'you could easily pass for a private eye.' Agata takes this as a cue to ask if there might be other things, she should know in case Mama hasn't...

'Please stop right now!' Mama's anger sends a shiver through the jungle above Agata's head. Where does this selfishness come from, Mama wonders aloud. This reckless insistence? Besides, after the war was over, she and Dad renounced the whole idea of blood which Agata seems so crazy about; they rejected anything to do with race, religion and all that. They hoped that the world had moved on.

'And where did those noble ideas get you? Locked up by your party comrades, that's where they got you,' Agata retaliates, succumbing once again to her childish belief that if Mama had loved her better than the communist party, she wouldn't have got herself locked up. No, her mother would have stayed home with her like the other children's mums.

'See?' Mama sighs. 'You always twist the argument.'

'And you always fob me off.' Agata's voice is now as thin as a strand of hair she sometimes pulls between her fingers to smooth out the frizz. And as tight. 'You claim everyone's dead, there's nothing left, not a single picture…'

Mama sits up, making her bed creak. 'I've already told you. I remember telling you that someone saved some photos in a box for me during the war, you never listen.'

'Ok.' Agata climbs over the potted greenery. 'Where are they then, those pre-war photos? Show me.'

Mama isn't sure. They could have gone missing while she was in prison. Or maybe the police confiscated them during the house search. Or they may be hidden under some stuff, how is Mama to know?

'So where is the logic in this?' Agata cries. 'Either you have those pictures, or you don't.' Her fury is futile. Because this has nothing to do with logic, this has to do with grief. And with grief, logic is of no use.

*

The sound of metal scraping the pavement wakes her up. She lifts the corner of the blind and peers out. Seeing the dustmen hoisting bins into the truck reminds her that they forgot to take out the garbage last night. Careful not to wake Mama, Agata slips into her baby blue dressing gown – too short but it will have to do – grabs the rubbish bin from the kitchen and calls the lift. By the time she emerges into the yard the truck's flashing lights are fading into the morning mist. The dawn is breaking, it must be around five. As Agata readjusts the handle to carry the bin back, the odour of decay hits her nostrils. She looks around. A few windows are already lit – here people go to work much earlier than in London. She separates an apple core from the mush of tea leaves and the remains of tinned sardines, and brings it to her mouth. The taste of the fluffy mould that has grown around the edges of the apple's shrivelled skin makes her instantly choke. She holds her breath. Then she opens her mouth and, still doubting her next move, deposits the core on her tongue and starts to chew. It tastes of nothing in particular. Willing herself to swallow Agata reaches back into the bin. This time she picks a piece of stale bread with strips of carrot peel glued to it together with a limp lettuce leaf. She chews quickly, suppressing an urge to retch. Morning chill begins to creep around her naked ankles, Mama's dressing gown pulls at her shoulders. Like the girl in that psychoanalyst's lecture, Agata has no idea why she is doing this. Yet, once she has started it doesn't seem so bizarre. She breathes on her cold fingers, rummages inside the bin again and brings out a piece of cheese. The night before they argued about it. Agata claimed there was mould growing on it, Mama claimed she was making it up. Now even her mother's failing eyesight couldn't miss the dramatic change it has undergone. As she chews, the yielding texture coats her teeth before sliding slowly into her throat. Somewhere above a window opens and a face in a silver helmet of curlers watches her gag.

Back in the flat she holds the shower to her mouth, laps the hot stream burning her gullet. It makes her feel better. Careful not to wake Lily, she tiptoes into the sitting room. She pulls the handle of the drawer where Lily found the wedding photo last night. Locked. She tries the drawer next to it, where Mama keeps her keys. Also locked.

10

Their visit puts Mama into a permanently elated mood. She takes them to the theatre, to eat in restaurants, they go to 'The Hall of Laughter' where a maze of mirrors shows them bizarrely warped and twisted. And they are to accompany Mama to Teplice, an old spa town in the north of the country. A local historian is going to show Mama some interesting details for her upcoming book *Music composed in Bohemian Spas*. 'Everyone raves about Karlsbad and Marienbad, but Teplice is more special,' Mama says to pre-empt Lily's protest. 'Beethoven started his famous 7th symphony there: *tumm ... tummm... ta... tummm...* Wagner, Chopin, Liszt – they all adored Teplice, we're staying in the same hotel as them.' Instead of making a face, Lily asks if Ilona can also come.

Unexpectedly, Julia gives her permission, even for her to spend the night in Mama's flat so that they can start early in the morning. Ilona arrives looking bright, but equipped with a list of forbidden foods. Bread, cakes, a range of dairy, and most of the fruits. They pull out the underside of Lily's sofa to make a bed for her. This leads to outbursts of laughter and jumping around during which the girls manage to break a glass. Which results in one minuscule drop of blood on Lily's finger and another one on Ilona's. To Mama's silent disapproval the girls rub them against each other, shouting, 'Now we are sisters!' Being already at the cusp of womanhood doesn't stop Ilona from happily submitting to Lily's childish games.

Once again, they are on a coach; Agata and Mama sitting together, Lily and Ilona in front of them, Prague's suburbs receding beyond the glass, and with them, the topic of Father's first marriage. There are some young Italian tourists on the bus and Agata overhears them asking the driver in English where to get off for the camp, although she can't see any tents or sleeping bags. As soon as they are on the road, Mama opens her newspaper.

'Look,' she says under her breath. 'Those idiots claim that the demo was financed by émigré centres. Unbelievable, how stupid they are.'

In front of them, the girls are chatting, Ilona in her classroom English and Lily cheerfully correcting her. Listening to them, a wave of joy sweeps over Agata and she leans forward to kiss their heads; first sniffing Lily's burned wood smell, then Ilona's nutty one. When Lily turns to stick her tongue out at them, full of inexplicable gratitude, Agata bends down and kisses Mama's hand. Whereupon Mama smiles and wryly taps her forehead.

They enter a town with long streets of imposing buildings, in urgent need of repair. Swallows flitter close to the ground, almost scraping it with their white bellies, announcing that it may rain soon. In a park, late autumn blossoms edge the gravel paths, and leaves on the trees are turning rusty pink as if breaking into a nervous blush.

'I spy, I spy with my little eye something beginning with…' glancing out Lily notices a large cross looming against the sky next to a huge metal Star of David. 'S!'

'Sky!' shouts Ilona, just as the driver announces, 'Terezín! Theresienstadt!' He repeats for the Italians' benefit.

'Is this…?' Agata gasps. 'I never imagined it looking like a town,' she whispers to Mama.

Her mother orders her to calm down. 'The town was built as an army garrison, everyone knows that.'

The coach stops by some ramparts enclosing a collection of one-storey buildings. Several tourist coaches are already parked by the entrance gate. *'Malá pevnost!'* The driver shouts.

The Italians collect their things and disembark.

'Ciao! Ciao!' The girls wave at them like film stars.

As the coach moves on a tall chimney comes into view. Agata is relieved to see that it belongs to an ordinary factory. Of course! What did she think? Terezín was only a transit camp, not an extermination one.

'Next stop is where they created a museum inside the barracks,' Mama remarks, sotto voce. 'They invited me for the opening, but I don't have to see everything, do I?'

Hazy hills on the horizon, the same hills seen by those in the camp. How old was Mama's mother when she was made to lug her allowance of fifty kilos through these streets? By then Jews were not allowed to buy any fruit, pulses, jam, cheese, fish, poultry, meat, so what was there left? Did Mama's granny make the journey alone or was she with Mama's mother? And what about her two daughters, Mama's sisters? And that little grandchild, that boy Hugo, did he have to trot next to them, or was he sent somewhere else? Agata glances at Mama's profile. Does she know?

'Where are we, Babi?' Lily looks back.

'Terezín, darling.'

Lily has never heard this name before, but registering something in her grandmother's voice, she turns to Agata. 'Everything all right, Buster?'

And Agata, instead of saying, look out Lily, this is the ghetto where your Babi's mummy and daddy and their family were kept with hundreds of thousands of others and from where they were packed in cattle trains to be gassed, only smiles and winks at her. What a coward she is!

The coach sways round the corner and Agata hears Ilona saying to Lily, 'I was here with school. We saw film about how *Židi* was happy here.'

'What is *Zhidi*?' she hears Lily ask.

'They are… It was…' Ilona searches for English words. 'How you say? Funny? But it wasn't true.' She turns to them. 'Can I show it to her?'

'Oh yes. Yes please!' Lily says.

*

Much against Mama's protestations Agata and the girls get off at the next stop. Mama carries on to her appointment in Teplice and they will get on a later coach to catch up with her.

The museum is housed in the same barracks where the Jews had been interned. Ilona navigates them straight to what she liked best: the reconstructed dormitory. Its whitewashed walls, three-tiered wooden bunk beds smelling of beeswax – a single child's vest hanging on a line, an open book on a blanket, a violin case under the bed – almost give off an air of friendly homeliness. Impossible to imagine the young and old packed like sardines in those cots, dying on top of each other from hunger and illness. After that, skipping happily past doors painted in cheery red and windowsills overflowing with blooming geraniums – the ladies who sold them the tickets must take pride in jollying up the place – Ilona leads them to a darkened room.

The film made by the Germans is called *Truth and Lies* and the inmates cooperated in its production believing – wrongly of course – that it would save them. Luckily, there are English subtitles so that Lily too can follow this elaborate charade. And indeed, apart from the fact that everyone carries a star pinned to their breasts, everything looks normal, even idyllic: people are making clothes in a workshop, lectures are delivered by men in proper suits, women have their hair coiffed and their brows pencilled; they chat to their friends, knit sweaters or water vegetable gardens. Stripped to their waists, men play football in front of an enthusiastic audience, and no one even looks noticeably thin. At some point, unable to bear this any longer, Agata quietly heads to the floor above, where room after room document the real life in this massive prison camp: the daily humiliations, illness, starvation, executions, the ever-present fear of the transports.

She returns to find the girls still in front of the screen: a woman is lovingly shaping a vase on a potter's wheel; young lovers stroll around hand in hand; children play in a sand pit; men splash in a shower – an eerie reminder of the showers that awaited them further east. In each new face Agata searches for a sign of familiarity; she even catches herself thinking that if only Mama were here, she could help. And yet – the possibility of her mother spotting someone she knew, maybe even someone close to her, is a vile, sickening thought. She keeps glancing at the girls: Ilona peering at those shortly to be murdered with much the same curiosity with which Agata remembers her peeking out from under the hood of her baby pram. Absurdly, she feels a flash of resentment of her ready chuckles and her forget-me-not blue eyes that, as someone pointed out in the video upstairs, could have been her life ticket. And here is Lily, her skinny Lily, hunched at the edge of the chair, shooting Agata dark furtive glances that fill her with regret.

*

'Here! Over here!' Two figures are waving at them across a cobbled square: Mama and her friend Dr Peterka. The pink dusk turns the details on the baroque fountain into a decorative lace, the clouds speed above as though blown by a heavenly breath, ripples of piano music drift from an open window. Hard to believe that only a few kilometres away lies the town of Terezín. Perhaps Mama is right, there is something wrong with Agata, why else drag Lily through that hell and then try to remedy it by buying everyone a double portion of ice cream? It's a relief to be back with Mama and Dr Peterka in his tailored velvet coat and his cravat. He has already shown Mama a few things and the next attraction on the schedule is the castle park where Beethoven, promenading here with Goethe one day, nearly collided with the Empress herself. *Let her step aside*, Beethoven said to Goethe, but the great poet had already moved out of the way, hat in hand. 'Oh how Ludwig despised Wolfgang's servility!' Dr Peterka trembles with indignation as though he himself had witnessed the offending incident.

In the castle, a group of Americans are already waiting, all the way from Prague, Oklahoma, in search of their roots. Once everyone pulls on giant felt slippers over their shoes they skate after Dr Peterka across parquet floors, past period furniture, Venetian mirrors and Dutch still lifes, Lily and Ilona tripping each other in a parody of a slapstick comedy.

'Ladies and gentlemen!' Dr Peterka halts them in front of an armchair of faded upholstery. 'You're looking at Giacomo Casanova's favourite chair from a nearby castle where Giacomo worked as a librarian.' Everyone pushes to get a better view of the white spindly legs.

'Waidaminute!' A man in a cowboy hat scratches his chin. 'This guy Casanova who chased broads, wasn't he supposed to be a made-up character. Like Don Juan?'

Dr Peterka finds Mama's eyes. For a historian in a lesser known spa which, although endowed with musical history, happens to be located in the middle of an ecological disaster, even such a lowly assignment as a tourist guide isn't that easy to come by.

Next their leader stops in front of a pianino on which Frederic Chopin and Franz Liszt are believed to have played. He raises the lacquered lid and looking at Mama gestures towards the stool. 'Madame?' Caught by surprise, Mama only wags her finger. 'Well, if you will allow me then…' Dr Peterka lowers his bony backside, but before he touches the seat, Ilona bolts forward.

She runs her fingers over the precious keyboard with ease, as though they were made of air; one hand skipping away in a playful staccato, the other one running after it. Ilona's twitching head gives the performance a slightly comical twist. What is it? Mozart? Bach? They listen, captivated. After a few minutes of this brilliance Ilona stops as abruptly as she began by crashing her forehead on the keyboard. The resulting cacophony makes everyone gasp. What's wrong? Has she fainted? Agata is ready to panic. Could it be that double portion of ice-cream Agata bought them after the museum ordeal? What if she comes out in a rash? Only when one of the Americans begins to clap, to everyone's relief Ilona jumps up and bows; it was just a joke, a theatrical gesture.

During their time in the castle a sulphurous fog has enveloped the town, thwarting Mama's plans. To identify the house where Richard Wagner used to lodge, they have to trek back and forth several times. They never find the house where Schumann visited his mother. As they pass a line of nursery children, their faces covered by masks, from somewhere above a loudspeaker blares out that, because of the inversion, everyone has to stay inside with the windows shut. Inversion? 'It's when the polluted air bears down rather than up,' someone informs them. 'Happens all the time.'

They dine in a hotel where the imperial splendour of tattered wall panels and dusty chandeliers survive from Franz Liszt's time, and a live band plays in the restaurant. Never did two meals, including several forbidden items from Julia's list, disappear so fast. Then, to Lily's consternation, a young man of about twenty with a smear of moustache appears by their table and asks Ilona for a dance. She accepts instantly. And later, when Mama sends Lily to fetch her back, Lily finds the two of them in a clinch by the loos.

In the morning the air is as clear as a freshly rinsed glass. By unspoken agreement, when their coach navigates on their way back through the town of Terezín, none of them look out.

11

On their last day in Prague they take a tram to the town centre to buy a present for Richard. When they get off, Mama points to a shop across the street. Her rich uncle owned it before the war, they are still selling jewellery there to this day.

'Wasn't it there, Babi, that you punched that horrible cousin of yours?'

'Yes,' Mama smiles. 'It happened when my mother worked for them, but you know what Lilinka? It must be two, maybe three months ago, I was walking along here and what do I see? A shiny foreign car parked outside. Wouldn't surprise me if those Frankels were here trying to get that shop back.'

'They were greedy, weren't they, Babi?'

'Mama,' Agata murmurs. 'Why do you have to speak to Lily this way about your relatives?'

'I don't care,' Lily says. 'I'll never meet them anyway.'

'Exactly. I don't know why you defend them; they treated my mother like she was dirt.'

'But you told me yourself how your aunt bought you and your mother tickets for the whole season at the opera,' Agata protests. 'She didn't have to do that, did she? It was generous of her.'

Mama stops to stare at her. 'What's up with you? You'd say any nonsense, just to argue.'

'Babi is right. Tell me again, Babi, I love how you socked that stupid girl.'

'Well, one day I came here to see my mother, and...'

Just then Agata notices a dark blue Saab pulling up in front of the shop. An elderly man in a camel-hair coat gets out and disappears inside. The car has an English registration number. Absorbed in her story Mama goes on about how, despite it snowing heavily on that day, she overheard her cousin Ruth order her mother to go out and pull up the heavy shutter to take something from the window for a customer. So Mama slapped her, and said *you go get it yourself*.

'Oh I love Babi,' Lily chuckles.

The man in the camel coat reappears and, clutching some papers, leans into the waiting car. Agata cranes her neck to see who is there. 'Mama, would you recognise them?'

'Who?'

'You know. Them.'

Mama glances up. 'It was a different car. Different colour.' The man turns, and even from that distance Agata sees that in contrast to his grey hair, his eyebrows are strikingly dark. He checks his watch and re-enters the shop.

'I think he's arranging something,' she says. And is met by Mama's mocking brows, dark under her grey bob. The man re-emerges.

'Hello?' Agata tries to attract his attention. 'Excuse me!'

The man glances around, then gets inside the car.

'Excuse me?!' Agata steps into the road. Grabbing her arm, Mama pulls her back, but Agata shakes her off. 'What if it's him?' The Saab starts to edge forward, waiting for a gap in the passing traffic. 'Mr Frankel?' Agata waves. As the Saab enters the flow, she glimpses on the passenger's side a fur collar. 'Mrs Frankel?' She dives into the road. There is a squeal of brakes. She carries on regardless, zigzagging between the cars. Horns honk. Several drivers can't resist sharing their unflattering views about her gender, but Agata doesn't heed them. The traffic lights ahead change to red, she still has a chance to catch up with the Saab. She keeps its roof in her gaze and only loses it when there is a deafening roar and a blast of heat as a giant truck lurches forward.

'Aaa-gaa-taa!' A low-pitched growl rips the air. Agata would have never guessed Mama capable of such an animal sound.

*

This time Mama isn't the only one to be appalled by Agata's conduct. Lily readily adopts her tone, jiggling her head, muttering *Izz, Izz*. To get over the shock, Mama invites them to a nearby café where they have a Sachertorte each. Then Agata excuses herself on account of a headache, she needs to walk it off she says. Fortunately, Mama doesn't object; finally, on their last evening in Prague, she can have her granddaughter all to herself.

Agata isn't far from the jewellers when a freak snowstorm breaks out, as if a bag of semolina has split open. Within seconds the streets resemble a pointillist painting. In an uncanny repetition of more than half a century back, Agata makes out in the blizzard a figure wrestling with the heavy shop shutter. 'We're closed,' the young man warns her, pulling the shutter down. 'Closed,' he repeats when she hangs about the door. And then the snow-caps rapidly accumulating on their heads soften his resolve and he lets her in.

The shop must have been recently modernised. Miraculously, the till is exactly in the spot – to the left of the door – where Agata has always pictured Mama's aunt presiding over the family business. 'How can I help you?' The young man breathes on his wristwatch to let her know he is in a hurry. She asks him if he remembers the elderly English gentleman who has come here earlier on. Around midday. The gentleman in question wore a Cary Grant camel coat, she adds, in an effort to spark his interest. Grant camel coat? The sales assistant is much too young to be familiar either with the fabric or the Hollywood star. Now the caps on their heads are trickling into their collars.

'He has an expensive car,' she tries again. 'Dark blue Saab.'

'900 Turbo.' The sale assistant snaps his fingers. 'Sefton.' Knowing little about motors she waits for a clarification. 'His name,' he fills her in.

'Not Frankel? Are you sure?'

'You don't forget the name of a customer who spends 400 000 crowns for a bracelet for his wife, and then buys a Rolex for himself.' They are sorting out his export duty. And a few other things.

Sefton, Rolex, end of story. She marvels at the breadth of detail this young man is willing to reveal, sadly none of it of any use. To show her gratitude she keeps him company throughout the locking up procedure, entertaining him by trying to guess Mr Sefton's profession that earns him this sort of cash.

'Lawyer,' the young man says. 'Doing business in Poland, here and Hungary.'

And suddenly here is a plausible explanation: what if Mama was right and this Mr Sefton is making enquires on Franz Frankel's and other Eastern European clients' behalf? There is glasnost and perestroika now, and a hope of a new social order that would reinstate private enterprise. What a stroke of luck! Does the sales assistant happen to know, by any chance, where Mr Sefton is staying in Prague?

*

Hotel Danton proves to be one of those soulless seventies buildings fronted by a canopy of brown tinted glass. What Agata doesn't expect is to be greeted by Monsieur Danton himself. With a theatrical swish of his Napoleonic hat he ushers her into a dimly lit subterranean lobby. Not a top league establishment then, despite the masquerade.

'Mr and Mrs Sefton?' she inquires at the reception.

'Room 49, fourth floor.' The receptionist barely glances at her, and once again Agata is surprised by this lax attitude to security. Rattled by the speed of it all she asks if the receptionist shouldn't notify Mr Sefton of her presence. To her astonishment she is told that Mr Sefton is expecting her, the only explanation being that the shop assistant has notified their client.

Agata locates the lift and when the door closes checks in the mirror whether her mascara has survived the snowstorm. She won't take much of Mr Sefton's time, she'll apologise for approaching him in this unusual way and explain that she is looking for a relative who might be a client of his, reclaiming his family property. Fourth floor. She advances along the lengthy corridor with walls thickly padded by brownish fabric as if to restrain unruly guests.

Room 49 is at the very end. After a moment of hesitation – there is still time to turn back – she knocks on the door. No response. She tries again.

Nothing. She turns almost relieved, when behind her a male voice growls 'Come on in.' The door is now partly open. She enters just as a man in a striped city gent's shirt and no trousers lands on a messy bed, stomach down. The air is dense with the smell of alcohol. Even from where Agata stands she recognises the man she saw by the jewellery shop. 'Shut the door,' Mr Sefton commands, rummaging inside the duvet for a wet towel to press over his head. The Cary Grant coat lies rumpled by the bed. No sign of Mrs Sefton.

'Mr Sefton,' she pipes, keen to clear up a possible confusion. 'I came here to ask if...'

'Hosannah! Finally someone speaks the lingo.' Sefton trumpets into his towel. 'At last that idiot Ladislav caught on that punters these days want more than a pair of tits. Sing us a song, will ya?'

Having entered this phantom reality, Agata re-assesses the situation; it's well known that Prague hotels regularly turn a blind eye, even supply prostitutes to their guests.

Surprised by her silence, Sefton lifts his head. 'What the...! Is that bastard scraping the barrel already?'

'I'm not a whore,' Agata adds, for clarity.

'Jeez, little lady, who's ever mentioned trollops? We import per*for*mers. Chardash! Polkaaa! Mazuuurka!' Sefton twists his hairy legs.

The girl she sees tottering from the lift on her way out, isn't much older than Ilona. Under her coat Agata glimpses a skin-tight top and bright pink leggings with a space in between to show off her puppy flesh. 'Please don't go in there,' she begs her. The girl cracks her bubble-gum and, giving off aroma of violets, advises Agata to go lick her own ass.

12

'My old primary school,' Agata points the grey painted building out to Lily. In the front seat Mama checks her watch, then repeats to the taxi driver that she is taking her girls to the coach to London, and they mustn't be late.

*

While Mama was locked up, it was Agata's father who walked her to school. As soon as Mama came back, she took over; and every day she and Agata strode hand in hand, Mama singing her brave, spirit-building morning song: *Hey presto pronto quickly, let our journey pass ever so swiftly.* It was no good. The closer they got, the more Agata would give in to odd rumblings inside her until she had to squat by the kerb and let the sick gush out. Mama would hold her forehead with her warm hand – the best part of that ordeal – and afterwards wipe her tears and blow her nose. Yet turning back was never an option; they pressed ahead no matter what. At the school gate Mama smoothed Agata's hair, patted her cheek and left her there.

Separation anxiety was Bobbie Greengrass's term for her permanent state of panic should Mama vanish again. Mama called it a funny tummy. Now Agata creates out of that misery an musing story for Lily. She describes their fractious journey, sings their song; *It's my story too, so let me*, she silently pleads with Mama who casts her disapproving glances. Finally Mama's patience snaps and she hisses in Czech, 'A bit short-sighted, pushing such ideas into your child's head. Isn't it, Gatushka?'

'Oh Babi, please!' Not speaking the language doesn't stop Lily from catching what's going on. 'Many girls in my school puke. They do it on purpose.'

'What? They vomit on purpose?'

'It's an illness Babi, it's called bulimia.'

Mama shakes her head. 'People in the West,' she mutters, 'making up imaginary illnesses.'

'Seriously. Anorexia and bulimia are imaginary, are they Babi?' Lily sneers. 'This place is so behind!'

At the coach station the drivers are already standing by, sipping coffee from plastic cups. Mama eyes their rumpled uniforms suspiciously, their stubble as thick as the layer of dirt on the coach windows. They look as if they haven't slept in years.

At the last minute, after they have kissed and hugged and said their goodbyes, Mama pulls out a large brown envelope and slips it under Agata's arm. Agata feels the shape of the packet. 'Carlsbad wafers, is it?'

'Stop asking stupid questions.'

Mama waves and they wave back, watching her tiny figure lurch a few steps forward before fading away behind the grimy glass. Will Agata ever see her again? The moment she is gone, Lily feels famished. No funny tummy for her. Swallowing tears, Agata digs out from the food bag a tub of potato salad and Wiener schnitzels wrapped in silver foil, all Lily's favourites. She leans her forehead against the window and chews her food, watching the park where, as a girl, her Babi used to gawk at the legless war veterans, the supermarkets that are springing up at every corner, the crumbling walls with pipes sticking out, the dismal city sprawl. While she eats, Agata runs her fingers over Mama's envelope. Definitely not Carlsbad wafers. She peers in, fishes out another envelope and she is holding a handful of small black and white photos, their edges neatly deckled as if nibbled by a troupe of trained mice.

A couple sits on the grass, middle aged, on a blanket. He is in a shirt, thinning hair, moustache. The woman wears a summer dress. Her face looks set. Next to the man's folded jacket lies a bunch of wild flowers they must have picked earlier, and next to this a small basket and a Thermos flask. In that meadow their city clothes seem out of place. On the other side of the photo Mama's handwriting says, *Matka a otec circa 1936*. So this is Mama's mother, Agata's grandmother. Stern. Not very pretty. Not like Mama. *Grandmother. Grandfather,* Agata samples the words. *Grandparents.* She studies their features for a trace of Mama, or of herself, but the picture is too small to show any detail. Then something about the position of the hillock behind them and the way the branches dip towards a slope, makes her recognise the spot – a clearing in Wild Šárka, a large nature reserve on the outskirts of Prague. The very same place where Mama always took them for their family outings.

Without turning from the window Lily stretches her hand for another Wiener schnitzel.

A young woman in a summer dress, sandals and white socks. Handsome, resembling Mama, but with eyes further apart. A chubby toddler in shorts holds her hand. Freckle-faced. Cheeky. Wearing adult wellies. Behind them a gravel path stretches to a garden pavilion, its contours bleeding into the sky. *Sestra Laura a její syn Hugo.* Sister Laura and her son Hugo. Cousin Hugo.

A different young woman. Slim. Laughing. Arms linked with another. *Annetka a kamarádka.* Mama's younger sister Annette with a friend. More of Annette: in a swimsuit, leaning against a bench by a lake, her arms graceful, strong. Annette – her other aunt, aged about seventeen, squinting into the sun exactly the same way Agata does, with one eye. Again with the same friend on the street, both in smart coats. More of freckly Hugo, this time wearing galoshes in the snow, gazing at a young man in a skiing hat. *Hugo a Franz*. Franz Frankel? Then, folded in half, a densely scribbled page. For a brief moment Agata could swear that she wrote it herself. Then she sees that it is in German.

Liebe Ante... Probably one of Mama's old letters, their handwriting is similar. The printed heading says, *Frauen Koncentrationlager Ravensbrück. Nr. 11074, Block 7/A*. The date: *July 1942*. In 1942 her mother was already in Argentina. Resurrecting the scraps of her school German Agata scans the text:

Dear Aunt, hope you got my letter... some news... about mother... What are Friedrich and grandmother... Financial help... Regards to Laura and her husband... Any news from Doris?... Ach how impatient, how curious I am!... Write soon... Annette.

Mama's little sister Annette writing from a concentration camp.

Outside, the clouds are dark at the bottom, as if lugging a burden. Next to a dusty building site, a line of statues stands wrapped in protective netting that makes them look as if they are in mourning. Mourning whom? Here and there torn plastic bags hang from a branch, shards of colour flapping in the wind – a foretaste of Christmas.

'Mum, I'm full.' Lily hands Agata back the rest of the schnitzel.

13

At Victoria Station, the minute they spot Richard, Lily rushes to press a fridge magnet with a view of Prague castle into his hand. How anxious our daughter is to let her father know that we haven't run away, Agata says to herself. During the drive home Richard's mouth is set in a permanent smile, a novice at the art of grinning. His face seems a little sallow and Agata notices a muscle twitching in his jaw.

'Anything exciting happened while we've been away?' she asks cautiously.

Nothing much. Oh yes, Richard's brother stayed overnight on the way to Dover, him and the family.

'Any plans to stop on their return?'

No, they timed their crossing to drive back home in one go.

'Pity. It would have been fun to see Uncle Roy, Aunt Kim and your cousins again, wouldn't it, Lily?'

The tension in Agata's voice prompts Lily to say that she literally isn't bothered about those boys from up north, who talk funny.

'Whoa,' Richard says. 'Although, those kids do look a bit daft. A bit like you, Lil, when you plaster your fringe with gel.'

'Dad!' Lily kicks his seat.

In the house Richard ceremoniously takes their hands and guides them towards the cellar. Together they stagger down the stairs. The transformation renders Agata and Lily speechless. The walls are now covered with shelves and colour-coded boxes for tools and right in the middle stands a shiny new washing machine. One of these days, Richard promises, he'll tile the floor from one end to the other and it'll be a proper utility room. Having time to himself, Richard had a chance to consider a few things around the house; take the bathroom for instance, always crammed with lotions and creams. Well, Richard has reduced their number to six and feels better for it. Surely, six is a reasonable amount.

'You're fibbing, aren't you Dad?' Lily races up the stairs to check. 'Mum!' she yells from the bathroom. 'I'm on the loo and there's no loo paper!'

'We're buying no more loo paper, Lil!' her father yells back, still smiling but blinking fast, a sure sign of something controversial coming. 'Smudging faeces around your bottom is an unhealthy habit. Seriously, better to clean yourself with water. More hygienic. Cheaper. Arabs do it. And the Turks.

Otherwise, why have a bidet?'

'Mum? Has Dad gone bonkers?' Lily calls again and Agata registers in her voice an undertone of despair.

*

She wakes up in the middle of the night. In Prague, Agata hadn't cried in her sleep, not even once. And now her pillow is wet again. Next to her Richard is snoring softly. She gets up. When she returns from the bathroom Richard reaches out and grabs her. 'Don't you ever fucking dare do that again,' he hisses in her face, squeezing her arm. Making her squirm. 'Dragging Lily away.'

And Agata is almost relieved that the storm has finally arrived. Throughout the night Richard is silently twisting and turning and towards the morning he tells her that while she and Lily were in Prague the biologist in charge of the Reptiles, Invertebrates and Amphibian exhibition checked into rehab. As a result, the exhibition has been put on indefinite hold, and so has Richard's job. Richard offered to keep the frog, but the biologist smuggled Xena in with him. So where Richard's miniature female companion used to float and follow his every move Richard now faces an empty jar full of murky water. And aside from worrying where the next contract might be coming from, Richard now has an additional worry: is that piss-head capable of organising a steady supply of live worms? Keeping the temperature of Xena's blood above a fatal low?

Feeling sorry for him, Agata strokes Richard's chest, her arm still sore where he gripped it. Her anger is gone; it is not the first time she has been on the receiving end of his lashing out, not unlike the mute fury that sometimes uncoils inside her from who knows where. Is that what makes them such a complete couple?

At breakfast, Lily's eyes dart from one to the other and they know that she heard their small-hours interlude. For Richard's benefit, she acts out the funny bits from the skating around Teplice castle, even from Ilona's dramatic performance, although nothing about the visit to Teresín. Laughing, she hauls Richard and Agata from their chairs and kissing them in turn, pulls them together and makes them prance around, cementing their togetherness.

The following night Agata can't sleep again. Despite the darkness, the world doesn't seem totally black, just warmer or cooler tints of grey. Only the digital clock glows in red, the branches outside swaying to its silent count; bits of furniture occupy odd corners, everything familiar yet as if nothing in these rooms truly belongs to her, as if Agata is no more than a temporary presence. She fetches her journal and heads for the cellar. Once she is there, she closes the door behind her without turning on the light and, accustoming herself to the darkness, taps her way to the new washing machine. She runs her fingers inside the metal drum and feeling its cool bumps, remembers how much she used to enjoy using the laundromat. She liked that there was a woman in charge who always smiled despite her missing teeth and called everyone 'pet'. Leaning against the spin-driers, feeling the warmth on her back, she watched people folding their underwear and felt their instant camaraderie. *Everything will be fine*, she assures herself. Richard will get another job and, in the meantime, he can have a rest. Tomorrow she will buy a batch of loo paper and hopefully, adaptable as she is, Xena too will cope.

The chilly draught creeping under her nightie makes her think of Annette: Annetka, her curious young aunt who Agata never met, who squinted into the sun the same way as Agata, and whose handwriting resembles her own. When Lily asked who the people in the photos were, Agata slipped them back into the envelope without a word. Is she turning into Mama? And where is Ravensbrück? Germany? Poland? In the gloom of the cellar she tries to conjure up Mama's sister Annetka. She sees her in a long cold barracks, a shadow of the smiling young woman with swimmers' arms. If Agata were to write her a letter, what would she say? She pulls a pen out of her pocket but instead of her journal, directs it to the place on her left forearm where the skin is the softest. There is no thought, just an impulse. When the nib pierces her, she sucks in air against the rush of pain: to be branded like a beast, is that how Annetka felt? Agata's fingers are now sticky, if with blood or ink, she can't tell.

Back upstairs, she disinfects the mess on her arm, covers it with a plaster. Then she fishes Mama's photographs out again. How tiny these snapshots are, the size of a biscuit; having so much wanted to see them, now Agata can hardly bear to look. As she returns them to their envelope her fingers find something else: a folded sheet of paper, thin and yellowed with age. The text is in German and after skimming through it briefly, though not fast enough to avoid the horror of what it says, she quickly folds it up again and slips it back into its dark corner behind the photos. Then she crams it all into an empty file.

FAMILY she writes on the label. Family, but she already has a family – Lily and Richard – not that Agata keeps a file on them, they are alive. She crosses out FAMILY and writes GRANDPARENTS. Then she adds, AUNTS. And what about that chubby little boy in oversized wellies? She writes COUS… and runs out of space.

14

Next morning Agata phones the Red Cross. After being kept on an endless hold, then redirected to several different departments only to get lost in the exchange system, she has to start over again, only to be told that to log a search for her mother's cousin she'd have to visit their office in person, fill in the relevant forms and provide as much information as possible: if not Franz Frankel's last address, then at least in which year they have lost contact. And of course, the accurate spelling of his name is a minimum requirement. So that's that.

On her way to her session, passing the Christmas baubles twinkling in the shops, she is instantly flooded by the old perennial dread. Dread at not being able to provide a large gathering of people with similar hair, similar eyes, similar noses. Bobbie Greengrass is the only one she could tell about the wretched envy she felt seeing a woman in the supermarket the other day squeezing turkey breasts.

'Big enough for fifteen of us, Tony?' the woman asked her husband.

'Eighteen, you forgot Mark and his lot.'

'Oh yes, Mark, Mandy and what's-his-name?'

'Merrick, but don't fret love, it'll soon be over.'

Today Agata has something else to talk about. She pulls at her sleeve to cover the plaster on her forearm and fishes her journal out of her bag. Today she wants to read Bobbie Greengrass what she has translated from that yellowed document in Mama's envelope. Not the whole thing, just a couple of sentences, that will do. Bobbie Greengrass only says, 'No need, it's for your own record.' Hiding her disappointment Agata stuffs the notebook back; perhaps Bobbie Greengrass is right, perhaps recording things for oneself is enough. 'You remember the worry radar I mentioned last time Agata?' the counsellor asks. 'Please jot down something that made you switch on that radar recently.' She hands Agata a sheet of paper, then discreetly aims her gaze at the window above.

Reconciled to Bobbie Greengrass's methodology, Agata quickly scribbles something down. 'Shall I read it to you?' This time Bobbie Greengrass nods. 'My mother phoned this morning unusually early, at seven. She has that tone, that foreboding tone and at the same time insanely brave, which always scares me. I was sure she was about to drop on me some kind of a bombshell, like she's terminally ill.'

'In other words, your catastrophic thinking,' Bobbie Greengrass is visibly pleased by Agata's willingness to cooperate. 'And you, Agata? Have you managed to challenge your negative thought pattern, like we discussed?'

Negative thought pattern, catastrophic thinking… What on earth is Agata to do with this? 'Yes, I have,' she dutifully reports. 'I've told myself that my mother's call is probably only about a house plant problem. My mother has a close relationship with her plants.'

'Good! Good example of your compassionate voice.'

When Bobbie Greengrass smiles a promise of a dimple appears on her cheek and Agata always wishes to give this dimple more of a chance. Today she has to disappoint her; while having breakfast in her Prague kitchen Mama heard on the radio about the catastrophic train disaster at Clapham Junction and, despite the fact that neither Agata nor Lily nor Richard ever go anywhere by train, Mama instantly assumed that they were all dead.

'I see,' says Bobbie Greengrass, searching for the bit of fur on her rabbit's foot.

'So,' Agata demands, 'please tell me what chance do I have, when catastrophic thinking runs in my blood?'

She spends hours in front of the TV watching men in yellow jackets hacking through mangled train wreckage, searching for casualties; some have to have their limbs amputated right there and then. When Agata hears one of those burly firemen say, 'It's sheer bloody hell, but we treat each person with respect, even if they're dead,' she feels great admiration for him. No, actually, she falls in love with this ruddy-faced man and keeps returning to the news just to see him again. She had once seen a documentary clip about how the Germans who lived near a concentration camp, respectable looking men in thick winter coats, womenfolk with hair done in plaits, were ordered as a punishment to collect the corpses and bury them in mass graves. She was horrified to see them dragging the naked skeletons by their limbs, knocking their heads on the ground like footballs. And now Agata imagines that, had this valiant fireman been there, because of his decency, his simple kindness, he'd have instantly put an end to it. She could swear to it.

In the evening she phones Julia, just to hear her voice. 'I'd so much like you and Ilona to come to us for Christmas,' she says, knowing full well that this is impossible, as even Mama is only allowed to leave the country because Agata married a British citizen. Julia sounds weary. Ilona lied to her, she complains. She said she was staying overnight at a friend's house but went to Miloš, her dad. Julia doesn't know what he gave her to eat, but Ilona came back looking pale. So Julia took her to a faith healer.

'Oh Jesus, Julia!' Agata sighs, her neck suddenly clammy.

'No, seriously,' Julia goes on, 'the other day, when I was out, Ilona almost fainted, and my mother didn't even call a doctor. She simply doesn't take Ilona's condition seriously, no one does.'

*

Why did she agree to meet Klaus Tuttenhoffer this afternoon? Well, she had. He proposed a Covent Garden pub, a popular meeting place for London gays, so Richard tells her. Anyway, Klaus is nearly half her age.

When she arrives, Klaus already occupies one of the alcoves, looking smart in his tweed jacket, a couple of wine glasses in front of him. '*Servus*,' he raises a glass ceremoniously, head bowed.

Servus? Agata hasn't heard this ancient form of *at your service* since childhood, and then only from someone from an older generation.

'We're compatriots from the old Austro-Hungarian Empire, aren't we?' Klaus says, offering her a wineglass. 'Practically brother and sister. No?'

And again Agata can't tell if he is serious. He thanks her for making time to meet him in this busy month of Hanukkah and when she appears a little befuddled, Klaus is quick to apologise if he has miscalculated *Kislev*. He follows it by saying something about lighting of *menorah* candles and she, having no idea what any of this means, remarks that the only thing she'd be lighting this month will be the Christmas tree.

'Oh! You don't keep the old traditions in your *mishpoche?*'

Agata does know what *mishpoche* means, it's one of the few Yiddish words she has picked up from Mama. It means family, but hearing it from this blond Austrian with a pinched nose and flushed cheeks makes it sound comical. The pub is packed, and they end up sitting close to each other, their tête-à-tête interrupted only by Klaus's frequent trips to the bar. Despite his slight build, his ability to consume large quantities of alcohol is impressive and she wonders if he misses the grassy banks of the Danube with their picturesque villages and medieval wine cellars. As soon as she mentions Austria, Klaus makes a face. 'Forget the yodelling and pretty scenery,' he scowls, 'the place is an *Arschloch* full of Nazis. Herr Waldheim our president is the worst.' She had intended to ask what his grandfather did to provoke his mother's nocturnal frenzy, garden destruction but after his comment, she thinks better of it. Whatever his *Opa* did, Klaus Tuttenhoffer can count himself lucky to have had a grandfather at all.

Whenever Klaus heads for a top-up, Agata studies the ornate décor, the gilded mirrors, the mahogany woodwork. She thinks of jotting something about it in her journal, but the upholstery keeps sucking her in, and she lacks the energy. When she finally manages to stand up, lurching about unsteadily, she suddenly wants to quote to her Austrian friend – why him rather than anyone else? – from that yellowed document in Mama's envelope whose contents she has memorised, and thus is now able to recite, even in her present state.

'The heading said *Sterbeurkunde*. *Sterbeurkunde* means death certificate in German, right?' she checks with Klaus Tuttenhoffer as the two of them stagger towards the Tube station.

'Correct.'

'The name of the deceased: Gisela Kraus née Weiss. Born 2 December 1901. The time of death 6 November 1942, at 10 o'clock 35 minutes. Identification number 33634, address Auschwitz, *Kasernenstrasse*. *Kasernen-strasse,*' Agata crunches the sharp syllables in her teeth. 'They named the bloody rows of huts as if they were streets in a town.'

'So… this Gisela Kraus, who was she?' Klaus asks, slowing down.

'Not sure. Probably one of my mother's aunts.'

'Your great-aunt?' He spins to Agata so abruptly that he trips over his own foot.

'They filled it all in carefully by hand, you know. In black ink.' Agata carries on, pretending she hasn't noticed that Klaus is now hobbling. 'Whoever that clerk was, he or she took great care to finish every word with an elegant swirl. Even used a ruler to cross out the *free of charge duty fee* and write -,60 *Reichsmarks*. They charged that poor Gisela Kraus -,60 Reichsmarks for that obscene piece of shit.'

Klaus comes to a standstill, so Agata also stops. 'And did they…' He peers at her through his misted specs. 'Did they put in the… the cause of death?'

'Take a guess,' she says. Then noticing the tip of his nose turning a little pale she takes pity on him. 'No. They must've thought it an unnecessary detail.'

15

Two days before Mama's flight to London, a Boeing jet falls from the sky at Lockerbie. Agata begs her to postpone her departure, Christmas or not. Yet if there is one thing Mama has learned in life, it is never to go back on a decision.

In the meantime, Agata spends days reading the phone directory. She has dialled all the Franks, the Frankelles, the Frankleys and so on, gone through dozens of useless conversations – the net result is zero. On the other hand, those were only London numbers, so there is still the rest of the UK to investigate.

Just as Agata is about to fetch Mama from Heathrow, Professor Chalabot's secretary calls with the latest news. Having learned that, despite her several cancers Mama is still alive, the professor is now keen to check her blood first. ASAP, before it's too late so to speak. As Mama has already expressed her views about testing of Jewish blood, partaking in Professor Chalabot's research would now require cautious diplomacy.

At the airport, Mama looks minuscule. Every time she arrives, there seems to be less of her. Seeing her shuffling behind the baggage trolley, lower lip jutting out as if keeping lips together at the same time as putting one foot in front of the other demands too much of her, Agata's resentment instantly morphs into an overwhelming pity and fear. As soon as Mama spots her she becomes her old self again: smiling and waving, pointing to the bag bulging with presents. 'You know what?' she whispers to Agata even before they embrace, checking around that no one listening. 'That Lockerbie disaster was caused by a bomb made from Czechoslovak Semtex, Gatushka. My neighbour in the plane, a top explosives expert, told me in strict confidence.'

*

For Christmas Eve, Agata lays the table with a hand-embroidered tablecloth, someone's heirloom that she spotted in an antiques shop. She polishes the wineglasses until they glimmer. The logs in the fireplace crackle and she has prepared a perfect meal. Lily and she even put on heels, and Lily daubs a bit of blusher onto her cheeks.

Now the four of them sit in front of the decorated tree, watching over the burning candles. Genuine candles in metal holders, clipped to the branches of a genuine fir tree. The holders come from Prague, the pine tree from Lily's friend's aunt who grows them in Scotland. They paid twenty pounds for it, but

Lily claims that her friend's mother had to pay her sister the same.

'Her own sister doesn't give her a tree from her forest for free? *Tzz, tzz...*' Mama wiggles her head. 'These English!'

'Babi, it's nothing to do with being English!' Lily protests. 'It's just business.'

'Really? Is that what Christmas is?' Mama tests the waters again. 'Anyway, I never understood the habit of stuffing presents in a sock. I think it lacks poetry.'

'I agree, I hate the poetry of Christmas.' Richard says, and three faces look up to watch him scratching his back up and down against the door frame, something Agata has begged him to refrain from in Mama's presence. 'Why can't we give presents in, say, May instead?'

'Oh, come on, Richard, it's a custom,' Mama backtracks in a conciliatory tone. To Agata she murmurs in Czech: *Let me handle him, Gatushka.*

'Babi! Stop whispering to Mummy, it's rude,' Lily cries in a show of solidarity with her father.

Mama, determined to dilute the atmosphere, gives herself *one, two, three* with her fingers and begins to chant: '*Oh mistře! Hej mistře!*' A traditional Czech carol she sings every year, and every year they have to wait until she runs out of words.

'Anyway,' Richard interrupts, blinking rapidly, 'this year being as it is, I'm not giving any presents.'

The effect on Lily is instant: 'But that's not fair!' she wails. 'Mum! Did you hear that?'

'Don't you worry, Lilinka. Your mummy and I have more than enough presents,' Mama jumps in before Agata has a chance to respond, pretending that Richard has ceased to exist. 'Gatushka be so kind, put on some music.'

Without warning Richard kicks a chair. 'Gatushka, Lilinka, Babeenka,' he barks at them. 'I've had enough of your trio.'

'But Ricardo, Mr Ricardo! Not a trio, a quartet! We are four. One, two, three, four!' Mama tries to stop him, but Richard has already slammed the door behind him, making the tree decorations tinkle. They sit in silence, Lily chewing on her lip. After a moment Mama leans to Agata and whispers, 'Poor Mr Ricardo. He worries about his work too much. I'll go and talk to him nicely.'

The door is thrown open and Richard marches in with an armful of artistically wrapped packages. 'Can't you tell when I'm joking? You are so easy to fool, you three.' They all make a show of laughing, especially Lily. From then on everything proceeds without a hitch. Agata's potato salad is a major success. The *carp au bleu* doesn't taste at all muddy, the vanilla pastry Mama brought from Prague melts in their mouths. Richard has triple helpings of everything and Mama, who eats like a bird, not only doesn't arch her eyebrows and say *tzz... tzz...* she declares that the blue fleece Richard is wearing 'befits him handsomely'. And when it comes to unwrapping the presents, there is an overwhelming abundance under the tree, especially from Richard, who never ventures further than their local WH Smith, via their local chemist's. Lily receives each of his gifts, each book, each highlighting pen, each self-adhesive sticker with rapture. Mama and Agata too make noises of appreciation about their year's supply of anti-wrinkle creams. Richard then mixes them each a cocktail of their choice, even Lily.

'Now Dora, this will interest you,' he grins at Mama while sipping on his cognac. 'I heard about some research where they got people of different blood groups to listen to music. And guess what they discovered?'

'No idea. Tell me, Mr Ricardo,' Mama plays along.

'Blood group A preferred harmony, Os were keen on a melody, and As and Bs went for Bach. Do you think there's something in it?'

'To be frank? It just shows that people need excuses: it's their blood... the stars... their parents...' Mama dispatches meaningful glances to Agata, but Agata doesn't mind. Richard and Mama are getting along, that's what matters.

At five minutes to nine Mama turns the TV on: 'I have a surprise for you. Just wait.'

And sure enough, after the main news, there is Mama on the screen, her very own self, her Liberty scarf, a birthday present from Agata, jauntily flung around her neck, being interviewed amongst the ancient tombstones of the Prague Jewish cemetery. She talks to the BBC correspondent Agata and Lily met in Mama's flat, about the rich pre-war *mélange* of cultures and languages that spilled into the music, her favourite Imre Lilosh being an excellent example.

'But I don't recognize myself.' Mama stares bewildered at the tiny woman drowned in the sea of stones jutting around her as if dropped from heaven. 'Is this really me?' she keeps asking, rubbing her eyes.

'Yes!' they yell. 'It is you, Mama! You Babi, Dora! You're famous!'

Mama leans closer to the screen. 'Is your TV out of focus?'

They exchange puzzled looks. Then Agata notices that the white of Mama's eyes appears shockingly red; and now Mama admits that yes, she did feel a little pressure in her eyes earlier on. She didn't want to spoil their Christmas, so she didn't say anything.

Repeating, 'You were great Mama, really great,' Agata leads her to her room, Lily in tandem, shadowed by Richard. Once they are there Richard picks Mama up and deposits her gently on the bed as if she had twisted her ankle, making her sigh with surprise, almost delight. Agata pulls off Mama's shoes, Lily runs to fill her glass with fresh water, then offers to rub her face with Richard's new anti-wrinkle lotion, while Richard, uncertain about his further use, hovers by the door.

'Just let me rest. I'm sure I'll be alright in the morning,' Mama assures the impromptu party around her bed. She waits for Lily and Richard to leave, then lifts herself up and whispers to Agata, 'Have you noticed, Gatushka, how my stupid eyes made Mr Ricardo finally feel the man of the family?'

*

In the morning Mama can barely see. Agata drives her to Moorfields eye hospital where they join a queue struck with various afflictions, one man's eyes swollen to such a degree that you would be forgiven for thinking that he wore a sausage where others wear glasses. It is Christmas Day, so there is only one doctor in attendance. When they finally call Mama's name Agata ignores her mutterings that she is perfectly capable of managing the consultation by herself, and follows her in.

The doctor who receives them has the velvety face men with dark hair get with stubble. He doesn't bother to introduce himself although his manner is polite, and behind his black-rimmed glasses, his eyes stir in Agata the emotion she often feels around short-sighted men. Her father wore glasses all his life and Mama claims that they were the main reason why all his female patients kept falling in love with him. Ever since then Agata has secretly associated short-sightedness with sex.

After finishing his examination, the doctor explains that Mama has a bug in her eyes. An eye bug? Mama peers at him sceptically, she knows for sure it is an infection. In fact something similar happened to her not long ago and this is what her doctor in Prague, who by the way happens to be a professor at Charles University, had diagnosed. Unperturbed, the Moorfields doctor says he is going to give her some drops and a tube of cream. Nodding in Agata's direction he adds that to avoid passing the bug to someone else her mother must be careful not to share her towel. Little does he know about Mama's complicated towel habits.

On their way out they stop to wait for the prescription. When a nurse brings it out Mama folds it in half and, shaky with the effort, fumbles in her handbag for the special zipped pocket. Agata's offer of help is again rejected on the grounds that Mama lives alone and is therefore trained to cope with life's adversities. While this is going on Agata observes the receptionist filing some papers into a folder. As she closes it Agata gets a quick view of its cover. And what it says scrawled in thick red marker is: *Dr Frankler's Clinic*. Frankler, not Frankel, but near enough.

In the car Mama entertains them with how the world appears to her through the fog in her eyes – the skyscraper skyline reminds her of snow-capped mountains, the furry pompoms of street lights, the traffic swirls around them, and as they cross Waterloo Bridge, the river turns into a giant lizard about to rise and shake them off its scaly back, and Agata busies herself with devising scenarios for how to approach Dr Frankler.

16

Agata imagines they'd be sitting in the dark, her chin wedged against the metal of the apparatus, their noses almost touching. Reflected in his spectacles she'd glimpse the orange inside of her retina. *Tell me again,* Dr Frankler would say, having instructed Agata to look towards his left ear, then towards his right, *what exactly is your complaint?* Would this be the moment she'd ask him if anyone in his family came from Prague, or would she carry on a little longer with her charade about the flashing lights marring her vision, the zigzags. Though once she is face to face with him, Agata might ask him straight away.

Except the reality is different. The reality is that Agata is once again sitting in a crowded hospital waiting room and the receptionist can't even guarantee if it will be Dr Frankler who will see her. And then, when she least expects it, there he is, Dr Frankler himself striding out of the surgery in a winter overcoat, looking tired and shorter than Agata remembers. She stands up and follows him into the corridor.

At first, Dr Frankler has no recollection of them meeting, but when Agata reminds him of her mother here on a visit from Czechoslovakia, he nods finally. A perfect moment to enquire if, by some remote chance, anyone in Dr Frankler's family comes from Prague. 'Forgive me this personal question,' Agata apologises, 'it's just because your surname is similar to my relatives – although I'm not sure about the actual spelling.' To which Dr Frankler remarks in his faultless Oxbridge English that the spelling of his name is neither here nor there, as back in Vilnius, Lithuania, which his folks had left at the turn of the century, modifying your name every few years had been something of a local custom.

Agata returns to the receptionist to cancel her appointment. And then, by pure chance, she catches up with Dr Frankler again by the hospital entrance. They step out at precisely the same moment. It is snowing now, but only slightly, the snowflakes dissolving as soon as they touch the pavement. Enough to generate in the passers-by an air of fellowship; of giving each other looks as if they are participants in an extraordinary, festive event. She and Dr Frankler also incline their heads towards one another. 'It won't last long,' he points to the sky. 'I'm popping round the corner for a pint. Would you like to join me?'

She had expected a long wait at the hospital, so having time on her hands, Agata accepts his offer. Dr Frankler orders a beer, and she settles for a G&T,

proud at being so worldly. They talk more about Vilnius where Dr Frankler, on his only visit, witnessed a good ten inches of snow. He says he has a house in Suffolk, that he shares with his wife and children, and during the week he stays in a basement *pied-à-terre* not far from here. And Agata thinks she hears in his voice a hint of sadness or maybe even an invitation? He has a full fleshy mouth and when he talks, he briefly brushes his hand against hers and Agata notices his slim fingers, no doubt a bonus for an eye surgeon. The scent of his aftershave reminds her that she finds glasses on men attractive. When he takes them off his face becomes instantly softer, as if it lacks contours, and Agata imagines how it would be to make love with someone practically bearing her family name – perhaps it would feel like with a cousin. While she wonders if Dr Frankler is circumcised, the pager in his breast pocket goes: a man has fallen through a glass roof with not a bone broken, but eyes full of splinters. Rushing back to perform an emergency operation Dr Frankler takes leave of her by Old Street station and again she feels a pang of sadness, though now she knows that the pang is hers. She wouldn't have minded having this doctor, with his fingers covered with fine black hair, for a relative.

*

The moment she opens the front door she hears Mama shouting, 'I just put the eye drops in, someone get the phone!' Agata picks it up, just in time.

'Hello, this is Nigel Hartley from the BBC. I'm calling from Bonn. Sorry to disturb you, but I understand that Doris Weiss is staying with you?'

'Yes, she is. Mama? It's the BBC man from Bonn.'

'Hello Nigel. Hello!' Mama is already pulling the receiver from Agata's hand. 'How are you, Nigel?' Her genuine warmth with casual acquaintances attaches them to her for life. 'Oh that was my daughter Agata. You met her in Prague, remember? We watched your brilliant reportage, it was unbelievable and… Sorry Nigel, who saw the programme, who phoned you?… Stoloff? No, I don't know anyone of that name… Aha. Her married name, I see… Hmm… hmm…' she keeps nodding. 'Yes, Renee Kraus. Yes, of course, she's my cousin. On my mother's side.' Mama makes an impatient face at Agata, and her voice begins to chip. Agata feels as if air is being sucked out of her chest. *Mama's cousin on her mother's side.* The novelty, the utter novelty of those words. 'Just a minute, Nigel,' Mama gropes around. 'I have to look for, have to find…'

'Do you want me to write something down for you?' Agata whispers, handing her a biro. Mama waves her off. *She is my cousin,* her mother said. *My cousin on my mother's side.* Crouching on the sofa, clutching the phone, Mama listens to the voice from Bonn passing her the news about her lost family. Her expression betrays nothing. Fearing her own reaction, Agata quietly takes herself to the kitchen. And only after she closes the door behind her she allows herself to succumb to an onslaught of sobs. It is true then, it is true. Someone, a relative, is alive.

When Mama eventually comes in, she thrusts a scrap of paper into Agata's face. 'Here.' She hisses, her bloodshot eyes glaring at her. 'You wanted a family, so now you have one. Happy?'

An out of London phone number. Next to it a name scrawled in shaky letters: RENEE STOLOFF.

'Who is she?'

'You heard – my cousin, my aunt's daughter. Not the one who married the man with the jewellery shop, the other one, the one who was psychiatrist in Berlin. She saw me on TV and phoned the BBC.'

'A doctor in Berlin? I don't think I ever heard of her.'

'No, that was her mother, aunt Gisela, Gisela Kraus. Her daughter, my cousin Renee, she came here in the *Kindertransport* after their family escaped from Berlin to Prague. They stayed in our flat. Her parents ended up in Auschwitz. Like everyone else in that flat.'

Gisela Kraus – the name on the Auschwitz death certificate. 'But Mama, I was under the impression that they had all died in concentration camps.'

'You and your impressions! The problem with you is that you don't listen.'

'But…' Agata can't stop herself, 'if you knew she came here, haven't you ever tried to find her?'

'I'm telling you; she was only a child. I don't know what happened to her, I hardly knew her.' Mama almost yells at her. She grabs a glass yet can't manage to turn the tap to pour herself some water, her hands tremble too much.

'Ok, ok Mama,' Agata extricates the glass from her fingers and fills it up. 'It all happened a bit fast, don't worry, everything is going to be all right.'

'Who's worried?' Mama snarls.

'Of course you're not worried. There's no problem, nothing the two of us can't handle.'

Mama passes her a look of contempt. 'What are you blabbering about, your brain's gone soft?'

Ignoring her, Agata suggests that she would make them something warm to drink. And a little something to eat. Joy rushes through her with such force, such ferocity, that she can't stop grinning. Yes, they should have tea. And crackers. And cheese. Maybe some marmalade. 'And then let's call her, shall we Mama?' She bends down to kiss Mama's cheek.

'You call her,' Mama growls.

*

The phone is answered by a light male voice. Agata introduces herself as the daughter of Doris Weiss, she asks to speak to Renee Stoloff.

'That's my wife,' the voice says and Agata hears him shout, 'Renee! Renee! It's your cousin Doris who vanished! Renee will be thrilled to hear from you. Are you calling all the way from Prague?'

'No, it's my mother who's your wife's cousin. I'm calling from London.'

'*London?* What are you doing in London?'

When Agata tells the man that she has lived in London for many years and that her mother happens to be here on a visit for Christmas and is in fact sitting right next to her, right now, he exclaims, 'What a shame that we didn't met sooner! Imagine all the arguments we could have had around the Christmas turkey!'

'Yes, yes imagine!' she laughs, avoiding looking at Mama who bears this outburst of jollity with a blank face.

'Renee has bad flu, she's been in bed for weeks,' the man tells Agata. 'The other evening, she switched on the nine o'clock news and suddenly there was Doris. She recognised her immediately. 'Harry, she called me, I've just seen my cousin Doris.' And of course I thought she was running a fever, poor thing. Here she comes, here's Renee! Darling, they're in London.'

'Hello?' A tiny, soft squeak. Agata presses the receiver into Mama's hand.

'Hello, this is Doris. Nice to hear you, Renee. How are you?... Na yah, I'm also happy to talk to you, do you want to speak German?... English, you prefer English, I understand. So Renee, how old are you now?... I see, I see. And what do you do?... Yes, in life.'

To hear Mama speak to her cousin as if she were still a child makes Agata instantly choke up. The manner in which her mother perches on the sofa, one shoulder raised, an elbow awkwardly sticking out, her bob ruffled, reminds her of the wretched creatures stranded on the beach after an ecological disaster. And all she wants to do is to warm Mama with her own body, to wrap her in a blanket and carry her to safety in her arms. Instead Agata makes her way back to the kitchen; the last thing Mama needs are her tears – Renee is Mama's lost cousin, not hers. What would this Renee be to her? A second cousin, someone twice removed?

When Mama finally appears her face is ashen.

'What did she say, Mama?'

'Nothing much,' Mama shrugs. 'No real profession, just a bit of social work, something like that.'

'Any children?' Mama shakes her head. 'Oh, maybe she will adopt me,' Agata suggests, laughing. A bloodshot eye darting her way leaves her in no doubt that was a wrong thing to say. How crass of her! 'So when are you two planning to meet?' This might be a bit difficult, Mama replies, since her cousin lives somewhere near Oxford. 'Oxford! What's difficult about living near Oxford? Oxford isn't far, I love Oxford!' Another piercing gaze from Mama. 'What's that place they live in called?'

Mama silently hands her a piece of paper.

'Chislehampton,' Agata reads out. 'Chislehampton.' She fetches the road atlas, scans the index. 'Here it is. Chislehampton, what a fun name.' *Slow down, just slow down,* she cautions herself, but her feet want to dance. 'It's not far at all, let's go to see them tomorrow.'

'Out of the question,' says Mama. 'Renee has flu and I with my eyes… We agreed to phone. Maybe in a week.'

'A week? You haven't seen each other for fifty-odd years, you didn't even know you were both alive and you're going to wait a whole week?'

Agata takes the atlas with her to bed. She has already reported everything to Richard and Lily during the dinner, gone over all the details again afterwards, until they begged her to give it a rest. Now she makes herself comfortable next to Richard who is absorbed in a book. She opens the atlas and looks up Chislehampton again: *Chislehampton, Easington, Tiddington, Littlemore* – her tongue fondles those homely, old-fashioned words. She runs her fingers over the pale green *Designated Area of Outstanding Beauty,* traces the blue meanders of the Isis. 'Ricky?' She tugs at Richard's arm. 'That Chislehampton place, it looks idyllic. Don't you think?'

He glances over his reading glasses. 'How can you tell from a map?'

'Easy,' she says. 'Look: here it says *little* wood, here it shows a *little* road winding through *little* villages – who knows, one day Lily may study in Oxford and drop in on them in Chislehampton and…'

'Why would Lily drop in on them?'

'Because they are almost her aunt and uncle, of course.' Agata has never called anyone aunt and uncle before. 'They sound really charming,' she gushes on. 'Harry, Renee's husband, he's Russian, he told Mama. Well, his great-grandparents were, and he has a business restoring icons, he could give Lily one for her twenty-first birthday. He may even know some people who organise exhibitions who could commission you…'

'Hey Agu, steady on.' Richard interrupts her. She smiles, leans against him and he goes back to his book. While she… she decides that from now on things will change: this will become a happier house; they will have the Stoloffs around for meals, it will be a regular thing. She kisses Richard and reaches to stroke him under the cover. Richard removes her hand.

'What?' she asks.

'I can't stand it when you get like this,' he says.

'I'm not *like this,* I'm just happy.'

'Ah, madam's happy, so the whole world has to stand to attention.'

'Not the whole world, just you,' Agata tries with her hand again.

'Sorry, no.' Richard murmurs, turning from her. She laughs and hugs him from behind; somehow the existence of Renee Stoloff has made everything lighter.

*

Bobbie Greengrass proposes that Agata should try to visualise her caring, compassionate image. This is supposed to activate the parts of the brain that make her feel good. The first image that pops in Agata's head is their neighbour's kitchen from her childhood. While Mama was in prison, what Agata wished for most was to be invited to play with her friend next door, where the stove was always hot from baking and the lino on the floor shiny as butter; that kitchen was an oasis of safety during those motherless days and weeks and months, when the world seemed permeated by gloom. If this isn't exactly what Bobbie Greengrass has in mind, her next question about what feelings would a *compassionate image* generate is easy to guess: words like warmth, love, comfort… all words that Agata can't bring herself to say – such words seem as alien to her as if she were asked to speak Chinese. Instead she announces, 'I have news.'

'Ehum?' Bobbie Greengrass nods non-committally.

'My mother's cousin has turned up living in England. My mother never told me about her, though she must've been aware of her existence. So, either she genuinely forgot her, which I find hard to believe, or… or my mother simply decided not to ever mention her.'

Bobbie Greengrass takes a bit of time to respond. 'Well… Let me ask you: how does this make you feel, Agata?'

'Awful,' Agata admits, yesterday's lightness gone. 'Awful. And ashamed.'

'Ashamed?' Her counsellor observes her with a sad grimace. Trying to avoid her gaze Agata focuses on the naked heating pipes she'd noticed the first time she came. What more is there to say? That she is mad at Mama for keeping her cousin from her? That she hates her?

'Seems to me, Agata,' says Bobbie Greengrass after another moment of silent rumination, 'seems to me that your mother has projected onto you her own shame and guilt for having survived, while others in her family were killed. Maybe that's why she wiped that cousin out of her mind. Because that cousin too dared to live.'

'Please don't say that. Please don't.' Agata begs her, tears dripping onto her hands. 'Can't you see that my mother was a victim herself? She endured so many tragedies with so much courage. The least she can expect of me… the very least I should be able to…'

'Agata, listen to me!' Bobbie Greengrass stops her. 'Your mother has suffered, but you are not guilty,' she says. No, she instructs Agata, her voice maddeningly kind. Warm. *Compassionate*. 'You didn't cause the Holocaust.'

'Didn't I?' Agata glares at her. 'What makes you so fucking sure?' It is important, vitally important to let Bobbie Greengrass know how crazy, how preposterous she finds her pronouncement. How accurate.

'You didn't cause Auswitch,' Bobbie Greengrass adds for emphasis.

For a second or so Agata remains speechless. *'Auswitch?'* she spits out. 'Has no one ever told you how to say that word?' As soon as she hears herself, she is mortified, as if knowing how to pronounce Auschwitz grants her a special status, a permission for righteousness.

'Au-schwitz,' Bobbie Greengrass corrects herself, colouring a little. 'My mistake. Forgive me.'

They spend the last few minutes in uneasy silence.

*

She finds Mama clutching a nail brush and a bar of soap in an effort to restore a plant that Agata had recently chucked in the dustbin, infested with mites. 'You poor old thing, look what they've done to you,' Mama talks to the plant, her eyes red and sticky. 'Getting rid of you as soon as you're not well.'

As she listens to these accusations, Agata has a distinct feeling Mama knows that she has spoken about her to Bobbie Greengrass. 'Mama, don't you remember that the doctor warned you not to do anything strenuous?'

'Why? There's nothing wrong with me,' says Mama. 'While you were out, I edited a whole chapter about Dvořák. Then I listened to the news. There was another demonstration in Prague, mainly students. The police attacked them with tear gas. How's this going to end?' She sighs, rubs the soap on the brush and, heaving with exertion, resumes scrubbing the leaves. 'Now that's better, isn't it? Now you can breathe again. Muuuch better.'

Watching rivulets of sweat dribbling down her mother's neck, staining her blouse, Agata can't resist a feeling of satisfaction, even of revenge. *Serves you right, serves you right*, pounds in her head. *Had you put more effort into gathering the shreds of our family, you wouldn't have to beg plants for love.*

17

Days fly by while waiting for Renee's call. In the meantime, Agata's friend Evie, her boyfriend Uli and daughter Sarah arrive from Munich.

After Mama was let out of jail and the whole family returned from their exile, most of Mama's friends were terrified even to say hello on the street, but Evie's parents invited them to share their cramped Prague flat. It took three whole years before Agata's family was allowed their own apartment. For Agata and Evie, their cohabitation was a lucky turn, they each gained a ready-made sister. That's why, according to Mama, the moment Evie appears Agata goes bananas and everyone else might just as well cease to exist.

Uli turns out to be considerably younger than Evie, and almost twice her height. Every time Uli's paw strokes Evie's head, which just reaches his chest, Sarah averts her eyes. How come both Agata and Evie have ended up with large blondish men, so unlike their fathers? Evie is four years younger than Agata and Agata remembers how, in the middle of the night, she would sit her sleeping friend up, watch her lolling head, inhale her hot breath and feel a strange thrill.

Now, at night, the top floor of the house groans and creaks with Evie's muffled cries of love. During the day it rattles with her laughter. When she doesn't give herself over to lovemaking or laughing, Evie scrutinises the world, her eyebrows two saffron husks, her eyes dizzyingly green and wide as if in a state of constant astonishment. With a face like that, how could you ever be unhappy? Evie recently qualified as a psychoanalyst and, besides Uli, there is now another new fixture in her life: a couch from which her patients confide their secrets. Agata can't wait to tell her about the astonishing, the unexpected emergence of Renee, her newly-found relative, but Evie rarely leaves Uli's side and even during mealtimes she sits on his lap, so it is anyone's guess if their nods and grunts relate to the food or to some hidden sensations in their flesh. On the rare occasion when Evie leaves the room, Sarah quickly climbs on Uli's vacated lap and presses herself against his large torso.

'That girl seems very disturbed,' Mama whispers to Agata when they find themselves alone. 'And her name! What made Evie give her that name?'

'Why? Isn't Sarah a perfectly regular name?' Agata pretends not to understand.

'To be called Sarah in Germany? *Tzz, tzz*... What does she need to prove?'

When Agata asks what she means, Mama pins her with sad, reproachful eyes.

Evie brings Agata a few snapshots from their shared childhood, she has a full box of them in Munich, she says.

In one photo, Agata is bent under her young friend's weight, giving her a piggyback ride. In another, Agata is sprawled on the grass balancing the laughing Evie on her matchstick legs, their respective characteristics already there: her friend's disarming beauty, her sweet disposition, Agata's dogged perseverance.

They set about exploring the town. Agata would prefer to spend more time with Evie alone, but Evie claims that Uli would get jealous. What can she say in the face of such devotion? Clearly, he worships Evie, and huddles in her shadow, no mean feat for someone of his build. Despite her eye condition, Mama too refuses to be left behind. Forced into an uneasy friendship, Lily and Sarah track behind them, a silent duo. Agata hopes that with time Lily will become fond of Sarah, the way she learned to love Ilona in Prague. Richard, who isn't keen on socialising, stays put in his studio.

One afternoon they undertake a pilgrimage to Evie's guru's house in Swiss Cottage. While Mama, Uli and the girls watch a video about Sigmund Freud's life, Agata and Evie inspect his famous couch. Standing in front of it, Evie spreads her arms, gauging its size. 'About one and half meters, none of my clients would fit.' And after checking that no one is around, she crawls under the rope to stretch herself on the legendary piece of furniture. 'It's weird to be lying here, where it all began,' she reports. 'Come and try it, Gatushka.'

Not as daring, Agata speaks to her from where she is. 'Dear *Fräulein*, do tell me about your infantile sexuality. Or shall I massage your chest first?'

Amidst bouts of laughter – is there no limit to how much her friend can laugh? – Evie tells Agata how much she hated her when they were children, because Agata bossed her around. And, curiously, sometimes she still feels like that, after all these years. Evie has never dared to tell her until now, from this couch. Before Agata can match her friend's bravery and admit the resentment that she felt, and perhaps still feels, about Evie's striking beauty, but mainly to tell her about the wondrous, the utterly unexpected appearance of Renee Stoloff, Lily runs in. 'The film's finished,' she announces. 'That Dr Freud liked dogs best.'

On their last evening her friend sits Agata and Mama on the sofa to show them a video of her belly dancing troupe *Sisters of the Desert*. 'I'm afraid she's confused, poor Evie,' Mama whispers to Agata as they watch Evie, unrecognisable under her gaudy make up; one of twenty or so Bavarian maidens shaking their tummies, jiggling their tasselled breasts to the accompaniment of wailing music. 'A person with her issues, curing others? And that Uli of hers – so much younger and so tall. A proper Aryan type. Poor Evie, she laughs so much, it must be a nervous tic.'

As for Uli, save for muttering endearments in Evie's ear, he remains mute. Agata wonders if his reluctance to speak has anything to do with the scar she noticed near his lip, though when she looks closer it seems more of a minor irregularity than an injury that would affect his speech. And as for Sarah, the first time she opens her mouth is when Agata drives them to the airport to catch their flight back to Munich. '*Die Autobahn… die Wolke…*' Sarah comments on the view in the window, visibly relieved that their visit will be soon over. '*Die Sonnenkäfer,*' she whispers, gently removing a ladybird from Uli's hair.

Outside, England is passing: tidy fields, trimmed parks, cemeteries with strict rows of grey stones. 'I wouldn't be seen dead under one of those,' Agata remarks, and she and Evie give each other a look only they understand. When they all lived in Evie's flat, Agata used to drag her little friend to watch funerals in the local graveyard. Their parents had no inkling about those trips. Holding hands they would join a procession of mourners, listen to the priest, wait their turn to throw clumps of wet earth on the coffin. No one ever asked where those two girls came from, perhaps because of Evie's angelic looks. She was too young to make out what was going on. But for Agata, knowing that there was a dead person in the box, the fantasy of it falling open, was irresistible. Carved on tombstones she read the cryptic stories: *born, died, tragically taken away…* Mesmerised, she watched the other children misbehave in their Sunday clothes: *shhh… shhh… it's your grandmother, your uncle, have respect*. Apart from her parents, whom she knew to be immortal, there was simply no one for Agata, not even a distant uncle whom she could bury and mourn. No fresh graves to mess around. No chance of ever wearing those fancy dresses.

*

She returns to a hollow house. Mama and Lily have laid the table for dinner, there are napkins and fresh flowers in a vase. The first thing Agata notices is the frown on Richard's face. Has he grown so fond of her friend that now that Evie is gone, he feels the same emptiness that she does? She suggests they go for a drink afterwards, just the two of them. Instead of replying, Richard removes the vase from the table. Mama brows lift in an arch: in Mama's books, a flower arrangement on a dinner table equals culture. Her silent disapproval impels Lily to inform her that her father suffers from hay-fever. As soon as they sit down Richard gets absorbed in something else: sliding the straw mat until it lies parallel to the edge of the serving dish. Dead parallel. His task achieved, as if possessed by an urge to master every object in sight, he positions the mineral water bottle to the centre of the table. The very centre.

Having read somewhere that such obsessive behaviour is typical for those who fear losing control, Agata assumes there is still no news about the frog-lizard exhibition.

'How about having some music with our dinner?' Mama proposes to break the spell of Richard's tidiness. 'Put on the Lilosh string quartet, Gatushka, it's a new instrumentation.' Nothing can save their meal. Every time the cello's sonorous sound builds up to something resembling a tune, it is crushed by the modernist lament of the fiddles. As they silently chew their food, Richard tells Mama that he is not surprised that her daughter, brought up in an atmosphere of cultural snobbery, now needs psychological help.

Agata kicks him under the table, but it's too late, they are headed for one of those flare-ups. Mama's response is swift: 'Nowadays everyone believes in all this psychologising coming from America,' she says. 'Even children. While we in *Mittel Europa* rely on common sense. Yes, common sense and healthy instinct.'

This Lily takes as a prompt: 'Babi,' she barks at her grandmother. 'Don't you know that Mum literally lost any healthy instinct, like, ages ago? Tiptoeing around you, and now with Dad.'

Mama gives Agata one of her plaintive looks. 'Lilinka, that's no way for a young girl to speak about adults. You don't know how lucky you are. You have a nice family, nice house, nice garden…'

'Oh shut up, Babi!' Lily shrieks. 'You just pretend that everything's fine, even when it's not. You always, always do that!'

In the ensuing silence Mama looks stony-faced and Richard flutters his eyelids as though he has just woken up. He gets up, announcing he is expecting an important phone call. The moment he is gone Mama leans closer to Lily. 'Now listen well, young lady,' she says in the same insistent whisper that used to terrify Agata. 'No one, not even you, my granddaughter, will address me in this manner – like they talked to me in jail. Never again. Please remember that, Lilian.' Lily endures her speech with head bowed, eyes glued on her half-eaten dinner.

Later that evening Agata finds Mama on her bed, raising and lowering her legs, her exercise routine adjusted for a restricted space. 'Mama, I hope you know that Lily didn't mean it, nor did Ricky. We all love you and want you to stay with us as long as you want.'

'Stop selling me your mad family,' Mama mutters, bending her legs first to the right shoulder, then to the left one, neck straining with the effort. 'The main thing is… the main thing is that I'm self-sufficient. I know many much younger who can't even do *pi-pi* by themselves.' To mark the end of her routine Mama kicks her legs playfully in the air, then lets them fall with a loud exhalation, the raised corners of her mouth letting Agata know that all is well again. Perhaps a suitable moment to mention Professor Chalabot.

Instantly, Mama's eyes become startled pins. '*Hereditary* research?' She spits out each syllable as if a razor was cutting her gums. 'I'm sorry, Gatushka, but I already told you, I'm no laboratory rat.' And to let Agata know that the topic is closed she shuts her eyes, her nose sticking out pale and sharp, like on a death mask. What is in store for them? Will Agata one day have to hold a cup to Mama's mouth, comb her hair as if she were the child and Agata her mother? Those small, mundane acts Mama never had the chance to perform for her own parents. How will it end? Will Agata be there? All this is as unimaginable, as far-fetched, as the cessation of the sun.

*

The call comes just as she is beginning to lose hope. 'Helloooo!' The chirpy voice belongs to Renee's husband, Harry. 'Bad news I'm afraid. Renee has lost her voice. Perhaps it'd be better if we meet next time your mother comes.' Next time? Next time Mama is coming will be in the summer, Agata warns. 'What a shame.' Harry chuckles.

'So what if we come just for a little while?' Agata suggests. 'Just so that the two cousins see each other.'

'To see her?' Behind her Mama rubs her swollen, bloodshot eyes.

Could Harry put her on to his wife? Agata politely demands.

'Of course, of course! Renee dear, it's Agatha for you. Or is it Agathé?'

'It's Agata.'

'Of course. You must forgive me, you're so new to us. Here is Renee. Here she comes.'

'Hello my dear.' A wisp of a voice.

'Hello Renee. I'm sorry to hear that you're not well, but we've been so much looking forward to meeting you. We wouldn't stay long.

'Oh it's not that, dear. It's... oh I don't know how to say it. When I spoke to Doris, I felt...' Soft, tiny gulps of air.

'I understand. Speaking to my mother after such a long time must be very emotional.'

'I heard some resentment in Doris's voice,' Renee interjects in a halting whisper. 'I have a good ear for that sort of thing.'

'Resentment?' Agata glances at her mother ostentatiously examining her nails. 'You must be imagining this, Renee.'

'Perhaps it's been a bit too quick,' Renee says. 'When we made the call, we never thought that Doris would be just an hour away. So I've come to a decision that...'

I mustn't let her go on, must stop her right now, Agata tells herself. *I must make her forget what she was about to say.* 'There is no problem, Renee. Mama, I mean Doris is staying another week. It's amazing, isn't it, that you're in Oxfordshire and I've been living in London all this time.'

'I think we should exchange letters first,' whispers a voice from far, far away.

Damn! Agata tightens her grip on the phone. 'Renee? Renee, I do very, very much want to meet you,' she says, deliberately avoiding her mother's stare. 'When you feel better, please contact me, will you?' Silence at the other end. 'Renee?'

'My dear, Renee told me to say that we wouldn't dream of letting a cousin disappear again.'

'What's the problem?' Mama asks, when Agata puts down the phone. Gently, she breaks the news to her: Cousin Renee doesn't want to meet her, not yet. She'd prefer a letter. *Tzz!* Mama shrugs, glancing out the window. 'People write to me every day asking for this and that. I've no time to write letters.'

'So you're not going to write to her?'

'I already told you, I'm very busy. I have a lecture about Janáček to prepare. And millions of other things.' Seeing the expression on Agata's face, she softens. 'Look, Gatushka, I'm not saying I'll never write to her. You must understand, she was a child when I last saw her. I'm glad that you now have family here, but she means nothing to me.'

But she is your blood! Your fucking blood! We share that stuff with her! Agata wants to scream at her. She does nothing of the sort.

*

Richard has at last been promised a show, called *Time Instruments*. And Mama was right: the bomb that blew up the plane over Lockerbie was indeed made with Czech Semtex, but to Mama, the most astounding news is that in Poland, Solidarity has forced the government to promise free elections. Unbelievable! Does this mean the end of communism? And what will come next? How will it work? Mama's eyes lose their angry redness, and she is ready to resume her life back in Prague.

Agata is already beginning to miss Mama as she drives her to the airport. It is early morning and though the branches are glittering with frozen drops, the misty sun is already thawing the road. The steam rising from every surface makes Agata feel as if they are floating through a gigantic alchemical laboratory. Mama doesn't seem to notice, she sits folded into herself, her mind, no doubt, already storing the good moments they have had, all the happy times. To distract her, Agata tunes into a classical music station and as an operetta duet bursts into the car, she tries her luck. 'It's Lehar, isn't it?'

'Offenbach.' Mama pats her arm. 'Near enough, darling, near enough.'

At the airport, as they come to the point where Mama will have to leave Agata behind, Mama announces, apropos nothing, that she has become a member of a church choir. 'I haven't converted to Catholicism,' she chuckles, when Agata looks startled. 'It's just that I like singing and they need new members. The woman who signed me up was so happy, she gave me a bottle of Vino Santo!'

'Great. You can have it after your TV supper when you get home tonight.'

'No, I'll keep it for when Petr comes.'

'Petr? Which Petr?'

'Don't look so worried, Gatushka.'

'Worried? Me? What about?'

'Aha!' Mama laughs, gives Agata a quick hug and a brief peck on cheek, then marches off. Agata watches her showing the passport, disappearing behind the grey partition then briefly reappearing to send her bag through the X-ray. She balances on her toes to catch the last glimpse of her: trundling through the detector gate, exchanging a few words with the security guard, turning to collect her handbag. It brings them temporarily face-to-face, but Mama is now too far away to see her.

18

'And then she vanished. Safer for me not to know that she was locked up, my father decided. Unwise of him, perhaps, but the political trials were in full swing, and friends of my parents were sentenced to death by hanging. So I was told Mama was away because of work. I was six and had just started school. The dinner ladies used to sit me in the kitchen to feed me, they must have guessed where my mother was.' Agata pushes her fingers under her thighs. Sits on them. Grins at Bobbie Greengrass. 'As my mother says – one should never feel sorry for oneself.'

'Why not? What's wrong with feeling compassion for that child who missed her mother?'

'That year my father sent me to a summer camp, where a siren would wake us in the middle of the night, and they'd march us in a dark forest.'

'Something like Brownies or Scouts?'

'No, we were rehearsing for the war.' Bobbie Greengrass probably never had to play war games in a scary night forest, and there are no deep forests in England, at least Agata hasn't seen any. 'While I was in that camp, my father wrote me a postcard telling me that we were moving to another town. A beautiful place, he wrote, where dinosaurs used to roam. Dinosaurs! What was I to make of that? I remember worrying about how Mama would find us in that new place. How would she know where we had gone?'

Bobbie Greengrass checks the clock on the wall. 'Today, Agata, we are going to consider your *worry process* again.'

'Can I read you something?' Bobbie Greengrass sighs, but Agata has already opened her journal. 'After my mother returned from prison, every day she made me a sandwich for school. During the break the other children ate theirs, but not me. *Have you eaten your sandwich?* she'd ask when I got home. And I always said yes and promised myself to eat it next day, and next day there was a new sandwich in my satchel, and I didn't know which to eat first. So I didn't eat any. In the evening my mother asked again. And again I lied. I wasn't aware that to buy the ham or the cheese for my sandwiches, my parents had to skip their lunch.'

'Not aware and yet you knew. Freud called it *the blindness of the seeing eye.*'

Agata duly scribbles it in her notebook, not that Bobbie Greengrass has ever asked her to make notes during the session, but it helps; in fact these days jotting things down has become something of a habit. Agata carries her notebook around with the same dedication angina patients carry lifesaving nitrate spray.

'The sandwiches piled up, and every time I opened my bag they reminded me of my crime,' she reads on. 'Soon a green mould started growing on the bread and on the decomposing cheese and ham, and in my stupidity, it never occurred to me to get rid of them on my way from school. At home I transferred the sandwiches to my toy cupboard, but then, the day arrived when my mother noticed the strange stink hanging around there. '*Ven,*' she commanded, '*V šechno ven!* Meaning *everything out*. So I started to pull my toys out. Very, very slowly. One by one. *Out!* My mother demanded, noticing I was dragging my feet. I felt her eyes in my back and wanted to die; anything to delay the discovery of that pile of rotting filth, as filthy as I felt. My terror was such that I started to whimper for forgiveness well before reaching the end. The end was always the same: my mother's sad eyes and her silence. I wished she'd hit me, but she never did, just silence that lasted forever. It was her throat, she explained to me since. No proper sound could pass.'

Bobbie Greengrass shifts in her chair. 'It seems to me as if…' She pauses to gather her thoughts. 'As if you were caught up in something rather frightening. A sadomasochistic game you were compelled to repeat. Both of you.' Seeing a look of alarm on Agata's face, the counsellor quickly adds, 'Not of your doing, Agata. You were only a child.'

No use in resisting. The sobs shake her with such ferocity that Agata worries she might throw up.

*

Klaus Tuttenhoffer keeps phoning. '*Servus,* Agata. *Shalom.* When are you coming to look at my dissertation?' None of Agata's excuses seem to put him off. Mama has been gone for two weeks, and Renee hasn't yet called. So she finally agrees.

Klaus occupies the top floor of a sprawling Victorian house in Tufnell Park. He warns her that Duncan, his landlord, is a psychoanalyst so they must keep *stumm* on the stairs. Usually there's nothing, just people coming and going, although once Klaus heard a woman bolting out, shouting *I fucking hate you, Duncan.*

In Klaus's flat the slanting ceiling and the wooden beams running across the room leave barely an inch or so of clearance. To avoid bumping his head, Klaus demonstrates a bent-knee shuffle. Besides stacks of books, there is a futon, a rail with a few clothes hangers, a chipped mirror, one chair and a bright red punch bag, probably belonging to Duncan. The general impression is of a Spartan encampment, but the kitchen has a working kettle and on the counter a spread of pastries awaits them; Klaus has been to a kosher patisserie near Belsize Park especially for her. What would she like first? *Hamantaschen?* Or maybe *Rugelach*, if *Hamantaschen* is too rich. *Mandelbrot* is also supposed to be good.

Balancing a plate on his knees Klaus offers Agata the chair and settles on the mattress. The moment her plate is empty he jumps up to bring her another bite of *Rugelach* or *Mandelbrot* or whatever those pastries are called; the names mean nothing to her. What's more, they taste like ordinary Czech biscuits. And yet, no one has ever shown such keenness to please her, such ardour, not even Richard.

After they finish, Klaus gets out his dissertation. He reads for a long time. He reads how the second generation's parents often look at their children as if searching their faces and gestures for someone else, someone who hasn't survived. He reads how this makes the children feel as if they were not good enough to be loved for themselves, for who they are. He reads about the second generation's fascination with the Holocaust which sometimes becomes an obsession. 'It's the guilt,' Klaus says, 'their parents guilt carved deep into them, as deep as a physical wound.' The quiver in his voice and his missionary zeal make Agata uneasy, so when Klaus pauses, she thanks him for his hospitality and suggests that she should head home.

Klaus takes off his rounded specs, buffs them slowly, sits them back on his nose. 'Agata?' he says. 'You haven't asked me, yet.'

'Asked you what?' She says, pretending not to know what he is alluding to.

'You haven't asked me what the vegetable gardener did in the war.'

She glances towards the skylight where the pale moon is already visible, and thinks of Mama's photos. Of how much she wanted to see them, and then, she didn't. *Who asks too much, learns too much*, warns an old Czech proverb. Resolutely, she brushes the crumbs from her lap and stands, her shoulder grazing the punch bag, making it swing. As she tries to steady it, she notices several pairs of shiny boxing gloves lined up on the rafter like freshly baked buns. She picks one up and, to her amazement, it is heavy, much heavier than she'd expected. 'Do these belong to Duncan?'

The gloves belong to Klaus. Klaus Tuttenhoffer, with his funny specs and spindly wrists poking out of frayed shirt cuffs, the last person you'd expect to see in a ring.

'You want to try them on?'

Klaus picks a pair and taking great care laces them up on Agata's hands. As soon they are on, and even before he shows her where to stand or how to hit the punch bag, she delivers the first blow, and has to hop on one foot to wait out the pain, not only in her knuckles, in her shoulder too.

'Let me show you.' Klaus pulls the second pair onto his hands. 'Lift your arms,' he instructs her. Agata does as she is told. Klaus thrusts a hip forward and plants himself in front of her. 'Now hit my right hand with your left glove.' She hesitates, but not for long. As she follows his command, Klaus calls out *one!* Then he orders her to aim at his right glove with her left hand: *two!* His right hand with her right glove: *three!* 'And again: one, two, three! A hook, a jab and a cross punch! And now we change: one, one, two! Now two, one, three! Bravo!' While punching his hands, Agata glimpses their reflection in the mirror: two creatures waving about their tentacle-like arms, weighed by grotesque blobs. 'Three, one, one! *Drei, einz, einz!*' Klaus keeps calling out. 'Chin down! Steady your hips! Come. Come!' Heaving with the effort she obeys his diktat like an automaton, she pummels his fists with as much strength as she can muster. Once or twice she sees Klaus falter and wince, her blows making him nearly lose his footing though he shows no signs of wanting to stop. Instead, he receives her blows with stoic determination, almost gratitude. Her pulse quickens and she detects in herself a disturbing undertone of pleasure. She wants to yell at Klaus: *Whatever your grandfather did, it's not your fault. Defend yourself!* Except she isn't Bobbie Greengrass, and this is not a therapy session. Klaus's face glistens with sweat and he keeps raising his arms higher and higher. Then it happens. As she delivers her left jab, her glove slips and crashes into Klaus's glasses. And almost instantly, a thin trickle of blood appears, running down the side of his fine nose, where his glasses have dug in.

19

No news from Renee Stoloff. Agata doesn't dare to leave the house for fear of missing her call. And she keeps postponing informing Professor Chalabot of Mama's veto. When she finally phones the hospital, she only tells the secretary that her mother won't be able to give blood for the simple reason that she lives abroad. The secretary phones back the same afternoon: the Professor would like to see Agata next Monday at three o'clock. She is elated. So, it'll be her blood the Professor will analyse. It will be her, Agata, who will establish a network for those linked by blood. How this will come about she isn't clear; all she knows is that she has been entrusted with this special task.

For some obscure reason she finds Professor Chalabot's office in the dermatology department. 'The professor has been delayed, I'm only a temp,' says the woman who opens the door, holding a kettle. 'She is running late.' *He,* Agata silently corrects her, the temp has probably started only this morning. The woman pours water from a kettle in a mug. 'You can't hurry pot noodles, or they crack between your teeth,' she says, inhaling the rising steam. 'Pot noodles teach you patience, they really do.'

When Professor Chalabot breezes in, clad in a tight-fitting tiger-striped suit, she is a woman indeed. Exuberant smile, mahogany hair. 'It's pretty straightforward, Mrs Upton,' she says after introducing herself. 'This is the needle.' She takes a plastic syringe out of a small cardboard box. 'You unscrew this, stick this on, draw the blood, then break this off and it's sealed, right?' She fits the syringe back in the box and pushes it towards Agata.

'Do you expect me to do this myself?' Agata asks.

The Professor glances at her, surprised. 'Oh no. I don't expect you to take this personally all the way to… where is it your mother lives again?'

'Prague.'

'You send it there by post. Your mother shouldn't find it a problem to get a nurse there to do it for her. Once the blood is taken I must have it back within twenty-four hours. You ask my secretary, there is a special service for that. It's important for our research, we're testing for a predisposition in women who have already have breast cancer, like your mother.

'And if you find this predisposition, then what?'

'Then…' The Professor crosses her legs. Elegant, pointed pumps. Soft green suede. She brushes them gently against each other to brush off a tiny mark. 'Well, she already has the illness, so apart from regular screening there isn't much we can presently do. What I mean is – not yet – we're learning every day, Mrs Upton, I myself attend many international conferences.'

Agata dumps the box in the first litter bin she finds. Then after a few steps she turns back and retrieves it. At home she hides it in her underwear drawer, where she also keeps her notebook.

*

Lily goes away on a school trip and Agata spends hours staring at herself in the mirror, wondering if there will be any resemblance between Renee and herself. It now strikes her that so much of who she is, perhaps most of it, has been passed to her from generations before, people she has never met. She remembers reading that after a certain age, everyone is responsible for their face. So she only has herself to blame for the two deep lines above her nose. Arching her eyebrows makes them disappear, but who can walk around with their brows permanently arched? And how thick those brows have become. The older she gets the more hair she seems to sprout. She is in the middle of inspecting her roots when Richard knocks on the bathroom door. 'Agu? I just remembered that a letter came for you the other day, but I forgot where I put it, I'll help you look when you are out.'

She finds it under their bed, inside the pages of the weekend Guardian. *Chislehampton, Oxfordshire*, she deciphers the rubber stamp. *Chislehampton!* Her heart quickens. She tears the envelope open and pulls out a map sketched in multicoloured felt tips. Right at the top, like on a child's board game, a caption says in large letters: *START. YOUR HOME.* From there a black line runs across London towards an orange motorway with exit numbers scrolled in red, until it merges with a blue line heading towards *Willow Roundabout*. The blue then skips along through several twists and turns until it hits a green rectangle: *STOLOFFS' COTTAGE. WELCOME! Lunch at 12.30.* The date is tomorrow.

Renee Stoloff is inviting her to her house for lunch! She says *WELCOME*. Agata hurries to the chemist to buy a hair dye. Since they don't have her usual colour, she gets a slightly darker shade and when she examines herself in the mirror afterwards, she is horrified; her hair now looks like a muddy wig. She drives straight back and buys the *Sun Kissed* hair lightener *number 2*.

Next morning she sets out with her hair restored. As a gesture of support, after taking his Friday sandwich out of the freezer, Richard makes her a cappuccino. A proper one, for which he mixes coffee essence with sugar, then pours it into milk that he expertly whips into froth. After checking there is enough petrol, he stands by to observe her departure. It adds gravitas to her expedition. At the last minute Agata rushes back to change from a blazer to a cardigan to look more girl-like for her very first aunt. Strictly speaking Renee is more like a second cousin, though Agata has already decided that she'll call her *aunt*. On the way she buys flowers – a nice bunch, not too formal, not too modest. She drives with the window open. The sky is cloudless, the new leaves on the chestnut trees lining the road sway in the warm breeze like dancers' skirts.

Two hours later she pulls up by the Stoloffs' cottage. For a moment she stays in the car to savour the view: a wooden gothic front door with a brass knocker; latticed windows framed by velvet curtains, on the windowsills freshly cut garden flowers and various bits of china, everything she hoped for.

A short stocky woman in purple corduroy jeans and a cardigan opens the door. In contrast to her telephone voice she seems surprisingly sturdy, down to earth. Her shy smile and mildly bucked teeth make her instantly endearing to Agata. *Agata – Renee*. Renee's hand is small and light, her skin a little rough. From toiling in the garden Agata assumes, holding on to it a little longer, relishing the moment: her aunt's hand in hers. How utterly amazing to be touching a blood relative. How sweet. And there really is a familiar air around Renee, making Agata wonder if there is such a thing as genetic scent – unless Renee uses the same eau de cologne as her mother. They pause to examine each other; Agata searches Renee's features for something that would remind her of Mama. Whose features is Renee searching for in her?

'I look more like my father,' Agata warns, in case Renee is disappointed. 'Your eyes,' she says, returning Renee's hazelnut gaze, 'they're lighter than my mother's, but they have a similar expression, sort of...' She tries to think of a word.

'I suppose one would expect that with cousins.' Renee's smile is muted, but reassuring, like the comfortable clothes she wears. Agata likes the way she guides her inside, holding her elbow as if they already know each other.

'Depth,' Agata says. 'Depth is the word I was looking for.'

'Are you suggesting that Renee has depth? Darling our new relative must be a poet!'

Harry is the more exuberant of the two. Bony, with greying pomaded hair. Beaked nose. Bright yellow foulard inside his shirt collar. A lukewarm handshake, but not limp. The least reserved is their black Labrador, Teerabula, who promptly wipes her huge tongue on Agata's face in a wet kiss.

While Harry is putting the final touches to the lunch, Renee shows Agata around the house. She meets every piece of furniture, every dainty porcelain basket, every polka dot on the tablecloth with cries of praise. And it isn't even an effort, Agata genuinely likes the calm, cosy orderliness that gives their home an aura of safety, of keeping the world at bay.

Ladling out the asparagus soup, it is Harry who takes it upon himself to describe how after *Kristallnacht*, Renee's parents packed what they could and the whole family travelled across the border to Czechoslovakia. 'No darling, that's not how it was,' Renee corrects him, gently. 'First, I was sent with Otto, our neighbours' son, because of the SS at the border. Mutti and Papi came later. We all finally met at Doris's parents' apartment in Prague.'

'And my mother, I mean Doris? Was she also there?' Agata asks.

Renee wags her finger in much the same way as Mama does. 'No. By then Doris was already at the Lyon conservatoire.' And then, while they were figuring out what to do next, Renee's parents had somehow managed to put her on the train to England. None too soon; a few days later the German army occupied the whole country. Now Renee's Mutti and Papi, together with Mama's family, were trapped.

'Here we are, ladies.' Harry serves the next course: cod in white sauce, new potatoes, French beans.

'I was only ten,' Renee says. 'I can't even remember how I said goodbye to my parents.'

'Oh you poor girl.' Harry pats his wife's hand. 'Parsley anyone?' He sprinkles the freshly chopped leaves over their plates.

What Renee remembers is that when she got to London a nice lady collected her at Victoria station, but it turned out that she was the wrong lady. Or Renee was the wrong child, but no matter: after a few days the right lady appeared and took Renee to Hove with her. For some reason it hadn't worked with that lady either, despite her also being very nice. That's why Renee was passed to yet another family.

'So what were they like, this family who finally took you in?' Agata asks.

'Very nice,' Renee is quick to answer.

'They loved you then?' Agata is still hoping for a happy ending.

'No, I don't think so, they were just ordinary folk who took me in,' Renee says. 'Mr and Mrs McNulty, remember Harry? You met them once.'

'Was that their name, are you sure dear?' Harry chuckles. 'Because the lady you introduced me to, I wouldn't call McNullity, not by any stretch of imagination.' He mimes a large chest. 'Mrs McWellendowed would be far more fitting.'

'Shush, Harry, shush!' Gazing at him adoringly Renee slaps his hand.

'We Russians can't help noticing, it's in our nature.' Harry winks at Agata and she is happy to be included in their teasing, they really seem to have a wonderful relationship, these two.

The trifle arrives with a generous helping of fresh cream and the rest of Renee's story. The McNultys sent her off to a boarding school where everyone was once again nice to her. The only snag was that when the school closed for holidays Renee had nowhere to go. Luckily, she had cousins in London.

'Cousins?' Agata pricks up her ears. Could Renee possibly mean that elusive Franz Frankel and his sister? Yes, Franzek and Ruth, Renee confirms. They too were very nice, but of course they had their own busy lives to live. 'That's incredible!' Agata exclaims. 'I've been looking for them all over the place.' Her enthusiasm is met with a distinct air of indifference. 'Of course Renee, I had no clue that *you* existed,' Agata hurries to add. 'Otherwise I'd have looked for you too.'

'I had letters from Doris throughout the war,' Renee says quietly. Mama wrote to Renee in England? First the news about the Frankels and now this? 'Oh well,' Renee shrugs, 'let sleeping dogs lie, that's what I always say, don't I Harry? By the way, the dessert was very nice.'

'Just a trifle, dear.' Flushed from the wine, Harry plops some more on Renee's plate. 'Go on angel, be a devil.' The tender exchanges between them make Agata wish she and Richard were more demonstrative to each other.

'After the war we had to learn terrible things,' Renee sighs. 'My parents were dead. And to poor Doris, only one person returned.'

'Renee, you're mistaken,' Agata corrects her. 'All my mother's immediate family were killed.'

'I heard from Doris that her sister Annette came back from the camp.'

'Her little sister came back?' Agata has to grip the seat of her chair, on the tablecloth the polka dots blur. How is it possible that Mama kept something like this to herself?

'Yes. Annette was poorly. There was a young doctor who was supposed to help her, but she's never recovered, poor lamb.'

Agata closes her eyes, the red dots now vibrate manically under her eyelids.

'So you didn't know. I suppose it was too painful for Doris to mention. She stopped writing. No more letters, not a word. Well...' Renee sighs.

'She couldn't write. She was locked up in prison.' Agata jumps to Mama's defence.

'In prison?' The two of them gape at her. Surely cousin Doris wasn't a criminal? Agata mentions the fifties, the cold war, the Stalinist trials. None of it dispels their look of incomprehension, of disbelief.

'I understand,' Renee finally murmurs. 'I also had many things to deal with.' Girlishly, she smiles at her husband. 'Didn't I, Harry?'

'I refuse to be referred to as a thing. Agathé here may think you're being rude, dear.' Amid high-pitched giggles, Harry winks at Agata, and keeps a permanent grin on his face as if his wife's life depends on it. And maybe it does.

Agata's thoughts churn. Annette, Mama's little sister Annette, survived.

That's why her name was missing on the wall of Pinkas synagogue. Yet Mama never told her. Just as she never told her about Renee's existence. Why did she keep it a secret?

'When I think of what you Jewish people had to endure, it's just too much, too much. It makes me want to cry.' Harry's voice is now brittle, his eyes in danger of welling up.

'No point prying into the past, I live for the future,' Renee warns, as her chin begins to shake.

What now? Now it's Agata's turn to do something, anything, to hold back the grief from invading their sunny kitchen, threatening to drown them, otherwise her new relatives may never ask her back. Folded in her handbag is Renee's mother's Auschwitz death certificate. Agata won't give it to her today, perhaps next time. Perhaps never. 'Thank you for a lovely lunch,' she says, smiling brightly. 'The trifle was terrific. I wouldn't mind the recipe.'

Afterwards, she and her new cousin, whom she doesn't dare to call aunt, sit on the sofa with Renee's family album between them; one half on Renee's knee, the other half on Agata's, Teerabula by their feet. Together they leaf through Renee's assembled childhood: a plump toddler in an old-fashioned pram. In a garden, wearing a frilly dress. With Mutti and Papi in the Alps. With a gathering of smiling adults by a lake. In the snow. Little Renee, their much-loved cherub, each picture lovingly inscribed by Papi so that one day their darling daughter will remember who was who. And then, unexpectedly, here is a photo of someone Agata recognises: a girl of about fourteen, teeth gleaming in a tanned face, one leg precariously poised above an Alpine ravine as if she were a cabaret dancer. The first photograph of Mama as a child that Agata has ever seen.

'Here you are, ladies!' Harry pushes in a trolley with coffee cups and in an imitation of Mama's daring prank, throws his arms up, kicks a leg back. 'Cousin Doris who vanished, ta-daa!'

'Oh cut it out, Harry,' Renee teasingly prods him with her foot.

They sip their coffee and carry on turning the pages: Renee growing, keeping her cherub smile, her body swelling up from all that food her parents piled into her before sending her off to England, just a small rucksack on her back with the few things they packed for her, including this album. Their cherished treasure, their *Schatz*, now too big for her age, too awkward to worm her way into some English woman's heart.

The time has passed quickly, outside it's already dark. Repeating how much she enjoyed being with them, Agata invites Renee and Harry to come for lunch and meet Richard and Lily, any time they wish. Once again it is Teerabula who appears most saddened to see her depart, she accompanies Agata to her car with heart-wrenching whines, before scampering back to her masters for a consoling head scratch.

'Goodbye and thank you!' Agata calls once more to the small group silhouetted against the glow from their fairy-tale cottage: her new family and their dog. Then she remembers she hasn't asked how to get in touch with the Frankels.

Her enquiry seems to take Renee by surprise. Ruth died some years back, she says. And Franz? Well, they haven't been in touch for ages, his crowd never really suited them. Also, he divorced his wife Ellen in a rather... how should Renee put it? In short, he left her for her best friend. In fact Ellen is the only one with whom they still exchange Christmas cards.

'So... to contact Franz, how would I do it?' Agata asks, aware of stepping on hazardous ground.

Renee gives it a moment's thought: 'I suppose through Ellen, although I'd have to go and check if I still have her phone number.' Would Agata care to step back inside?

No, Agata thanks her. 'I'm happy waiting here, it's a beautiful night.' She is drunk with exhaustion, her jaw hurts from smiling all day and she fears that if she were to go back, she wouldn't find the strength to leave, and her new relatives may feel obliged to put her up in their guest-room and who knows, even stroke her head good night, like Teerabula.

Renee returns apologetic: Ellen's number would require a more substantial search. She promises to phone Agata within a week.

*

Next morning Agata writes a thank-you-for-a-lovely-lunch card. She picks from Richard's collection of art postcards a colourful eighteenth-century Japanese print, *Minamoto no Yoritomo Fighting Enemies Bravely* by Kokunimasa. Richard assures her it is virtually impossible to go wrong with something of that ilk. Afterwards she follows Richard around, bragging about how wonderful Renee and Harry are, and how they both can't wait to meet the rest of the family. When Lily returns from her school trip, Agata repeats it all again. Later, when she glimpses Lily conferring with Richard by his studio door, her daughter's face crinkled with concern, she wishes she hadn't allowed herself to get quite so carried away.

In truth, neither Renee nor Harry expressed any such sentiments. Nor did Renee show much interest in Agata, and even less in Richard or Lily. Some people are like that, Agata explains it to herself; too tactful to ask personal questions. She keeps her spirits high. She tells Richard she has invited her new relatives for a meal, and is looking forward to inviting the rest when she meets them; it'll be quite a gathering, even those who are not on speaking terms might make up again. She doesn't say anything about Mama's little sister Annette returning from the camp. If Mama decided to keep it a secret, so be it. All the same, she indulges in a fantasy that Annette lived long enough to fall in love with that young doctor Renee mentioned, and he with her.

Days fly by and there is no phone call. One afternoon, Agata dials the Stoloffs' number. It is Renee who answers the phone. They exchange polite formalities, bridge awkward pauses; Agata can almost hear their brains ticking along their separate tracks. Finally she plucks up the courage to inquire if Renee has managed to locate Franz Frankel's first wife Ellen's phone number.

'As a matter of fact I have,' says Renee, 'though I had to go through the whole pile of old Christmas cards. You wouldn't believe the dust.'

Agata thanks her, then asks if Renee has by any chance found time to phone Ellen on her behalf, not that she expects it from her, of course. There is a lengthy pause. 'Listen, dear,' Renee finally says, 'I'm afraid you won't like what I'm going to say. I've decided not to go through with it.'

'Oh, please don't worry,' Agata assures her. 'I'd be happy to phone Ellen myself.'

'No dear, you misunderstand. I'm not going to give you Ellen's number.' Renee then explains her theory. More than a theory, a certainty: Agata's wish to meet the rest of the relatives is bound to bring unhappiness. Someone might get hurt.

'But who'd get hurt and why?'

'Someone might, you must believe me.' Despite her birdlike voice Renee sounds steely. Is she implying that meeting Agata has actually hurt her? Agata tries to point out the absurdity of her claim.

There follows a little intake of air, a little rasp. And then, a soft 'Yes. It has.'

'How? Please tell me how?'

'Some things you said…'

'What things, Renee? What things?'

'Questions. Old wounds that shouldn't be opened.' Renee murmurs. 'Besides, I have a premonition about this.' A premonition? 'A hunch,' Renee explains, in case Agata isn't familiar with that word. 'Harry knows that I'm always right with my hunches.'

'I'm not Harry!' Agata protests.

'I'm sorry dear, I've noticed that you can't take no for an answer.' Renee's grave tone confirms that Agata's very presence, not only in their cosy cottage, but even now through the telephone, causes Renee Stoloff acute discomfort, maybe even pain.

Everything inside Agata contracts in disbelief. 'You can't do this, Renee; you can't play God!' she pleads. 'I never had any proper relatives. You don't know how important this is for me. Please, Renee. Please! I beg you!'

Renee excuses herself for a moment and Agata can hear her whispering something to Harry. She returns listing a catalogue of disasters Agata's unexpected appearance might provoke: marriages might get rocked again; memories disturbed; relationships between generations upset. No, Renee could not take on such a responsibility.

Now what? What do you do when your first and only relative is mean to you? It is time to swap tactics.

'In that case,' Agata announces, masking her despair. 'In that case Renee, I'm sorry, I'm going to search for Franz Frankel by myself.'

'That's up to you, dear,' says Renee. 'But I must warn you. After the war he adopted a new name.'

20

The morning starts with rain that abruptly turns into hailstones. A moment later the sky is blue again. Mama loves comparing her Prague weather with Agata's. It is Agata's turn to call her: one week she phones, one week Mama, to spread the cost. She picks up the phone and hears Richard saying, 'One of these days she's bound to…' It is met with a sigh, much like one of Mama's *ach yos!* This is so unexpected that Agata quickly replaces the receiver. She regrets it immediately, picks it up again and says loudly, 'Who is bound to do what?' The phone is dead. What was Richard talking to Mama about? Their phone did not ring so it must have been he who made the call.

She dials Mama's number. 'Morning Mama. Have you just been talking to Ricky?' Mama responds by laughing as if Agata has told her a joke. 'Zora the azalea produced thirty-two buds,' she informs her. All Mama's plants have names, and Zora is prolific. Last year Mama counted twenty-eight buds, so that makes it four more. 'Maybe it's what's in the air this year.' Talking about plants, Mama often smuggles in a political innuendo. She lowers her voice as if whoever is tapping her phone would be hard of hearing. 'Your BBC, did they mention that our you-know-who dramatist is out of prison?'

Agata takes a deep breath. 'Mama, I went to see that cousin of yours, Renee.'

'Aha.' As brief as that.

'Renee and Harry invited me for lunch and Renee showed me an album with a photo of you as a teenager. I didn't know you were so pretty.'

'Don't exaggerate. Anyhow, I got a letter from her, she mentioned their new roof. I know nothing about the woman, and she writes to me about different makes of roof tiles. *Tzz, tzz…*'

'Well, guess what, Mama. Renee told me that Franz *does* live in London. He had two kids, got divorced. Ruth, his sister, is dead, though.'

'I never liked Ruth,' Mama reminds her.

Agata puts all her effort into sounding light-hearted. 'I know that story Mama. When I asked Renee to put me in touch with Franz, she wasn't that cooperative. She is very discreet, you know. So I simply wanted to ask you if you could possibly write to her and…'

'Gatushka?' Mama's patience is rapidly evaporating. 'We've been through this before.'

'It's a different situation now.' Now that they know Cousin Franz is definitely around, all Mama would have to do is just mention him in her letter. In the silence that follows, Agata goes to stand by the window to watch the tiny hailstones falling again, Making the birds dash from one tree to the next as if struck by panic.

'Listen darling,' Mama's voice is as chilly as the day outside. 'If you want to contact him, you do it by yourself.'

'But Mama! He's changed his bloody surname and Renee won't give it to me!'

'So Franz has changed his name? Ha, ha,' Mama cackles. 'Typical.'

*

Harry Stoloff calls to confirm that despite Renee's unwillingness to help, they are, after all, coming for Sunday lunch. The date falls on Agata's birthday, but she asks Richard and Lily not to mention anything. Let it be a surprise when Lily brings in the cake with lit candles; Renee and Harry will be sorry not to have brought her flowers and a card, perhaps even a little present. Teerabula will bark with excitement and Agata will say that the best present they could give her was turning up. And they will put the date in their diary for next year, and all the years to come. Mellowed by their *en famille* spirit, Renee will jot down Franz Frankel's new name and kiss Agata in apology. And should it not go to plan? Well, you can't choose your relatives, even she knows that.

As the day approaches, Agata pores over recipes. Richard complains that she murmurs *poulet en croute* in her sleep. When she wakes up, *turnip puree with walnut topping and braised duck* is her first thought. This seems almost worse than her nocturnal grief to Richard. At last, Agata settles for chicken in wine, Dijon style, and sleeps well that night. On Saturday morning while they are still in bed the phone rings: 'Harry Stoloff here, apologies for calling so early. I have a request to make: could you please not serve chicken or turkey as the hormones they're fed caused a client of mine, a passionate poultry eater from Baden-Baden, to develop a pair of you know… Not a pretty sight on a man, pardon my French.' No problem, we don't eat poultry either, Agata tells him. 'Excellent! Till tomorrow then.'

Richard takes pity on her and offers to cook something else. Lately, he's been avoiding the studio, some days he doesn't bother to pull on his waistcoat or to shave, he even eats his sandwiches on the wrong days. Agata hopes that her new relatives will pull him out of his lethargy. For the day, she and *Mr Muscle* become inseparable, licking every surface, tackling the Venetian blinds segment by segment. Lily makes sure to keep out of the way, though it is she who answers the phone that evening: 'Mum! Some man, sounds posh. Says he's family.'

'Hello, this is your cousin Harry again. Bad news. Renee is still not quite well, the trip to London would prove too much for her. So I'm afraid we'll have to cancel. Hope you haven't already bought the ingredients.'

'No problem, we can do it some other time,' Agata assures him. 'Is Renee too unwell to call?'

'She's afraid.'

'Afraid?'

'You know, of hurting you.'

*

'They aren't coming,' she announces gloomily to Richard.

'Good,' he says, putting down his computer magazine. 'We can relax in a surprisingly clean house.' Agata feels the pressure building in her nose. 'You're not going to bawl, are you?' Richard scrutinises her face. 'Oh yes, tears, little tears, here they come again. Poor Agu, rejected by her folk, feeling sorry for herself. *Tzz, tzz...*' he finishes in imitation of Mama. When Agata accuses him of being mean, he says that Czechs don't get British humour.

She draws the curtains and crawls into bed. She thinks of Richard's readiness to be nasty, of the pleasure it gives him. 'At least I'm honest,' he once told her, which is more than he can say about Agata who is ever ready to suck up to everyone, like these new relatives, and even to her mother. And of course Dora is an expert in using that to her advantage. That cuts more deeply than anything else.

She hears a passing airplane and thinks about Mama returning from exile to an empty flat. And about the day Annette returned from the camps. Had she rung the doorbell unannounced? Had Mama, who was only a young woman then, recognise her? Was she recognisable? Was there hair on Annette's head, or only black scabs? Did Mama cry when she saw the baby sister she used to watch asleep in her cot, whose hand she used to hold when crossing a street? It was nothing short of a miracle that Annette came back. The battle to save her life must have begun on that day, the day of her return:

'Eat. Eat.' Mama holds a spoon to Annette's cracked lips. She is barely three years older than this bag of bones she is trying to revive. Mama is pretty, her skin is tanned. She had arrived only recently from Argentina, where she discovered what mangoes taste like. '*Jez. Prosím jez.* Eat!' she implores Annette, as the food is retched back. Is there nothing useful left inside, is there no stomach? And that young doctor, does he know how to help? *Please Annetka, eat. Eat away my knowing the warm air of the tropics, the shade of the palm trees, the sound of the sea. Damn it! Swallow that soup I've cooked for you. That ham. That cheese.*

Of course Agata has no way of knowing any of that.

21

'This gentleman, he left the country legally?' asks the Czechoslovak embassy official at the other end of the line. Agata explains that her relative left to escape Hitler. He later changed his name, and she is calling to enquire if they'd have his old name on their records. 'We don't keep such records,' the man answers. And even if they did, he'd be in no position to pass on such information due to the privacy laws. The only place he can suggest is the Red Cross, though he isn't very hopeful. 'Back home it'd be different, but here, where you can come and go and never register with the police, frankly this democracy is a bit of a mess.' *While back home,* Agata imagines retorting, *back home you get locked up for just having a thought in your head.*

Back to the telephone directories. Of the organizations starting with the word *Jewish* there are quite a few. She chooses two: a newspaper and a refugee agency. She is fortunate with both. The newspaper promises to send her an issue so that she can see how to word a search notice. 'There's always people looking for people, you write your shtick, and we publish, no problem.' Agata's mood improves; she isn't the only one, there are others on this trail. The refugee agency even employs someone to hunt for lost relatives. 'Mrs Sylber, a very dedicated lady, please call back on Wednesday.' Finally she is going about things in a proper, mature way.

The newspaper arrives with a note directing her to page seven, where she finds that for example, a certain *John (Jonathan) Zack Salem (Shlovsky), grandson of Ruth Shamemovska Verena/Vereny née Shlomova, whose cousin Chaim Shamemitch (Shemolo) born in the town of Vitebsk, emigrated to Sheffield prior 1914 is searching for relations. Please write to PO Box 34.* Single column of 65 mm (3-column page) is charged at £12. 48 mm (4-column page) is only £10. In comparison, her case seems boringly simple. She composes her text about Mr Franz Frankel from Prague who, after the war, changed his name and sends it off together with a cheque for the more expensive column. It's not every day that you look for family, she'd hate Franz to think that she was skimping. Besides, she entertains a little fantasy about one of Harry's Jewish business cronies, who he had mentioned during her visit, wrapping an icon for him in that very issue displaying her notice, and Harry bringing it home where it would catch Renee's eye and shame her for her lack of generosity.

While waiting for someone to reply, she chases after the elusive Mrs Sylber.

Each time she calls Agata is interrogated by a different voice. What is her name? What is she phoning about? Why exactly does she want to find this person? A relative? Aha! Why didn't she say? Under those circumstances Mrs Sylber, 'who provides her service free of charge, you must understand, is indeed the one who can help you, unfortunately she's in a meeting.' Oh no, no point in talking to anyone else, she's the one. Top notch. Wednesdays only.

Wednesdays go by, Mrs Sylber contracts the flu, after which she has more meetings to attend to make up for lost time. No reply comes to Agata's newspaper notice.

The longer she waits, the more she keeps being distracted by everyday life, there is also the vertiginous loosening up of the Eastern bloc. She feels useless. Momentous events are rocking the world and here she is, chasing after a lost cousin. Every Sunday Mama shares the latest news: 'The Poles declared the end of communist supremacy,' she whispers. 'Hungary is dismantling its border fence with Austria. Only here, everything is slow.'

One Wednesday, Agata has had enough of waiting. First for Renee and Harry to arrange another visit, then for Franz Frankel to turn up, and failing that, for Mrs Sylber to find him. On this particular day, Lily is performing in the end of term production of Animal Farm as a chicken. Agata warns her that she may not be able to attend.

'Mum! Oh please!' Lily has spent days prancing in front of the mirror making squawking sounds. Now she pecks Agata's shoulder with her nose. 'Please! Cluck, cluck...'

And Agata sees herself as a girl dancing the polka in front of an audience of parents, hoping against hope to catch a sight of Mama. What Agata remembers clearly is worrying that even if, miraculously, her mother were to sit there, she wouldn't recognise her. After nearly two years of not seeing her, she couldn't picture Mama's face or the colour of her eyes. The only thing she remembered was that Mama's hair smelled of nettles.

Agata goes to Lily's show. She makes an effort to engage in small talk with other parents, even the woman who always wears disturbingly sharp jewellery. She duly claps and cheers each time Lily clucks, each time she flips her elbows as wings. And only sneaks out after the curtain-fall.

The refugee agency resides in a sombre, Greek-columned, secret-handshake type of edifice. 'Mrs Sylber is expecting me,' Agata calls to the receptionist. 'Which floor please?' The receptionist politely summons her back. It takes only a brief phone call to find that Mrs Sylber has no appointments today. 'Impossible,' Agata protests. The receptionist passes her the receiver, and she pours into it the whole sorry chronology of her attempts to hook up with Mrs Sylber. And is met with a positive response: she is asked to sign her name in the visitor's book, has her bag searched, then she is sent off to buzz her way through a series of doors. By the last one is a petite creature in a dark tailored suit with a jolly red handkerchief peeping from her breast pocket – something you probably need when you spend your Wednesdays sniffing out persons lost in the chaos of the war – already waiting for her.

'Mrs Sylber?' No, this lady is just a helper. She ushers Agata into an office and disappears. A rather shabby black and white map of Europe covers the wall, the mishmash of furniture in contrast with the magnificently pillared exterior. Soon an elderly bespectacled woman makes her entrance.

'Mrs Sylber?'

'I understand you have no appointment, but since you are already here…' Mrs Sylber waves Agata to sit down. 'Is it a *Wiedergutmachung* you want to claim on behalf of this person? Or stolen deposits from a Swiss bank?' Her English crackles with German intonation, her dry cheeks dislodge tiny clots of fine powder onto her pleated tartan skirt.

Agata explains that she is looking for a relative who was originally called Franz Frankel, but then changed his name. Mrs Sylber carefully notes everything down, retreats somewhere, and within minutes re-emerges. No one of that name on the registry, she is sorry to say. The only one she found is a certain Charlotte Franklen, whose address in Wimbledon dates from 1926.

After all that waiting, all those phone calls, Agata feels badly let down. 'May I ask what kind of a registry you keep?'

'Microfiche.'

Agata can just see Mrs Sylber peering through her thick lenses at the microscopic text, missing a name here and there. Why should Mrs Sylber's myopia deprive her of a potential link to her family? 'Would you allow me to have a look myself?'

'Certainly not!' Mrs Sylber seems appalled by her offer. 'It is *my* job, and it is highly confidential.' She glances at her watch, then, perhaps regretting her briskness, says, 'Looking for people is an infinitely painstaking task, you understand?'

'So, have you ever found anyone?' Agata asks, trying not to sound sceptical.

'Oh certainly!' Mrs Sylber's face lights with unexpected gaiety. 'There have been many over the years. Mind you, no one ever calls back to say thank you. Only when they don't get their pension they call. Then they call, you can be sure of that!'

While buzzing her out Mrs Sylber says, 'There is always the Wiener Library, if you ever want to check the dead.' What library? '*Vee*ner.' Mrs Sylber repeats. 'Don't you know the *Vee*ner Library? They have a world class archive on the Holocaust,' she explains, her knotty hand patting Agata's arm, excusing her ignorance.

Back at home Lily and Melody are watching The Simpsons, chewing marshmallows. Everyone loved their chickens, they report, some claimed they were even better than the hens. The next play the school is staging is *The Diary of Anne Frank,* and this time Lily has decided to go for something more challenging than impersonating poultry. This time around, being Jewish may give her a head start over that snotty Katy Stuart-Frogart who always grabs the main part.

'Only half Jewish,' Agata is quick to add, Bobbie Greengrass's worry-radar kicking in. The carelessness with which her daughter bandies around such words, as if they mean nothing.

'Not by the Jewish law, Mum.' Lily firmly repudiates Agata's attempt to dilute her claim. 'I'm not half, am I, Mel?'

'No, Lil definitely isn't half. She's a British Jew like I'm Black British,' Melody declares with quiet authority. 'Actually, I'm going to audition for that Annie myself,' she announces, stuffing a handful of marshmallows into her mouth.

'Cool,' says Lily.

22

A friend falls ill, and asks Agata to take over her animation class. She is happy to accept; they need the money, but half term is around the corner, and Agata isn't sure what to do with Lily. During their Sunday call Mama announces that she is planning to go for a few days to Marienbad to research her book. She has been offered a gratis room in one of the plushest hotels there, hotel *Kontinental*. 'Not the same one where Richard Wagner was recuperating after composing the Ring, though still very *nóbl.*' This gives Agata an idea: how about if Lily joined Mama now that she is old enough to travel alone? To have Lily to herself? And in that *nóbl* hotel? There is nothing better Mama could wish for.

Fortunately, Richard doesn't protest. He has a new deadline.

Lily insists on preparing her suitcase by herself. After she packs her favourite tops, her books, her Walkman and cassettes, Agata squeezes in Professor Chalabot's cardboard box with a note inside: *Please Mama, arrange to have blood taken on the morning of Lily's flight back. Thank you. Your loving daughter.* What does she have to lose?

At the airport, the moment the stewardess trots in on her high heels, Lily glues herself to her, her parents now mere random bystanders. With an air of an important mission Lily strides away hand in hand with her new friend, the *Young Flyer* pouch with her passport swinging gaily around her neck.

Agata and Richard rush to the top floor of the car park to watch the plane take off. The clouds display an amazing palette, below them the aligned aircraft are connected to the giant tubes like cattle in a milking shed. When the plane carrying their daughter in its steel-plated belly rises above their heads they wave, Agata's hair whipping madly around her, her cries drowned by the roar of the engines. What possessed her to allow Lily to go alone? Her daughter, only a year older than Renee when her parents put her on that train, never to see her again.

*

'We're open every day, anyone can come and look at our books, no need for an appointment. Only nothing can be taken out.' The female voice on the phone has a reassuring foreign ring to it.

The Wiener Library turns out to be surprisingly small, almost like someone's living room. Bookshelves of dark wood line the walls, the sun floods in through the tall windows. A scattering of people are dotted around a long wooden table immersed in reading, occasionally jotting something down. Suddenly, Agata can't fathom why she has come. Didn't Mrs Sylber say this was the place to look only for the dead? Yet she is here, standing in front of the librarian's desk, wondering what to ask for, when her eyes fall on a couple of thick-bound volumes titled in large silver letters: *Theresienstadt*. Someone must have recently finished looking through them.

'Seems they've been waiting for you,' says the librarian, a pleasant young woman with a French plait and a birthmark on her cheek.

Agata carries the weighty tomes to the table. They consist solely of names of Czech and Slovak citizens who went through the Theresienstadt camp; the first volume runs from A-M, the second one from N-Z, over a hundred thousand names in total, each displaying a star next to the date of birth and a cross next to the date of death, if known. The Weisses fill three entire columns. Agata has no problem finding Mama's younger sister Annette. Annette Weiss: page 325. On page 325 she reads that Annette arrived at Ravensbrück from Theresienstadt on 25th January 1943. She was sent to Auschwitz one year later, a fortnight before Christmas. How did she survive the winter? Did she have anything to keep her warm, shoes to walk in the snow? Knowing that Annette managed to emerge out of this hell alive gives Agata a small taste of victory. And what about Laura, Mama's older sister, if only Agata remembered her married name. She decides to look for Mama's mother instead who, she is sure, was called Karla. There is a Karla Weiss on page 328: born 11th October 1885, who was on the transport from Prague to Theresienstadt on 15th May 1942.

In May, lilacs bloom in the Prague parks. Every year Agata used to bring Mama an armful of their perfumed blossoms. She goes back to the dates next to Annette's name. Were she and their mother in Theresienstadt at the same time?

From Theresienstadt, Karla Weiss was deported to Auschwitz on 6th September 1943. No cross next to her name, just another anonymous death. Agata examines the index again to find her grandfather. She vaguely remembers Mama mentioning him as Moritz. Moritz Weiss – there are several of them; but according to the dates each at least ten years younger than her grandmother. She doesn't recall ever hearing anything as scandalous so she must have made a mistake: her grandfather's name wasn't Moritz. One of the Moritzes was only nine years old when he was gassed.

Nine. That makes her pause, slow down. Turning the pages her fingers become clumsy and damp, which is odd, Agata rarely sweats. She goes to the toilet to let cold water run over her hands and sips a little from her palm.

Now she remembers that Mama's father's name was Karl, Karl Weiss. She finds several and copies their dates in her journal to see if they match her grandmother's. Except if her grandfather's name was Karl, it is unlikely that her grandmother's was Karla, Karl and Karla just doesn't sound right. Maybe her grandmother was called Gisela. Four Gisela Weisses, but only one with a date of death. Now Agata wonders if that Gisela was Mama's aunt, the one who married Franzek's father, the old Frankel. She looks up the Frankels, finds several Giselas before she remembers that, actually, Gisela was Mama's other aunt, her cousin Renee's mother. Of course – Gisela Kraus, she has her death certificate in her file. She closes the books. This is unforgivable. Worse than that – shameful. Monstrous. These books are of no use to someone like her who hasn't even bothered to retain something as simple as a few family names. What is she doing here? Appropriating a sorrow that isn't hers?

She needs both hands to lug the two heavy volumes back to the librarian's desk.

'You found what you were looking for?' The librarian smiles at her. Agata nods. 'Are you a Friend?' A leaflet is pushed towards her. 'A Friend of the library. Here are some programmes we organise.'

Something called *Generation Series* is going to take place soon. The name of the organiser is Dr Mark Ackermayer. Ackermayer. It sounds familiar. Wasn't that the name of the man Mama's older sister Laura married? Suddenly she knows: his name wasn't Ackermayer, but Ackerman. Anton Ackerman, the layabout with a broken nose, who raced sports cars. She saw the photo of their son Hugo in the envelope Mama gave her. She opens the book and within seconds finds all three Ackermans. 'Here they are.' She points them out to the librarian. And indeed, here they are for everyone to see, a whole chunk of her family: Anton, Hugo, Laura. Taken to Lodz on one of the first transports in November 1941.

In November Prague's melancholic gothic looks at its best.

Altogether twenty thousand were sent to the east, the book says. Agata has never heard about a camp in Lodz. Now she reads that Mama's sister Laura died there on 24th August 1942, at thirty-one, there are no crosses next to her son or husband. Agata makes a quick calculation: Hugo was eight when he arrived, Anton was thirty-five. He was an amateur boxer, who knows maybe he managed to protect his son. The transport to Theresienstadt left when the Germans were clearing the Lodz ghetto in the last throes of the war. The journey took days, the prisoners arrived in sealed cattle wagons without food or water. The inmates who pulled them out had to sort out the corpses from the skeletons still showing signs of life. Most of them went on to die from typhus, but a few survived. Hugo would have been twelve by then. In the photo he looks a strong boy; he would still be only in his late fifties, living who knows where. Perhaps in America. Perhaps in Israel, or even in the UK, oblivious that he has relatives. And Agata feels a sliver of hope. If her cousin Hugo Ackerman survived, he would have been old enough to remember who he was and where he came from, which could be useful if she tries to look for him. The librarian shares her excitement, together they comb through the long list of names known to be on that transport from Lodz: out of one thousand only four survived. Not an Ackerman among them.

On the station platform, Agata observes a small boy standing next to a man with dark hair who is drawing on the roll-up nestled in his cupped palm. The boy instinctively mimics the man's gesture. He looks like a smaller version of his father, except on the boy everything is still in the state of promise: his hair curling softly around the delicate folds of his ears, his eyes still translucent and tinged with deep green, their white with pearly blue. At the sound of the tannoy announcement the man gently slaps the child's cheek to pay attention, as if the destinations refer to some faraway places, rather than suburban London. Watching the train pull in, they comment in Greek, or maybe it is Turkish, on the number of the wagons or the type of the wheels, or the engine. Like fathers and sons do all over the world.

*

While Lily is visiting Mama, tanks roll into Tian'anmen Square. The world looks on in horror as the army shoots live ammunition into the protesting students, while people stand around shouting, 'You're killing our children!' In the Eastern bloc there are further rumblings, further demonstrations, further repressions. Having sent Lily to that part of the world, Agata follows the news with growing concern.

'The government is getting scared,' Mama whispers down the phone line when Agata calls the hotel.

After a week, Lily returns in one piece. Her big news is that Ilona has a boyfriend whom she allows to touch her bra, though this barely compares to Lily's time in the spa hotel. Not only had the lift boy in a red uniform always saluted her, but after every dinner Mama ordered *palačinky* for her, piled with canned pineapple and frozen whipped cream. And the waiters let Lily into the kitchen to show her how *knedlíky* are made, and Mama bought her a special porcelain cup, flat as if someone sat on it, with a protruding spout for sipping the hot healing waters.

The moment Lily goes to bed, Agata looks through her suitcase. She discovers the Professor's cardboard box next to the obligatory pack of wafers, and under a new blouse that had been unavailable in her size last time she was in Prague. Inside the box she finds the vial full of Mama's blood. She inspects the winy liquid against the light and careful not to agitate it, slips it inside her underwear drawer. Then she goes to report Lily's safe return to Mama.

'Gatushka! I'm so glad you are calling. Do you remember Igor? Igor and Žeňka Kadorsky, my friends who live in Reading?' Mama just heard through a common acquaintance that Igor has suffered a stroke, she tried to phone, but their number doesn't ring. She is very worried and wants Agata to find out if Igor is alright. Agata jots down the Kadorskys' number and promises to try to contact them. 'Good!' Mama sounds relieved. She and Lily had a great time, she reports. She even managed to squeeze in a bit of work on Mozart. Not Wolfgang Amadeus – his son, also a musician – who died in Marienbad. Mama suspects he was there seeing a certain baroness, married to someone else. 'You know, Gatushka, sometimes you need a bit of invention to nudge a story along,' she says. 'But you must never lose the kernel of the truth. And how do you know where that kernel is? You know, because it's where it hurts.'

'Thanks for sending that blood,' says Agata. 'When did you have it taken?'

'This morning of course, I'm not a complete idiot, you know. How's the blouse?'

'Fits perfectly. Mama, I know you don't want me to go on about it, but if you'd just write to Renee…'

'Relax,' orders Mama. 'I've already written to her, I even sent her the study about Imre Lilosh.'

'Oh that's wonderful,' Agata blurts out. 'And did you manage to ask her if she would…'

Mama sucks in air. 'You're beginning to get on everyone's nerves, Gatushka. Have you nothing better to do with your time?'

No! Agata would like to yell at her. *No.* Right now she has nothing better to do than getting hold of that cousin of hers, Franz Frankel or whatever his bloody name is! Instead, she does her utmost to keep her voice down. 'Why, Mama? Tell me why you don't want me to look for him.'

Around Agata the room has become darker and from the hall comes a faint rustling sound. She crosses the floor silently and in one rapid move throws the door open.

'Just getting a drink,' Lily jumps from the doorway. Agata covers the receiver and motions her to go away. 'Who are you talking to?' Lily mouths back and the way she twiddles the hem of her nightdress tells Agata she was listening behind the door.

'Hello! Are you there?' Inside the handset Mama's voice tickles her palm.

'It's Babi, isn't it? You've upset her again. You always do!'

This time Agata waves her away so vehemently that her daughter finally trudges off. Agata waits for her to climb the stairs and only after hearing her bedroom door slam shut, grips the phone and presses it to her mouth.

'Mama,' she whispers. 'Mama, I know that Annetka came back.'

23

The woman who opens the door to her this time is not the same one as before. This one instead of fiddling with Pot Noodles is holding a steaming tea mug. 'I'm here to see Professor Chalabot. It's rather urgent,' Agata says.

'Professor Chalabot is working in Barnet today. What is it about?' Agata explains that she is bringing a sample of blood that needs to be analysed ASAP. The woman takes a leisurely sip, then points to a desk on which a disarray of papers and unopened post, as well as a pair of scissors and a reel of scotch tape, are piled. 'Just leave it there.' Agata hesitates. Is she expected to leave Mama's precious substance encoded with her very essence – their shared essence – in a random spot like that? After glancing around for a safer place she repeats it is extremely urgent that Professor Chalabot gets it in time. The woman has a few more sips to think it over, then dials a number. When there is a voice, she passes Agata the phone. Agata explains who she is and that she is bringing her mother's blood fresh from Prague.

'Bravo Mrs Upton! Well done!' Professor Chalabot congratulates her. 'Please leave it with Margaret, she'll show you where.'

*

That particular Sunday they plan to go with Lily to Pizza Express and then to a movie. Having tried several times to reach Igor and Žeňka Kadorsky, Agata summons Lily to warn her that, unfortunately, she has to drive to Mama's friends because Mama needs to check they're still alive.

'Phone them,' Lily suggests, the practical child she is.

'Their phone is out of order,' says Agata.

'Oh why does everything have to be so bloody complicated around here?' Lily stamps her foot. 'Why can't you two have proper jobs like everyone else and go out on Sundays like all my friends with their families?'

'And why can't anyone around here appreciate I'm doing my best to put a proper family together?' Agata explodes. 'Why don't I ever get any credit for that?'

'What credit?' Lily gapes at her, confused. 'We have a family.'

'Yes, but it's incomplete.'

'Incomplete?' Lily turns to Richard who is buried in his magazine. 'Dad?!' When he carries on reading, she turns back to her mother. 'I don't get it. So who's missing?'

'How am I to know?' Agata snaps at her.

Lily's eye flood with tears. 'Oh I'm fed up! Fed up with you both!' She shrieks, bolting towards the door.

'Whoa!' Richard flings down his magazine, grabs Lily under her arms and starts spinning her around.

'Stop it, Dad!' She kicks the air. 'Dad! Put me down!' But already she is laughing. Then calling each other 'you guys', the two of them stomp around, and leave the house without saying goodbye.

*

Whenever she drives through this particular stretch of road Agata thinks that if she had to live here, she'd put a bullet through her head. Once these houses must have been considered luxuriously modern. Back then, no one imagined that one day a stinking worm of dual carriageway would burrow through their midst spitting filth into the atmosphere. Do people who live here sometimes pray for a major pile-up to end the din at least for a few hours? Or do they find the constant clamour as soothing as the murmur of the sea?

The weather is perfect, the billboards glide against the aquamarine sky like in a Midwestern movie, and everything seems to come up in groups: the road signs, the lampposts, and later, a massive comb of poplars silhouetted against the sky. They remind Agata of a painting, though she can't now recall the artist, of a man striding purposefully past a row of similar trees, he and his elongated shadow, both lonely and joyful. She regrets shouting at Lily. And yet, the last thing she wants to do is to eat pizza or sit in a cinema. No, she must carry on with the business of looking. Looking to find someone, anyone, Frankel or Kadorsky, she desperately needs some success.

She takes the next exit, hoping to retrace the route she drove to the Kadorskys' with Mama when Lily was still a carefree little girl and Agata a perfect mum. Then Žeňka Kadorsky took Lily's hand and said, 'Come up Lilinka, I'll show you something'. They all stepped into the spare room and Agata's eyes widened: on a table in front of them stood a perfectly scaled down house. Dainty light shone in every room, the kitchen was equipped with miniaturised gadgets, the fridge packed with mini food. Minuscule skirting boards ran along the walls, the table was laid with a dwarfish tea set, all the chairs had velvet-padded backs and every window fine silk curtains embroidered with yellow birds. Nothing was missing from the perfect home that Žeňka had patiently assembled and lit by hidden batteries. Nothing except its inhabitants: no dolls relaxing on the cosy sofas, no infants in the nursery. Born into a rich Prague household, Žeňka Kadorsky was the only one from her large family to return from the camps alive.

Now, guided by her memory, Agata combs the streets. Eventually she hits on a row of Victorian houses which look familiar. She parks the car and walks around. At the end of the street where a camellia has shed its red petals in a puddle, Agata notices curtains in one of the windows with an embroidered pattern of yellow birds. She steps into the front garden and rings the bell.

'Yes?' A frail, white haired woman, leaning on a stick, looks her up and down.

'Žeňka ?' The last time Agata saw Žeňka, the hair framing her thin face was jet black. 'I'm Agata, Doris's daughter.'

'Gatushka?' As if on tap, tears, Agata's faithful companions, make their entry. 'Oh my!' Žeňka gasps. 'Has anything happened to Doris?'

'No, Mama is fine. She just got worried about Igor. Your phone doesn't work.'

'Well, the phone's being repaired and so is Igor,' says Žeňka. 'He is losing his marbles, but to play golf you need just a few, so that's no problem.' Mama's friend's laughter sounds exactly as Agata remembers it: raucous. Only now it causes a major disruption to her balance.

While Žeňka busies herself with getting tea ready, Agata tells her about Mama's cousin Renee Stoloff and about Franz Frankel who has changed his name. And that, so far, despite her efforts she's been unable to find him. 'Oh you poor kitten!' Žeňka hobbles to give her a hug. 'So Doris doesn't want to help you? But she worships you.'

'Really?'

'She does! Every time we talk about our children, Doris always wins, hands down. If it's not you, then it's Lily or even your Mr Ricardo.'

Encouraged, Agata asks Žeňka if she has heard anything about Mama's sister Annette coming back alive. Žeňka shakes her head. No, Doris has never mentioned her sister and Žeňka never asks. 'Look here my darling,' she sighs, 'the truth is that every one of us… we each can only manage so much. I'll ask around, that's the least I can do. As for me…' She grabs Agata's arm for support and marches her across the room to an old-fashioned dresser where she pulls out a drawer overflowing with hand-written pages. 'See? It's all here. Everything that happened to me is here.' Before Agata manages to catch at least a few words Žeňka pushes the drawer back. 'I wrote it down for my children, all of it.' She cracks a smile. 'Well, you know… most.'

Agata drives home wishing that Žeňka was her mother.

24

'As a grandson of a Nazi, you may ask what right I have to speak about the trans-generational transmission of trauma?' Klaus Tuttenhoffer raises his eyes from the lectern over the packed hall to where Agata sits, right at the back.

The audience stays hushed, waiting. The Generation Series is taking place in a school gym somewhere at the edge of north London. Agata showed Klaus the leaflet from the Wiener Library, but he already knew about it, he is even presenting a chapter from his dissertation tonight. 'The second and third generation of both, the Holocaust survivors and the perpetrators, grew up in silence. Silence that paralysed them, that made them forever try to puzzle out their parents' secrets.' Klaus pauses to wipe his upper lip. 'Paradoxically, the perpetrators often present themselves as victims; they talk about hunger, being wounded, the bombardments. And on the other side, the survivors reject the idea of being victims and present themselves as superhumanly strong. That's why their children grow up believing that because they haven't suffered like their parents, they have no right to feel weak. Or angry. Or guilty. In short, that they have no right to any feelings, problematic or not.' The audience murmurs in agreement. Klaus dries his face again and even from a distance, Agata notices the nervous blotches on his face.

So finally she knows. Klaus's grandfather was a Nazi, not just a naïve country lad drafted into the Wehrmacht. By the time Klaus's speech is over she has made her mind up not to ask him any further details. His *Opa* is his problem. When he comes to sit next to her, she squeezes his hand. He squeezes hers back and doesn't let go, resting it on his knee; his fingers tremble so violently that she allows a few minutes to pass before reclaiming her hand.

The speaker after Klaus, Dr Mark Ackermayer, is a bearded American who peppers his lecture with terms such as *compromised individuation, sadistic super ego* and *embodied history*. Words as impenetrable as treacle, and as indigestible. Yet when, towards the end, Dr Ackermayer confides in them how everyday words like *transport*, or *wagon*, or even computer jargon like *select* or *save*, bring up the darkest associations in him, Agata knows instantly what he means. As soon as he finishes a man in a bulging pullover jumps up to say that although he isn't Jewish himself, he'd like to thank the doctor for sharing this and he'd like to share with them – here he bursts into tears – that he has a Jewish friend whom he loves as his brother. By now Klaus has recovered sufficiently to pull a face and tap his forehead.

The next speaker, a young woman in a blazer with lapels covered by mossy green velvet, launches into a lengthy exposition of the book she is working on. She is looking for an answer to why only a small proportion of women were raped by the Nazis in the concentration camps. Rape is a regular occurrence in any war, she reminds her audience, so its curious absence in the camps was an exception. Therefore she feels it's of great value to ask ourselves why this didn't happen more frequently? Were the women too ashamed to admit it? Or was it that they were considered subhuman and therefore not worthy of sexual interest? Or are we dealing with a lie?

The hall is growing restless, there are mutterings about the usefulness of such a question. Next to Agata, Klaus is also mumbling words like *idiotisch* and *dumm*. She lets her eyes wander around the walls lined with gym apparatus, and mats exuding the odour of leather and sweaty young bodies. And then, in the middle of one of the front rows she spots a familiar shape: a headful of brown hair, roughly cut, thin shoulders in a home knitted cardigan. From that moment on Agata's eyes stay pinned to the back of that head. How well she knows its slightest inclinations, nods and shakes, even its stillness. How accurately she can read what they mean. Nothing can escape her: protest, doubt, amusement... in spite of having practically zero knowledge of this woman outside their meetings, it is as if she knows everything there is to know about her.

The man who takes to the lectern next, speaks about healing. Even the briefest of therapies, he claims, can make a major difference. During the Q&A, Agata sees her counsellor's hand shoot up. In her professional experience, she says when given the microphone, a brief therapy can only be of limited help. This is because the trauma and guilt felt by the children of those who survived is extremely deep. As the latest neuroscience is beginning to show, it has been passed to them from their parents even through their molecules, neurons and cells. She speaks softly and though Agata doesn't catch every word, she feels an overwhelming surge of love for her; Bobbie Greengrass is with her. She isn't alone.

*

The beginning of summer turns out to be hot, with sudden monsoon-like rains. Within minutes the sky darkens, and ropes of water bend the trees. A flock of escapee parakeets torpedoes between the branches, adding to the illusion of tropics.

On her way to her session, Agata gets caught in one of these downpours. She runs into a supermarket, where a display of flowers inspires her to get a bunch for Bobbie Greengrass. She chooses a mix of freesias and white roses, and then it strikes her that this might be inappropriate, as inappropriate as letting Bobbie Greengrass know that she saw her in the audience the other night. Not only her, but the tall, slightly stooped man in a leather jacket who appeared in the aisle near the end. As soon as Bobbie Greengrass spotted him, she stood up and, apologizing to those she had to pass, made her way out. And when she reached him, the man smiled, bent down from his height and planted a quick kiss on her impossible haircut.

She finds Bobbie Greengrass in her green armchair, hands folded in the skirt that, unusually, bears a floral pattern. 'Looks summery,' Agata says, wondering if the tall man has anything to do with this new look. Today Agata notices how thin Bobbie Greengrass's arms are, peeking from her short sleeves like two pale asparagus spears. 'You've lost weight,' she says. 'Are you all right?'

Bobbie Greengrass only smiles. 'Today we're going to focus on how the mind works,' she says. 'Please close your eyes and picture something… for example a succulent roast chicken.' After Agata complies, Bobbie Greengrass asks her to focus on her physical response.

'Saliva in my mouth,' Agata reports.

Bobbie Greengrass nods, a customary dimple appears on her cheek and Agata feels stupidly proud that she has got it right. 'That's how powerful imagery can be,' says the counsellor. 'So we can employ a positive image to counteract a negative one.' Then Bobbie Greengrass invites her to read her a recent worry. The first thing Agata sees written down in her journal is how towards the evening certain buildings are illuminated with such intensity that they look as though they may cause a cosmic explosion, but this sounds too obscure, and actually, Agata can't wait to tell Bobbie Greengrass that her mother's younger sister Annette survived the war. And that Mama has never said anything and now that Agata has found out she told her mother that she knew.

'Oh I see. So your mother never told you. Any idea why she kept it a secret?'

Why indeed? *You and your secrets, Gatushka,* Mama said when Agata asked the same question. Bobbie Greengrass patiently waits and when Agata stays silent she carries on with her protocol. 'And your worry about revealing to her that you know, Agata? Your *feared outcome?*'

'My feared outcome? That I am… that what I do and how I behave… ' Agata finds it difficult to gather her thoughts. 'That I'm an awful person. A swine.'

'A swine?' Bobbie Greengrass scrunches her eyes as if in agony. 'May I ask why you speak about yourself in those terms?'

Perhaps the wrong word. Agata has translated it from Czech where *sviňe* is used to describe someone abhorrent, a despicable character. Which is exactly how Agata felt, even before Mama put the phone down on her.

'Something about me hurts my mother. I do this to her; I always cause her pain.'

'So that is your *feared outcome*,' Bobbie Greengrass surmises and Agata hopes the counsellor won't insist she conjure up her *compassionate image* to be soothed by it as promptly as a succulent chicken had made her salivate. And yet, after she heard what Bobbie Greengrass had to say in that school hall, Agata knows she won't. She feels there is now an unspoken connection between them. Bobbie Greengrass's voice, even her silences, now flood her with warmth.

'I think I understand,' Bobbie Greengrass murmurs, as though she could see into Agata's head. 'Separating from a parent, I'm talking about proper internal separation Agata, is always painful,' she states solemnly, checking if the rabbit foot is still there. 'How else are we to become ourselves?'

Separation. The word balloons in Agata's brain and squeezes out every other thought until it threatens to explode like those illuminated buildings. *Separation.* 'I think…' she starts.

'You think…?' Bobbie Greengrass echoes, and Agata notices how unusually delicate her hands are. Delicate, soft. This morning Agata got up early before the heat filled the air. Pushing the lawnmower about she noticed that whenever she ran over a lavender or a salvia stem, the crushed leaves released an extraordinarily powerful scent, more so than at any other time. Is everything sweetest when about to end?

'I am stopping my sessions,' Agata hears herself announce, this being as much news to her as to her counsellor. She can't think of any other way of leaving Bobbie Greengrass. Of parting with her.

'Just like that?' Bobbie Greengrass says, squeezing the root of her nose, her voice a little unsteady. Pointed fingers. No ring.

All Agata can muster is a nod. A tap on her shoulder. Blurred paper tissue. Taking it, their hands briefly touch. What if Agata kissed it? What if she asks Bobbie Greengrass for forgiveness, for what she doesn't quite know, but she's had plenty of practice with Mama. From a great distance she hears Bobbie Greengrass saying something about the need to distinguish between separation and running away. And though Agata understands, fully understands, she orders her legs to hoist her up and, resisting an urge to bury her face in Bobbie Greengrass's floral lap, she forces herself to traverse the stained carpet. Everything becomes hazy. Conscious of Bobbie Greengrass tracking her progress from her seat, Agata follows the ceiling lights, the air buzzing thinly in her ears: this is just a rehearsal, it whispers, a rehearsal for the mother of all separations, of all partings, the ultimate, the inevitable one; and suddenly there is a shocking sense of coherence.

25

The news catches up with her one evening. They are watching TV: in Poland, after more than forty years of totalitarian regime, an anti-Communist Solidarity supporter has become Prime Minister. Jubilant crowds are singing in the streets; the old order is on the brink of extinction.

'Hurrah! Hurrah!' Agata joins the celebration. Richard obliges with a thumbs up, before going back to his laptop; for him it's history, more than heart. Next item: the Romanian dictator Ceaușescu imploring the Warsaw Pact to send tanks to Poland to save socialism, like they did in 1968 in Czechoslovakia.

'You bloody bastard!' Agata shouts at the screen.

'You cunt,' Lily throws in. She waits for a reaction and when nothing is said, she adds: 'I meant count… Count Dracula.'

Agata has to laugh, has to hug her. More news: President Gorbachev renouncing the use of force against any Soviet-bloc nations. Wow! On the whole planet, there is no one Agata wants to discuss these momentous developments, no one more than her mother. Mama must have had the same thought because just as Agata is about to call her, the phone rings. 'Mama? Have you seen the news? Isn't it incredible?'

'Professor Chalabot here,' says a voice at the other end. 'Can I speak to Mrs Agatha Upton, please?' This is so unexpected, so utterly out of the blue, that it takes Agata a moment to remind herself who Professor Chalabot is. 'Mrs Upton, I'm calling to say that I have the result of your mother's blood test. It is positive, I'm afraid.'

At first, she takes this to be good news; it is the word *positive* that confuses her. Also, Professor Chalabot's matter of fact voice makes it sound like some casual information you impart to someone after dinner. 'It showed a predisposition for breast and ovarian cancer so, unfortunately, there is a possibility that it has been passed to you,' the professor continues. 'We're still in the research stage and there is a lot we don't know yet, it is important to remember that, Mrs Upton.'

The TV is now drowned by Richard and Lily arguing about homework. Through the Venetian blinds the red sunset draws a giant claw mark across the floor.

'So what do I do now?' Agata asks.

'Well, you are already doing all the right things, no need to do anything else for the time being,' Professor Chalabot assures her. 'Your mother has already had her treatments and you do come for regular scans, don't you Mrs Upton? Would you kindly remind me if you have any children?'

'Yes, a daughter.'

'How old is she?'

'Eleven.'

'Then we don't have to worry, we have plenty of time. The science is advancing tremendously fast.'

Agata has to support herself against the wall. This is so completely new that she doesn't know how to react. 'How dare you tell me this over the phone?' she whispers finally, her tongue as clumsy as if she were drunk.

'Excuse me?' Professor Chalabot seems genuinely surprised. 'I don't know why you're angry, Mrs Upton, considering that nothing has actually changed. And really, Mrs Upton, wouldn't you rather know, than not know?'

*

Is this what catastrophe looks like when it finally hits you? You can't predict it, you just find yourself inside it, like in an avalanche; as if it weren't bad enough that the generations before had to endure pogroms and lethal gas and now this – a hereditary curse. A deadly time bomb, that may be ticking inside you and who knows, perhaps also inside your child.

After everyone has gone to bed, Agata quietly heads to the cellar; where better to release this sound that she has been lugging around inside her, than in this bunker at the bottom of the house with the lights off, the door locked and everyone else out of earshot? All she has to do is to open her mouth so wide that its corners nearly crack, scrunch her eyes and fill her lungs. The howl she produces isn't particularly loud. Still, everything around her begins to vibrate, Agata even hears a metallic twang coming from the old paint tins on the shelf. In her head there is only one thought, clear and sharp: she must be ready. She mustn't get caught unawares, as were those before her. She, she alone, will have to take care of everything. Because there's no one else.

When, somewhere above her, the phone shatters the stillness for the second time that night, fear smashes into her with a force. The digits on her watch show 02:00. It has to be about Mama, something has happened to her. She hurries upstairs.

'Gatushka, is that you?' the voice at the other end asks in Czech. 'I'm sorry for calling so late. Did I wake you?'

' Žeňka?'

'Who else?' Mama's friend laughs until she makes herself cough. 'Now take a deep breath,' she orders. 'And have you something to hold onto? Ready? Gatushka. I... found...' Žeňka stretches the pause for an effect. 'I found your Mum's cousin!'

'What?' Agata nearly pulls the phone cable out of its wall socket. 'Žeňka? You're joking?'

Žeňka Kadorsky is not joking. She and her husband went to dinner with old friends; the man in the couple served in the Czech division of the British Army during the war, and, as soon as Žeňka asked him if by any chance he ever came across someone going under the name of Franz Frankel, he went: *Sure! He calls himself Fred Philips now, we were in the same battalion.*

'And darling, listen to this. Our friend, his name is Tonda, he picked up the phone and there, at the other end, there was guess who? Your Franz Frankel aka Fred Philips, himself. He expects you to call him *schnell*. ASAP.'

The two of them agree not to mention anything to Mama, at least not for now.

*

She finds Richard asleep in his Pharaoh position. 'Ricky!' She shakes him. 'Something amazing just happened.' Startled, Richard rubs his eyes. 'You know that Franz Frankel, Mama's cousin? Guess what? Žeňka Kadorsky found him.' Agata has to say it a few more times before the news sinks in. Before Richard demands that she stop making a racket and let him sleep.

Somehow, Agata endures what is left of the night. In the morning she tails Lily, repeating what Žeňka said, her voice raw with excitement. 'Such a coincidence. People I know are friends of people who know Mama's cousin. Isn't it crazy? Amazing?'

Lily doesn't seem impressed; Czechs, Jews, there's only a handful of them, it's inevitable that they should know one another. Anyway, she is late for school. And Richard is off for an important meeting; there is a possibility of the frog-lizard exhibition being resurrected with a different biologist in charge.

After they leave, Agata sits by the phone sipping tea. First, she ponders that thing Professor Chalabot told her, the bomb ticking thing – didn't the professor say that there is still time, and that the science will find a way out? When her cup is empty, Agata dials Franz Frankel's number. A female voice answers – hard Czech accent. Agata asks to speak to Fred Philips.

'Hello? Fred Philips here.' Another unmistakably Czech voice; how out of place they all sound, even after spending a lifetime here – like tourists just off the plane. Agata introduces herself and asks Fred Philips if he wants to speak Czech. 'Czech, English, German, *Französisch*...' To Fred Philips it's all the same. His manner is energetic and brisk and in complete contrast to the Stoloffs, he immediately invites Agata to visit. 'We live in Hampstead. Golders Green, to be precise. The only civilised part of London,' he explains. The day they agree on falls on Friday the 13th, but hey, Fred Philips likes to tempt fate.

'Just stick a rose in your teeth so I recognise you.' And Agata is already in love with his humour.

When Lily returns from school, Agata repeats the whole exchange to her. 'Shall I? What do you think? I think I might... I just might arrive there with a rose in my mouth.' She only slows down after noticing the expression of distaste, if not pity, on her daughter's face.

Later, she goes through it all again with Richard. 'Fred Philips? That rings a bell,' Richard says. Years ago a wealthy Czech man came to his college looking for someone to build him a replica of Tower Bridge for his garden pond in Golders Green. A mad idea, but for Richard, a penniless student at the time, his very first job. The man's name was something like Frank or Fred Philly.

The hair on Agata's arm begins to tingle. 'Ohmygod! What if it's him? Only his name isn't Philly, it's Philips. What's he like, Ricky? Lily, did you hear? Your Dad has probably already met him!'

'Who?' asks Lily.

'Mama's cousin, my relative. Your dad might have met him even before he met me! That's unbelievable, isn't it?'

'Not really,' shrugs Lily, but at dinner, when Agata steers the conversation once more to her favourite topic, she explodes. 'Mum! I can't believe how you are. Yelling and running around, annoying everyone because of some stupid relatives. Like you have no family! No Dad! No me! No nothing!'

Shocked by the ferocity of her attack, Agata tries to argue back. Tries to explain how she grew up, the only child with no extended family and how...

'Hey, hey! Bring out the violin.' Her daughter sneers. 'So what, you have no relatives. I have no sister; no brother and I manage.'

'But darling, I'm not claiming to be special.'

'Yes, you are! You are! You are!' Lily screams, her whole body now shaking. 'You just can't wait to meet those awful people Babi never wants to speak to! You pretend it's romantic and fun!' She doesn't bother to wipe the water dripping from her nose, her face contorted, arms strangely twisted as if she were in the throes of a fit. 'Of course Babi doesn't want to talk about her mum and her sisters. Because she can't! Babi is old! Don't you get it?' Lily sobs, thumbs dug into her clenched fists, sharp lines that Agata has never noticed before, raking both sides of her child's mouth. 'It's horrible, horrible to see your mother behave in such a selfish, such a cruel way!'

Throughout Lily's outburst Richard directs his gaze somewhere above their heads and when there is a moment of silence, broken only by Lily's desperate sobs, he slips out of the room as if giving up on them. Then everything in Agata seizes. This is what she's done. She's screwed up her child. And now it's too late to undo it. 'Ok, ok darling, I'm sorry. So sorry.' Agata stands up, the chair crashing behind her. 'Please Lilinka don't get upset, I'll call it off. I promise.' She throws her arms around her daughter, but Lily wriggles free.

*

She gets out at Maida Vale tube station. This season women are wearing peasant blouses with low necklines and a shoulder sticking out, and she wishes she too was wearing one of those; she left the house in a rush and now she is boiling in her sweatshirt. She breathes in the smell of the city in the late summer, the air made glassy by the heat mingling with the fumes. Everything is in bloom, the trees bent by the summer growth as if under heavy wigs. Agata moves carefully through the warm air as if any abrupt gesture might cause something inside her to break.

'I hate you!' Lily had shouted at her. How pitiful her daughter suddenly looked, and it's her fault; she is a useless mother. And it was Richard finally who wrenched them out of their misery, Richard who offered to drive Lily to Melody's, to buy her a hamburger on the way. They don't need her.

She recognises the house, the only one in the street hung with clusters of wisteria. She rings the bell and the man who opens the door wears sandals and has thinning hair in a ponytail rather than a Freudian beard. 'You must be Riva, you're a bit early,' he addresses her gravely, assuming she is his new patient. 'Next time could you please...' When Agata explains she came to see Klaus he seems amused. 'Oh, you're coming to see Herr Tuttenhoffer? Well, Tutten's all the way up, just give him a knock.'

She knocks on Klaus's door, but gets no answer, although she can hear the TV. While she stands there in the dark, the doorbell rings downstairs and she hears Duncan greeting Riva. Agata waits for their voices to fade away, then raps on the door again.

When Klaus finally appears he is only in a vest and boxer shorts, his legs thin and pale. The air that wafts from inside is as if he has opened a door to the Kalahari desert. He must have been watching the news from his futon bed, there is a half-drunk bottle of wine and a plate of leftover chips next to his pillow. Agata is embarrassed to surprise him in this way, yet when he reaches for a shirt, she says not to bother. The only chair in the room is piled high with things, so Klaus invites her to sit on the mattress. He doesn't ask what brought her here and she only mumbles something about the argument with her daughter. Nothing about Lily's clenched fists, her sad puckered forehead, the histrionics. Nothing about the devastation her child's unhappiness has left her with. When Klaus murmurs something about her enviable family history, Agata laughs as if he has cracked a joke, and then cries, dispatching Klaus to the bathroom to reappear clutching a roll of loo paper for drying her face, mumbling apologies.

On the TV, an endless stream of East German Wartburgs and Trabants crawls through the newly opened borders from Hungary into Austria, honking as if heading for a carnival. Others are fleeing the communist paradise on foot with rucksacks on their backs and children in their arms, passing barbed wires, the antitank barriers, the watchtowers from where armed border guards used to perfect their shooting skills on live targets.

Baked by the sun, the room is stifling, every surface oven-hot, even the bed-sheet. Sweat trickles down Agata's neck; she only has a bra under her top so at least she pops off her shoes. 'Sorry that the bedding isn't so clean,' Klaus apologises again, settling at a respectable distance beside her. 'If you want, I could put a *decke* over it. A blanket.'

Agata doesn't care about the bedding, she wants to stop thinking about Lily. Wants to guzzle Klaus's wine with him, share his chips and watch the miraculous loosening of the Eastern bloc. While to Klaus, the mass exodus to Austria, 'the shit hole' he swore never to set foot in again, seems rather... well yes – *komisch*. He kicks his legs for emphasis.

'What's that?' Agata asks, pointing to the pink patches around his shins.

'Psoriasis. Nothing you can catch. First time it appeared was after Mutti died.'

'Your mother? Was she ill?'

'For sure, we all are, but Mutti, one day she took some pills and a bottle of schnapps and went to a forest where she dug a hole in the snow, crawled in, stuffed the pills in her mouth and helped them down with that schnapps.'

'How could she?' Agata sits up, appalled. It's one thing to have rows with your children, but to leave them like that?

'Obviously zapping those vegetables wasn't enough.' Klaus pulls a face, and she notices, for the first time, his blond stubble; it surprises her, she has never imagined him growing a beard. 'You see,' Klaus explains, 'the real products of Opa's blood – Mutti, my sister and me – she couldn't dig us out. Couldn't burn us. Afterwards one of her brothers told us the truth: our nice vegetable gardener worked in a *Frauenlager* as a *Wachman*.'

Women's *lager* – Agata only knows about one exclusively female camp: Ravensbrück. Ravensbrück is where Mama's sister Annette was interned. Agata looked it up, it's in north Germany, near a lake. What is she supposed to do now? She read that some guards, male and even female, beat the women prisoners to death, just for fun. After the war, only a few were tried and executed. Klaus's grandfather must have been allowed to return to his village, marry a local girl, beget children, plant vegetables...

'*Ach Mensch*,' Klaus sighs.

In the skylight the stars are beginning to show and Agata wishes she could think of something to say. Something consoling. Maybe she could quote Bobbie Greengrass about cultivating one's inner compassionate voice? The heat is fogging her thoughts. Above them, the boxing gloves are perched on a beam like slumbering pigeons, beside her Klaus shuts his eyes. With one arm flung behind his head she can see the blond hair nestled in his armpit, the beads of sweat quivering with his breath; beneath his shorts she glimpses his penis curled to one side. She feels a sudden tenderness for him, assumes that being gay must be yet another reason why he ran away from the rolling hills of his home, where tradition rules, and transgression isn't an option.

*

The light is still on in Richard's studio, he opens the door as soon as he hears her coming in. 'Where the hell have you been? Lily was upset that you weren't here before bed.'

Lately, this has become something of a pattern between them – Agata's absences, Richard telling her off, though for years it was the other way round – her at home with Lily, and Richard out and about with his projects.

'Out for a walk,' she says. 'I bumped into that student I've mentioned, the one writing a dissertation about how trauma is transmitted from one generation to the next.'

'Transmitted?' Richard glances at her sceptically. 'How old is this guy?'

'Twenty-something.'

'Must be one of those New-Agey types who believe in telepathy.'

What Agata left out is that she fell asleep in Klaus Tuttenhoffer's bed. To fall asleep next to a stranger? It must have been the drink; she isn't used to it.

26

On Friday the thirteenth Agata stuffs an A-Z and a camera in her bag and tells Richard she is going shopping for a new pair of jeans. On the way to the station she buys a bunch of red roses.

In the underground she sits opposite a man in dark glasses who slides his finger briskly across the pages of a book, now and then chuckling to himself. The exotic-looking woman who replaces him has that sultry air around her that must have once driven men crazy, and it crosses Agata's mind that maybe this is how Franz Frankel's second wife, the one who broke up his marriage, will look.

In this part of London the streets breathe with unhurried tranquillity. The houses have windows that open outward like in a child's drawing, the front gardens not just a formality to pass through, but somewhere to put up a bench or a swing, maybe a sculpture. As Agata gets closer to Franz Frankel's – alias Fred Philips' – house, she notices a Jewish cemetery. She is a good half an hour early so she pushes open the heavy metal gate and surveys the expanse of flat grey slabs stretching in all directions like the rooftops of a sunken Middle Eastern town. No trees to break the monotony, no photos of the dead, unlike any cemetery she has ever seen; even the Jewish one in Prague, where Lily had once got angry with Mama for not being able to find her family grave. When they eventually stumbled across *their* piece of black marble, it was covered by cobwebs and dirt. Lily, appalled by such neglect, made them search their pockets for tissues to rub back at least some of its sheen. And yet, neither Mama nor Agata has a heart to tell her that, apart from Mama's grandfather who'd had the good fortune to depart from this world long before anyone had ever heard of Hitler, not one of those names carved in golden letters was buried there, the grave empty.

When the time comes to present herself at the Frankels, Agata pulls one rose stem from the bouquet and inserts it between her teeth. And only then rings the bell.

The first thing that strikes her about Fred Philips are his eyes. Large, dark, flickering, they are Mama's eyes. He is of a slight build with a mass of grey wiry hair. His handshake is pleasant, firm. 'Bára, meet Agata. Agata seems to be warning us that she's a vegetarian,' he introduces her to his wife. Bára, who is petite and fair, nothing like the woman in the tube, only smiles, while Fred and Agata roar. Sharing a humorous streak with one's family is a new experience, new and wonderful.

The tea is served in the garden. 'We're not very formal here,' Fred says even before they sit down and to demonstrate their new intimacy, he unbuttons his shirt to show Agata his pacemaker, so close to the skin that she can make out its contours. She sinks into the floral deckchair, inhales the pleasant fragrance of the freshly trimmed box mingling with the scent of Bára's perfume, lets her eyes wander. Everything seems perfect. Neatly kept shrubs. Plump profiteroles served on fine china, oozing fresh cream, the pink of Bára's nail varnish matching her lipstick, Fred's Lacoste t-shirt with a little green croc, even the way they observe her with their tanned faces. Only Richard's replica of Tower Bridge is nowhere to be seen.

'So Franz, I mean Fred, please tell me – how did you and your sister leave?' Agata begins once they are settled, perhaps a little more abruptly than she had intended.

'Leave?' They both gape at her puzzled. 'Leave where?'

'Czechoslovakia. Before Hitler occupied it.'

'Oh that.' Fred waves his hand dismissively. 'Can't remember. Why do you want to know?' Agata says she is interested. What is so interesting about it? Simply, one day Fred's parents packed him and his sister off, they were both adults already, and that was that. Did their parents have to pay anything for them to be able to leave? She probes. 'They probably did,' Fred sniggers amiably. 'Don't you know that there's no such a thing as a free lunch?' And then? Then nothing, they came here. The way Fred puts it, nothing about this seems out of the ordinary; he came to England, served in the British army in the war, went back to Prague to find his parents and everyone else dead, got married to a pretty girl – not this one, this one came later – who too had returned from exile in England. And when the commies took over, he bought his way out once again, with the gold bullion his father had cleverly hidden from the Germans.

'Where did your father hide them?'

'Where?' Fred glances at Bára. She shrugs; how is she to know, she was married to someone else at the time. 'Who cares?' The main thing was that Fred and his then wife, Ellen, beat it back to England before the commies closed the borders.

'And when you got here the second time, what did you do?'

'Bit of a nosy parker, this one.' Fred winks again at his wife. 'The first thing I did, I hooked up with my old RAF mates. We still meet once a year, and every year they read out a list of those who've kicked the bucket; and it's getting longer and longer. So last time I proposed, wouldn't it be faster to just read out who's still alive?' Fred laughs heartily and so does Agata, he really is quite something, this new relative of hers. 'I started a business with one of them,' Fred goes on. 'We had a warehouse in Brixton where the darkies live. I tell you in those days those poor buggers...'

'So, do you have any children?' Agata butts in before he expands his views; she so much wants to like her new-found uncle; it isn't as if she is spoilt for choice. Fred has a boy and a girl, Jessica and Jack, both married, three kids each.

While forking up profiteroles, hoping that Fred will suggest that she should meet her new cousins, Agata tries to think how to carry on without seeming too indiscreet, too prying. This business of meeting relatives is proving to be quite tricky – but fun – she started with no one, and now if they were all to meet, counting just those she has already heard about, they would make up a whole football team. It would take several supermarket trolleys to feed them, four chicken,s maybe five, an ordinary oven couldn't cope with the job.

'What about Doris then? What happened to her?' Now Fred is the one to move the conversation on.

Agata offers a carefully censured version of Mama's CV: her wartime escape from the Lyon conservatoire to Argentina, her politics, her incarceration, her musicologist successes.

'Jailed by the commies?' They both look genuinely baffled. Didn't Agata just say that Doris was a communist herself? As soon as Agata mentions the Stalinist political trials, the purges, Fred's eyes glaze over. Bára on the other hand enquires in a sharp tone if Mama is still a commie.

Here is a new dilemma. If Agata answered no, it would be as if she were siding with Mama's old enemies. Saying yes, would make Mama seem naïve. She attempts to explain the basic paradox of being a communist in a pre-war liberal democracy to being one in a totalitarian regime, but soon gives up. She swallows more of their profiteroles, gulps down more of their malt whiskey, then takes out her camera. Fred and she push their chairs closer and grin into the lens, his arm around her. *Fred and Agata. Cousins, God bless.* Then Bára replaces her by Fred's side and Agata takes their picture. In the lens she sees how Mama would see them: jolly, untroubled, monkeying around their cosy garden, pretending there was no tragedy. Traitors. Scum.

The afternoon is ending. Agata knows that she should leave, yet keeps thinking there must be more to talk about. More to find out. Does Fred by any chance know anything about Mama's younger sister Annette? She finally ventures to ask.

'The pretty one who made it back from the camp?'

'Yes, that one.'

'I heard she was expecting, then later I heard that she... well, passed away. So there you go...' he shrugs.

'And the child?' Agata asks, feeling a flush of hope.

Looking again to his wife Bára for assistance, Bára who has most likely never heard about any of them until now, Fred throws up his hands. *Keine ahnung*. No idea. Not exactly a spa she returned from, you know.'

Agata knows. All three of them do, that's what they have in common. Amazing: Mama's little sister, her aunt Annette, Annetka, possibly gave birth to a child. A child who might still be alive. Agata needs a little time by herself to absorb this astonishing piece of news. She asks if she can use their bathroom.

'Oh sure, sure, use the one downstairs.'

She sits on the wooden toilet seat warmed by the sun, inhales the pine air freshener and contemplates the unexpected possibility of having a cousin, a real first cousin this time, alive somewhere in the world, knowing nothing of her existence. A woman or a man? She doesn't mind, although she quite likes the idea that Annetka had a boy. A boy would be someone different from her, and yet similar. The girl she imagines more of a lookalike, and she isn't sure about that. Of course that boy would be a man by now, probably a bit older than herself. Why has Mama never mentioned him? Didn't he turn out well? Whatever became of him, deep inside Agata already detects a spark of fondness for that unknown man, her cousin; it is as if his mere existence clarifies something about hers.

'How many stuffed peppers are there left?' Fred's voice reaches her from the garden.

'Four. Why?' she hears Bára reply.

'I thought we could ask her for dinner, but if we only have four…'

'It's ok. If she and I have one each, you can still have two.'

She refuses their kind offer. As they part Fred holds her close to him and for a moment, she can feel the round edge of his pacemaker near her heart. Instrument against instrument. They promise to see each other soon. Well, some time.

*

The instant she walks in, she is confronted by Richard's gloomy face.

'Lily isn't well. She's been sent home from school.' Agata smells alcohol on his breath; she has noticed he has started to keep a bottle under his desk. She wants to rush upstairs, but he holds her back. 'She's asleep, and it's just a cold. Where's your shopping?'

Having prepared a plausible explanation for coming back empty-handed, a torrent gushes out of her: about Fred and Bára and their suede loafers, the chintzy garden furniture, their spiel about the commies. As she is about to launch into her major, her most important scoop, the one about that baby, her cousin, Richard whispers angrily, 'For God's sake Agata! Didn't you promise Lily you'd stop all this? But no, you carry on, never mind that you mess everyone up: your mother, your daughter – who you claim to love – even that old couple in Oxfordshire.'

'My daughter who I *claim* to love?' She stares at him, stunned. Does Richard actually believe that meeting her relatives could mess Lily up? Or for that matter, mess anyone up?

Richard does an imitation of a laugh. 'Don't tell me you haven't noticed how much you upset Lily. She's turning into a nervous wreck! It wouldn't surprise me if she's down with this cold because of all this.'

His words are lead poured into her, suddenly she weighs a ton. It is true then; she is a selfish fool. Who else would ignore their daughter's pinched knuckles? Slowly, she climbs the stairs to Lily's room. How much younger she looks clutching her favourite giraffe while she sleeps with her mouth open, her nose bunged up. Agata pulls up the duvet and, careful not to wake her, bends down to nuzzles her hand. As if she could feel her, Lily smiles in her sleep. The crease around her wrist from when her arms used to be cherub-pudgy is still faintly visible; the baby fat that fed those limbs, this rich hair, those teeth, the whole miracle that never ceases to amaze Agata.

Richard waits for her in bed. She quickly undresses, but before she slips into her nightie, he catches her waist. 'Hey Agu,' he whispers, pulling her to him. 'Don't be angry with me, *sla-ke-ser-ce*.' *Sladké srdce* means sweetheart in Czech, though back home no one would use it as a term of endearment. Those sounds, the syllables Richard has learned for her, so awkward in his mouth, never fail to stir her. She turns the bedside lamp off; Richard prefers to keep the light on; Agata prefers the dark. She runs her fingertips through his hair, then across his face. It has become a little battered over the years, but it suits him. He tracks her hand with his lips, his warm tongue caressing the inside of her palm. They don't speak, only now and then one of them lets out a muffled cry. Perhaps not everything is lost.

Afterwards, as they lie next to each other, their limbs entangled, cautiously, and only as if in passing, Agata mentions, though she can't be sure of course, that Mama's sister Annette had a child, possibly a boy. Possibly?

'That's really far-fetched,' Richard protests. 'And even if it turns out to be true, there'll be a perfectly valid explanation for why Dora decided to keep it to herself.' Agata shakes her head, and he insists, 'Everyone's entitled to keep some things to themselves. Usually for a good reason.'

Agata sits up. *What a cheat!* Hasn't Richard himself told her how much he hates it when Agata and Mama keep secrets from each other? Hasn't he accused them of playing stupid games? 'Makes me wonder, Ricky,' Agata pinches his thigh, 'makes me wonder if there's something *you* would rather keep to yourself... for *a good reason*.'

Richard takes a minute to mull this over. 'Hmm... What if there is? Wouldn't you rather keep some things to yourself?'

'I asked you first,' Agata says.

'OK. Let me think...'

In the darkness Agata can't see Richard's face. She senses that he is blinking – she can almost hear the flutter of his eyelids – it is enough for her to feel a tightness in her stomach.

'I'm waiting,' she says, keeping the tone playful. Richard stretches and yawns announcing he needs to pee. She hears him entering the bathroom, pottering around the kitchen, opening and closing the fridge. The longer she waits the more alarmed she gets. *What if Richard has been unfaithful to her?* It pops into her head out of the blue; if he has, would she really want to know? While considering this possibility, the phone goes off downstairs and she hears Richard answering it.

'It's your crazy friend,' he says when he reappears, a beer can in his hand.

'Agata! Ilona's been kidnapped!' Agata hears Julia shriek even before he passes her the receiver. 'He kidnapped her, my baby!'

'Who?' she shrieks back. 'Who kidnapped her? Julia?'

'Miloš! That bastard! Agata help me!' Then the line goes dead.

After the first shock, hoping that this is one of Julia's exaggerations, Agata dials her number. It is Julia's mother who answers. 'Our Ilonka! She ran away!' she wails.

'I wish you'd buggered off instead! You old witch!' Agata hears Julia scream, fighting to wrestle the phone from her, before it is slammed down again. By then, Lily is calling from her room, demanding to know what the commotion is about.

They both head up the stairs. 'Everything is ok, Lil.' Richard lowers himself onto Lily's bed, having a sip of his beer. 'All that's happened is that your friend Ilona went to live with her dad.' Glad that he has taken it upon himself to explain the situation, Agata lingers in the doorway.

'Ilona in Prague?' Lily sounds puzzled. 'How come?'

'Because her mother keeps winding her up, with her crazy stories about her, all those imagined illnesses,' Richard says.

Flushed and puffy from sleep, Lily gapes at her father, wide-eyed. 'But she is her mother. Ilona can't leave her. I'd never leave Mummy.'

'Of course you wouldn't,' Agata says, striding in. 'And I would never leave you.'

'Well, at times there is no other way,' Richard says. 'When for the sake of the child's own health it may be necessary...'

'Daaad,' Lily moans, her breath struggling loud in her mouth. 'That's not a nice thing to say, while I'm ill in bed with a cold, is it? It's mean.'

Richard glances from Lily to Agata. 'I don't see what your cold has to do with it, I'm just stating simple facts.'

'Mum, I feel strange. I feel like crying,' Lily mumbles.

Agata sits down and hugs her. How hot Lily is under her pyjamas, her temperature must have gone up. 'If you feel like crying, then cry,' she whispers in Lily's ear fighting back her own tears of selfish gratitude for having her daughter right here next to her. She kisses her wet cheeks. In return Lily presses herself against her so tightly that Agata feels each button on her pyjamas, each fold.

*

Agata was seven when her mother came back from prison. On that particular afternoon she was in the after-school club, where their teacher habitually entertained them with cautionary tales; this time it was about a small boy who kicked a ball over the garden wall and when he ran out to retrieve it, a woman dressed in black appeared and took his hand. And from that day no one ever heard of that boy again. Not until his father ordered a meal in the local eatery renowned for its tasty goulash and something tinkled on his plate: his son's golden ring. In moments like these Agata would plug her ears, though not too much, so that she could still hear about the man-size mincing machine in the basement. And then out of nowhere, her father stood right in front of her, announcing that a surprise is waiting for her at home. Agata hoped it was a *mrkačka*, the doll with moving eyelids, but when they entered the kitchen, there in the dim light she saw a ghost. It sat hunched on a chair, its ponytail roughly tied by a string, the kind you use on parcels. The ghost looked up and from its grey-yellow face two scary holes latched onto her. *Would you like to comb my hair?* the ghost asked softly. Unsure, Agata advanced a few steps. A claw of a hand rose, its nails gnarled and dark, undid the string and the hair fell over the ghost's shoulders like an old rag, without even the slightest whiff of nettle shampoo. Agata spun on her foot and ran to hide behind her father. Sure that this couldn't be her mother.

27

She has written a thank-you-for-having-me postcard to Fred and Bára with Dufy's painting of palms and an aquamarine sea, but she doubts they'll ever meet again. At least Fred gave her his daughter's number. In the last few days everything around her has gained a poignant quality. Everything catches her eye: the alarming colours of the book spines on the shelves; the vertiginous spirals in the wood of the floor; the sharp sheen of the spider's yarn, none of it exactly ominous and yet reminding her of a *before* and *after, but before and after of what?* No further calls from Professor Chalabot, no news about Ilona from Prague, nor from Renee Stoloff. And nothing more about keeping things to oneself, although every time Agata spots the slightest hesitancy in Richard's voice, or a flutter of his eyelids she pauses what she is doing, only to resume it with added watchfulness.

Unexpectedly, she is offered another animation class. While preparing herself, she comes across her old box of coloured pencils. It's been too long since she's held one and she has almost forgotten how it feels. She quickly draws a figure with outstretched arms, a Chaplinesque stick in one hand, a hat in the other, a comedian about to bow to an audience. She scans the drawing into the computer and traces from it four sketches. In each she raises the arm a little more, makes the hat jump up a little higher. She plays it as a loop: an arm is raised, it tosses off the hat, the hat flies in the air, the hand catches it back, again and again, the predictability of it soothing.

She begins her class with the usual, breathing a soul – anima – into an inanimate object. '*Enema*, is it, teacher?' a girl called Puni, asks. Agata instructs the students to draw an object and transform it into something else in a few drawings. Rush of excitement, burst of creativity: one student is changing a cloud into an angel, another one a cappuccino into a doughnut. Puni, who is metamorphosing a goose into a hoover – *correct, teacher?* – wants to know if there will be a coffee break soon.

During the break, Agata tries to call Julia from the office. The phone is quickly picked up. 'No one's here, I'm all alone,' her friend's mother wails in a pitiful voice. After the class is over Agata has another go, hoping that Julia has managed to talk to Miloš and the whole thing is being resolved. This time Julia's mother tells her that Julia threatened to do something stupid with a kitchen knife, so she called the ambulance, and they took Julia to hospital.

That night Agata has a terrifying dream. She sees someone lying in a coffin and when she comes closer the face is covered with a black cloth, looking like an empty hole, the surrounding tresses the same rich colour as Lily's. She wakes up and runs to check that Lily is still breathing.

When she returns Richard is sitting up. 'I thought all that was finished,' he points to her pillow. She stops in the doorway, mutters something about Julia and Ilona and how distressing she finds the whole thing. 'Fair enough,' Richard says. 'Though frankly, you should stop taking other people's problems so much to heart... it's not normal.'

'Julia isn't other people.'

Since the other night, she and Richard have been cautious around each other, meeting mainly at mealtimes. Now, out of the blue and apropos nothing Richard announces that there is something he's been wanting to tell her for some time.

She hesitates halfway to the bed. Should she climb back in or stay standing?

'Come here, Agu,' Richard taps the space next to him.

'I'm fine where I am,' she says, gripped by fear.

In the dimness of the room she hears him swallow a few times. 'I don't know how to say this. It's something about... well, about me and Dora.'

'You and Mama?' Agata gasps, incredulous.

'It's not what you think.'

What *does* she think? For the moment she prefers not to think at all. Her mind empties, her ears pick up the distant trundling of a train, then a sharp shriek from across the night gardens. A person, a fox? At this hour who knows? The faint sound of an ambulance. The city at night, thousands of stories, thousands of dramas.

'It started years back. We were sitting around the table, you, Lily, Dora and me,' Richard goes on, the bulk of him sinister against the wall. 'Lily said something silly, I can't remember what, and I felt someone kick me under the table. At first, I thought it was you, but it was Dora.'

'Is that it?' Agata asks, hopeful again.

It was, then, but another time Mama did the same thing, and this time, as a joke, Richard gripped her foot between his legs. Only briefly, no one else noticed. Except next time when Mama kicked him, Richard knew she wanted him to hold her foot again. So he did, although they never talked about it.

A sharp pain soars through Agata's chest. It's as if she's been hit by a wrecking ball: how far between Richard's limbs had her mother's foot travelled during their family dinners? And what was Richard's response, what degree of delight, maybe arousal was involved, who felt what and where? Questions too mortifying to think, let alone ask. She limits herself to something she heard on a film. 'You were playing footsie with my mother?'

'That's not what it was,' Richard protests, with an outrage that seems genuine.

'What was it then?' she barks at him. 'Is it because you're jealous of my mother? Because you couldn't stand yours and so you have to spoil what we have?'

'No! I carried on because I assumed it made her feel safe. Yes... that's what it was,' Richard says. Placing her foot between Richard's legs equalled Mama depositing it in a safe. It seemed like a minor thing that didn't cost Richard anything.

'Do you still do it then?' Agata demands.

'Sometimes,' Richard mumbles. 'When she wants it.'

'How can you? You make me sick!'

Next morning when Agata spots a stain on her pillow she feels almost gleeful – at least now her sorrow is legitimate. She contacts Bobbie Greengrass and asks if she could come to see her again, if need be, privately, but Bobbie Greengrass doesn't work privately. The only option, she suggests, is that Agata goes back to Dr Rupinda who had put her name on the waiting list, though Bobbie Greengrass can't guarantee who Agata would end up with. Agata listens for a hint of warmth and when she doesn't detect it, she wonders if this is what it means to be a professional. Or if simply what goes on between therapists and their clients is just as unreliable, as fraught as any other relationship.

28

'Jessica Blakely?'

'Yeah?' The voice sounds cautious.

'My name is Agata. Agata Upton. I got your number from your father Franz Frankel. I mean, Fred Philips.'

'Oh yes, my father did say something.' This is followed by a non-committal, 'He mentioned that you came to see him.'

No more than that. In the resulting pause Agata tries to guess the possible verdict on her visit in Fred Philips' household. When nothing is forthcoming, she offers, 'I would also very much like to meet you.'

'I see.' A note of surprise, almost a momentary panic. 'Well, that would be very nice, of course, but we're very busy. We have a young family, and my husband works as a financial adviser.' Agata says she understands and expresses a hope that a little time could be found. This provokes another pause. 'Tell you what. I'll talk to my husband and work something out. Then we'll call you back.'

She assures Jessica that she'd be happy with anything they care to propose. And, should Jessica's husband not manage to find any free time, perhaps the two of them could still meet. Couldn't they?

'Absolutely.'

She talks to Mama less frequently now, keeping their conversation to politics. By September thousands of East Germans have escaped to the West. In October another wave starts to arrive at the West German embassy in Prague, a splendid baroque palazzo with a manicured garden, where they camp in their hundreds, spoiling the flower beds. Prague citizens call it a Trabant invasion. Daily demonstrations in East German cities force the top party *apparatchiks* to be replaced by others who, even before they stick their name on the door, are kicked out. What began as unrest is rapidly becoming a revolution.

All this, even the anticipation of meeting Fred Philips' daughter is pierced, or rather dulled, by a pervasive all-encompassing sadness. These days, whenever she crosses paths with Richard a squabble erupts between them about something insignificant, like the house being a mess. As for Julia, she never comes to the phone. 'On strong medication,' her mother informs her.

She contemplates going to Prague. Didn't Julia ask her for help? But Agata can't face meeting Mama. Despite Richard's insistence that Dora placed her foot between his legs solely for the purpose of safekeeping, she feels betrayed. Then one day Julia finally answers the phone. The din in the background gives an impression of a party in progress. 'Ilona is back.' Julia sounds upbeat. 'Some people I know went to fetch her from Miloš. They're being wonderful to me, they made sandwiches and a cold buffet. Now I know who my true friends are.'

True friends.

*

Another secret expedition, this time to Finsbury Park. Everything goes according to plan: Agata told Jessica that she'd be wearing jeans and a stripy sweater, has curly hair, rather a lot of it. 'Tell me about it,' said Jessica. 'I drive a red car.'

The road is throbbing. Agata turns after every red vehicle; finally she is about to meet a relative of her own generation, someone with the potential to become a friend. At last a red Fiat Uno pulls up, and from underneath long eyelashes large charcoal eyes gaze at her. Franz/Fred's eyes. Mama's eyes. With her petite figure and dark hair, Jessica looks just like a younger version of Mama. It's uncanny; there are people alive on this earth, people you have never met and yet they look like family. As Agata shakes a cold, slim hand she has to smile at Jessica's boyish haircut. 'I see you solved the hair problem.'

Jessica passes her a shy look. During the short journey she asks Agata to explain how they fit together, but when Agata tells her that Mama's mother had two sisters, one of whom was Jessica's father's mother, Jessica seems to switch off. They pull up in front of the Blakelys' home, where husband Stuart is already waiting for them. A fleshy face under a shiny pate, shirt stretched tightly across a belly, a ready smile. Next to him Jessica appears agonizingly thin.

'I'm a sort of a relative,' Agata introduces herself.

Stuart Blakely puffs out his cheeks and firmly shakes her hand. 'There's no such a thing as a sort of a relative. Either you're one, or you are not. And from what I gather you definitely fit the first category.' Unlike Jessica, it is easy to take an instant liking to him. After filling their glasses with bubbly and fiddling with the security lock on his briefcase, Stuart takes out a notebook and a gold-nibbed pen. 'How exactly do you spell your name?' he starts his interview. 'Your mother's maiden name? Your father's? Your aunts'...?'

Agata does her best with the minimum she knows. It would be tempting to plug the voids with little improvisations but who does she want to kid? Stuart Blakely jots everything down, including the hypothetical existence of Annette's child and the uncertainty about its gender. His gentle prodding, recurrent eye contact and jovial asides, testify to his skills of handling clients under stress. As for Jessica, she slips off, as fast as a ferret, and they don't see her again until she re-emerges with lunch. By then, a skeleton of Agata's ancestral tree has sprouted in Stuart's pad, most of its branches ending in question marks. He kindly does a photocopy for her. It is only now that Agata grasps entirely that her and Jessica's grandmothers were sisters, that's how closely related they are.

Lunch is a brief affair of paper-white bread triangles laced with a paper-thin layer of ham. Agata was hoping to hear from Jessica how she grew up in England with her foreign parents, but the only thing Jessica mentions is her utter disdain for their muttering in 'strange gibberish' so that the kids won't understand. The way she flinches when Agata slightly mispronounces an English word, makes it clear that Jessica wishes to think of herself as devoid of any foreign past.

During the drive back to the station Jessica's run-down of the Blakelys' social diary clarifies that there isn't a single slot free, not for at least three or four months. Realistically, they are looking at next spring at the earliest. Before Agata gets out, Jessica apologises once more for the briefness of her visit due to their tight schedule. 'I probably shouldn't be telling you,' she says clutching the gear stick, 'your husband rang the other day.'

'My husband?' Has Jessica confused Agata with someone else?

'His name is Richard, isn't it?' Jessica smiles, and Agata is again startled at how much she resembles Mama, down to how she holds her neck. 'Your husband said he was worried about you, in case you arranged to meet us. He told Stuart you're suffering with some issues.'

'Issues? What kind of issues?'

'Oh I don't know. Psychological?' Jessica mutters, checking her side mirror from under her long eyelashes, her foot on the pedal. 'Please. You mustn't be embarrassed. If we can be of any help, now that you know where to find us...' She leans over and opens the door for Agata.

29

Agata transfers her journal with all the names and phone numbers she has collected to the back of the cupboard in Mama's empty room. Was the phone call Richard's idea, or is Mama pulling the strings from Prague? Are they talking behind her back? Veering between numbness and boiling rage, Agata decides not to mention anything to either of them.

She sends a thank-you-for-a-lovely-lunch postcard to Jessica Blakely. This one Lily bought at the Pinkas Synagogue tourist shop. It depicts *The blessing hands of the Cohens, detail of the gravestone from the Prague Old Jewish cemetery*. She doesn't have much to lose with Jessica, in comparison with Annette's child, she is only a distant relative, one of many by now. The thought of meeting her proper first cousin makes everything else matter less. Agata tries to imagine what he'll be like. In the photographs her aunt Annette looked tall and athletic, much taller than Mama. Yes, he'd be tall. For some reason she imagines that he is called Joseph, Joe for short. She thinks of him as an actor. After all, Mama studied music, and Agata went to art college, so there is definitely an artistic streak in the family. Not knowing his own history might have provided Joe with a talent for stepping into different roles. And if he plays in theatres in other countries, he probably never stays in one place long enough to start searching for his family. Now that Agata knows about him, she'll look for him, find him. If he exists that is, if he is alive.

She pulls open the filing cabinet to look again at the photo of his mother Annette and to her disbelief, finds the *grandparents, aunts, cous…* folder missing. Thinking that it must have slipped off the metal rails she takes out the contents of the whole drawer. Nothing. Furious, she rushes off to confront Richard; this is taking an interest in her too far.

The studio is locked. Since the night Richard told her about Mama's foot business, he rarely leaves the studio; he is on a new job – the one about the Time Instruments didn't come off, but there is an exhibition about urban regeneration on the horizon.

'Richard?' She bangs on the door. 'Have you taken anything from my filing cabinet?' Silence. 'Richard, I mean it!' She hits the door again. 'Have you taken any photos from my filing cabinet, yes, or no?'

'No, of course not! Leave me alone, I'm trying to think.'

Richard sounds genuine, so her next call is to Lily. As she climbs the stairs she is halted by voices from Lily's room.

'Hi Lil. Oh hi Tom. I like your... What?' Whisper. 'Tom! It's... sexy.' Whisper. 'Didn't I see you snogging Kelly?... Jealous? But Kelly's got buck teeth... I... I love you, Lilian.' Rustling. Whisper. Soft sounds. Agata throws the door open. Curled on the bed Lily hastily peels her lips off her thin arm.

'Mum! I asked you to knock before coming in.'

Not the best moment for a lesson about privacy. 'Lilian?! Have you been through my filing cabinet?' Instead of an answer Lily slips deeper under the duvet. 'I'm missing a folder with some photos. Have you seen them?' Silently Lily stares at the pattern of blue clouds and yellow suns on the bed cover. In the glow of the lamp her eyes looking frighteningly huge. 'Please answer me. Have you seen those pictures?'

Sliding her finger from sun to cloud to sun, Lily whispers, 'I chucked them.'

'You what?' With one move Agata yanks her out of the bed. Lily is wearing a green nightie with a line of white sheep across her chest, and Agata can't help noticing that the sheep are crossing two almost imperceptible mounds. 'Where are those photos?' She grabs her daughter's shoulder and shakes her.

'I destroyed them,' Lily murmurs, fixing Agata with her serious eyes.

'You destroyed the pictures of my family?' Lily nods, but Agata knows she is lying. 'How?' She tries to catch her.

'I...' Lily searches for what to say. 'I burned them.' Then seeing the disbelief on her mother's face she changes her tack. 'I flushed them down the loo.'

Had there been no sharp hoofs pounding her temples, Agata would have to laugh. Instead, she raises Lily's chin with her index finger, in exactly the same manner Mama used to raise hers. 'You hid them, didn't you?' She is met by an unflinching gaze; she's got character, her daughter, tons of it. 'Where did you hide them?' When there is no answer Agata marches straight to Lily's toy cupboard. She swings the door open, and the raid begins.

Out torpedoes Barbie, in a glittering evening gown, limbs chewed up by Mopsy, their old rabbit; a bunch of marionettes, their plaster faces that have endured years of mishandling by clumsy little fingers crack on the floor; furniture for a dolls house they never got around to buying; mechanical toys for toddlers that Lily insists on keeping; dolls' dresses stitched by Mama; battered building blocks, plastic animals that used to float in the baby bath...

Lily observes her mother's performance as if hypnotised, it is a first for her. The scene is agonizingly familiar to Agata, an uncanny replica rehearsed with Mama countless times. Once the cupboard is empty Agata sinks down amongst the detritus of Lily's childhood and weeps; another sad first for her daughter, who stares at her, blank with shock. Then Lily squats next to her and begins to rummage through the pile. After finding what she is looking for – a red plastic beach spade – she stands up.

Agata follows her down the stairs and into the night garden. Across an island momentarily bleached out of the darkness by the anti-burglar light, to the spot far back, where last year they buried Gingersnap, the hamster. Voices spill out of someone's house; shouts of hurray announce the first cut in the birthday cake. Somewhere a dog barks.

The place is marked by a small cross fashioned out of twigs and secured by a bulky stone on which several small pebbles have been carefully placed: a miniature Judeo-Christian memorial. Lily begins to scrape the soil away with her spade. It doesn't take long before the folder surfaces from its shallow grave. Without a word Lily passes it to Agata. Then, sensing that her mother is waiting for an explanation she says, 'I don't want to talk.' She wipes the spade on the hem of her nightie and heads back: a troll returning from her nocturnal travails, the light picks out her impish figure once more, before she vanishes inside.

Amazed by Lily's tenacity, in awe of her attempt to perform a farewell ritual, her resolve to 'put the past to rest', Agata brushes the dirt from the exhumed folder, chases a few beetles from between the photos, sniffs the smell of the rot, of the earth.

Back in the house she bumps into Richard. 'I can't concentrate with you two carrying on. What's up? What were you doing in the garden?'

'Nothing,' she says.

*

The temperature in the communist bloc continues to rise, daily demonstrations erupt in one city after another. Agata listens with only half an ear. Often, while in the middle of doing something, she stares from the window at the neighbours' house. When their back door is open and she glimpses one of their children – they have four – or one of their Alsatians, she feels hopeful. On the days the door remains shut she assumes they have gone out and feels abandoned. Is she missing Mama? Sometimes Agata pities her, at other times she hates her. What sensations, what fantasies did Mama entertain while her foot nestled between Richard's limbs? Limbs that move in a nonchalantly awkward manner, that Agata was the only one to notice, to love. At least, that was what she had believed.

One morning it occurs to her that she may be missing Renee Stoloff, which is absurd, since she has only met her once. Yet Richard sees his brother maybe twice a year and they are still family. She could ask if Renee has ever heard, even if only just as a rumour, that Annette had a child. Or maybe Renee knows something about the young doctor who helped her – he could even turn out to be that child's father, who knows?

'I have a favour to ask,' Agata says when Renee answers the phone. 'I'd like to photograph some pictures from your family album.' She needs to proceed with great delicacy, and this seems a plausible enough pretext.

Renee chews it over for a moment. 'What for, dear?'

Agata has an answer at hand: Mama would love to see the photos of Renee's parents, her uncle and aunt. And of course also of Renee as a child. Whenever it would be convenient Agata will bring a camera. The lengthy pause at the other end makes her wonder if there is a fault on the line. When, finally, Renee comes back she says that, unfortunately, they have been moving some furniture around and the box with the album ended up underneath a huge pile.

'Oh that's no problem, I'm happy to wait,' Agata assures her, seizing the opportunity to ask about Annette's child. A child? No, Renee knows nothing about Annette having a child, she only knows that Annette came back in a bad way. She remembers how sweet her cousin Annette was to her while they were still staying in Prague. 'As a child I wanted to be an artist,' she tells Agata in a unprecedented bout of cordiality. 'Annette gave me a box of pencils; the colours were arranged in a rainbow. I can still see the name on the lid: *Caran d'Ache*.'

'Oh what a coincidence. *Caran d'Ache!*' As always, when speaking to Renee, Agata injects her voice with a dose of jolliness. Here it is: another member of her family with a talent for art. 'I have exactly the same box, with a picture of a rainbow on the lid.'

'Mine showed the Alps in the snow,' says Renee. 'Sadly, they stayed behind with... well, with everything else.'

Agata allows a week to pass. This time Harry comes to the phone. After a few obligatory niceties she repeats her request.

'But Agathé dear, haven't you already spoken to Renee?' She has, and Renee told her the album was in a box underneath a mountain of things. 'There you go,' says Harry and it only dawns on her now that she was not to take Renee's excuse literally. 'I'm sorry dear, but Renee would rather you didn't photograph it.' Harry confirms her guess. She tries to reason with him, assuring him that she'd be extremely careful, wouldn't damage anything, no harm would be done. 'You mustn't take it personally,' Harry says. 'You have to understand, that album is the only thing Renee has left. Don't forget Agathé, you still have your dear Maman, but Renee has no one.'

That's ridiculous! she wants to object. Yet what right does she have to get angry at someone like Renee Stoloff? The girl who was torn from her parents to never see them again.

That night Agata dreams that Annette's son Joe has died. Though it isn't Joe's death that is so shocking, it's that Agata doesn't know where his funeral is. She is in a restaurant. Among the people at the next table is Renee, holding a menu – a long strip of paper looped around her neck as a wreath – poring over the dishes, taking forever. Plenty of other menus on other tables, but they won't do. Agata needs this one. It holds the vital information about Annette's son. Without it, she won't know which cemetery to go to. And her only cousin will be lost to her forever.

30

At the end of October Mama attends a demo in Prague. Her friends plead with her to give it a miss, there are fears that the police might intervene. And they do; next day Mama reports seeing a young man's head cudgelled just a few steps from her. A rumour spreads quickly that someone has been killed. Two days later a huge crowd of protesters hold a minute of silence in East Berlin for those who lost their lives while escaping to the West. Masses are on the move, marching through the streets, flooding the squares, demanding much more than freedom for foreign travel.

On Thursday 9th November, when Agata is at home alone – Richard has gone to Manchester to visit an old university friend and Lily is staying the night at Melody's, as she does more and more these days – Mama phones. 'Gatushka! Are you watching the news?' she asks, her voice raw with emotion.

'Why? What happened?' It is ten o'clock and Agata had decided to go to bed early.

'Turn on the TV!' Mama yells. 'Just turn it on!'

On the screen thousands are scaling a wall, those at the top pulling up everyone else, cheering and applauding the impromptu acrobats. People are chipping into the bricks with anything they can lay their hands on: metal sticks, hammers, pickaxes. Someone has brought a drill; they are all amateur masons. Slabs of concrete tumble down, everyone rushes to grab a piece. Loud music, flashing lights, an improvised disco. Wild dancing, everyone hugging each other, kissing, drinking. Tears. Euphoria. An era is over. Finished. Gone.

Agata dials the number Richard gave her. The phone rings for a long time before a young boy picks it up. Grandma is in bed, he says and everyone else went to the pub. Pity. Who to phone next? Agata calls Melody's house, she hopes that the girls would still be up; she knows that Melody's mum Charlene has a relaxed attitude towards bedtime, even on a school night.

'Is it something urgent?' Charlene asks.

'Yes! It's the Wall!' Agata shouts.

'The wall?'

'The Berlin Wall, they're pulling it down!'

'Oh,' says Charlene. 'It's just that the girls are watching *Honey I Shrunk the Kids*. It's nearly the end,' she adds apologetically.

Next Agata tries Žeňka Kadorsky. There is no answer. Then, just as she decides to celebrate alone with some crackers and leftover wine the phone rings. 'Agata, *mazel tov*!'

*

The moment she walks through the door, Klaus pops the champagne. The room is a mess, the bed strewn with crumpled t-shirts, odd socks and a selection of threadbare underpants, there is a bashed-up rucksack and a dirty looking sleeping bag. 'Berlin,' Klaus beams at her through his round specs. 'Getting an early train from Victoria. You coming?'

They install themselves on the mattress. Balancing glasses on their bellies they surf the channels, watch the same footage over and over: ecstatic crowds hacking off pieces of the wall, shouting, cheering, dancing. Relatives reunited in explosions of crying and hugging, disrupting the regular programs. '*Hurá!*' 'Bravo!' 'The wall is *kaput!*' '*Do prdele!*' '*Scheisse!*' Agata and Klaus join them, each in their own tongue. When the champagne is finished, Klaus fetches a bottle of Riesling. They are laughing so hard that Agata has to keep running to the toilet. Reeling back from one of these excursions she discovers that Klaus has rolled off the bed and is now crouched on the floor, head pressed into his knees.

'What's up?' She nudges him with her foot. 'Can't be the drink, surely?'

Klaus wobbles his head but doesn't budge.

'So what is it?'

He lets a few minutes pass before he murmurs. 'My *Opa*...'

What's new? Hadn't Klaus already tell her about his grandfather, doesn't she already know? She contemplates the crown of his head where his skin is showing through his hair, dusty and soft as a fox pup's fur and it crosses her mind that she could simply stroke it and say, *shush, all is well*. Instead she waits.

'He raped women. In that *lager*.'

The first thing that races through Agata's mind, the very first thing is – what if one of those women whom Klaus's grandfather raped was Mama's sister Annetka? For a hallucinatory moment this becomes almost a certainty. She never told Klaus that her aunt was a prisoner in the same camp where his *Opa* worked as a guard. It's too late for that now. Now, the only decent thing to do is to pull on her shoes, button up her coat, and get out.

'At the trial he claimed it was love. *Häftlings* loving a *Wachmann? Cha!*' Klaus is peering at Agata as if expecting a verdict. When she doesn't move or say anything he scrambles up, clenches his fists, but instead of attacking the boxing bag he charges the roof-rafter with his head.

'Stop it, Klaus! Please stop it!'

Klaus doesn't stop, he continues ramming his head into the beam shouting, 'Fucking liar! Fucking, fucking liar!' The hollow sound of his head-bashing in eerie contrast to the energetic chipping of the Berlin Wall. Not with hammers and sickles, as one of the TV reporters remarks wittily. Oh no, this time with hammers and chisels.

By the time Klaus finally stops, a dark bruise is blooming in the middle of his forehead, like a stigma. 'Agata?' He whispers, looking straight into her eyes. 'Agata, I've never slept with a woman.'

Unsure what to say, she turns to the TV screen where guards in heavy uniforms have dragged open a metal gate that used to be the East/West Berlin border. The soldiers hang about watching an endless river of people stream through: a laughing, shouting flood, saluting them in mockery, some even insisting on shaking their hands.

'So is that,' she says, 'is it because you are...?'

'No. I'm not a homosexual. I'm, you know, hetero – hundred percent.' Klaus's cheeks are now flushed, his ears too. 'But every time...' he wipes his nose with his hand, 'every time I find myself with, you know, in that situation, all I can think is what that old bastard did.'

Trauma is not known in words but in the body, Klaus once told her, and even then, she guessed that he was speaking about himself. Though now it is Agata whose head hurts, as if she, rather than Klaus Tuttenhoffer, had bashed it on the wood. Does Klaus expect her to be sorry for him, because he can't keep it up? A wave of rage rises inside her: *this has nothing to do with me, not my problem,* she wants to yell at Klaus. Then another thought takes root in her and won't go away: is she the only one thinking it, or is Klaus thinking the same?

She crosses the room. Turns the TV off. Except for the distant murmur of the traffic everything grows still. Through the skylight the moon looks down on them, but all she sees of Klaus is his back lifting and sinking with alarming speed, his breath making small heaving sounds. Out there the world is celebrating new freedom and here the two of them are, bound together as if they were twins.

*

She passes days in front of the news. Whenever there is a rally in Prague and she watches the riot police thrashing the protesters for shouting slogans like 'We only have bare hands,' she braces herself just in case she glimpses Mama's bloodied face. And every time she sees a jubilant crowd by the crumbling Berlin wall, she looks for Klaus. He told her that he was staying with some girl, and Agata wonders if he has put his newly acquired skill to use.

*

When she doesn't watch the news, she types on Mama's old Olivetti. She focuses on the relatives she has met and also those she has only heard about. Meticulously she notes down every detail: how she learned about them, from whom and where and when. Despite the few false leads and question marks she seems to hold in her hands something real. When Richard asks in passing what she is up to, Agata says, 'Just something for my animation class.'

Sometimes she calls Žeňka Kadorsky. During one of their chats Žeňka mentions that she has heard of people discovering relatives – cousins, aunts, uncles, even siblings they never suspected they had, by registering their own personal details in the database of the Shoah's victims in the Yad Vashem archives in Israel. To Agata, this becomes another incentive for organising her notes. On another occasion Žeňka tells her about her return from Bergen Belsen.

*

It was a summer day when Žeňka rang the bell of their old family apartment in the centre of Prague. The young woman who answered the door was wearing Žeňka's favourite dress: light blue with tiny red flowers. Permanently cold, Žeňka wore a coat – a tattered garment that had been with her throughout her ordeal; Žeňka had used it as a blanket, the scraps of lining provided her with a towel, a head scarf, sanitary pads, some of it she even ate. The woman was visibly shocked by the gaunt apparition reeking of ill health. Having spent the war years in the Žeňka's family's spacious rooms, cooked dishes in their pots, eaten from their fine china, and recently even spawned progeny in their eiderdowns, she shut the door in Žeňka's face.

*

Agata comforts herself with the thought that at least when Annetka came back she had her sister Doris and that young doctor to care for her. Regarding her other kin, things take an unexpected turn. One afternoon the phone rings and it is Harry Stoloff.

'Bad news, my dear...'

A week earlier he and Renee had gone to their local pub where the menu offered an excellent leg of lamb, but this time Renee ordered just a little salad. And the next thing Harry knew – Harry's voice fails him – the next thing he knew Renee's dear face fell in her plate.

'And now Renee is in hospital with a brain haemorrhage and the doctors can't tell if the poor girl will ever wake again.'

'Would it be possible to visit her?' Agata enquires, albeit with caution.

'Oh, Agathé dear, would you?'

It is her turn to look after Lily, but Richard agrees to take over. Despite the seriousness of Renee's situation, Agata is elated; the first time she's been invited to assist a relative in need, the first time ever.

It is an unusually chilly autumn; the freezing winds are blowing from the east, like the last blusters of the Cold War. Harry is waiting for her by the main entrance, cardigan askew, shirt collar crumpled, face unshaven. As soon as he sees her, tears flood his cheeks. 'So good of you to come, I'm sure poor Renee would appreciate it,' he mumbles, leading her to the ward where in the corner by the window lies a woman who bears a vague resemblance to the one Agata met before.

'Renee darling, Agathé is here.'

'Hello Renee,' Agata greets the slumbering face sunk in the pillow, the hospital gown dotted with a pattern of tiny black parcels as though anticipating an early Christmas.

'I'll leave you two girls to it,' Harry says, regaining something of his old chirpiness. 'While you keep Renee company, I'll nip to the cafeteria downstairs. Shall I bring you anything? Tea? Coffee?'

Agata has never seen anyone in a coma before, assuming that this is what it is. Next to the bed is parked a drip, the tube leading to Renee's arm, plump and weirdly pink, as if she were in the best of health. Another leads from somewhere under her blanket to a plastic bag half filled with orangey liquid. The other women on the ward languish on their beds in various stages of undress – the room is seriously overheated – a bare shoulder here, a glimpse of a fleshy leg there. Someone calls to Agata, 'Pull the curtain love, for privacy, like.'

Now she and Renee are secluded, the world behind the pleated curtain is reduced to a background noise. Agata pushes her chair closer. The bed has been cranked up in such a way that Renee is semi-sitting, head on her shoulder. Her breath makes echoing sounds, regular though much faster than Agata's when she tries to fall into step with her. Now and then Renee groans as though in the middle of a strenuous climb. In her open mouth Agata glimpses her fillings, and saliva sticking and unsticking to her lip like a piece of yellow chewing gum, but it is Renee's dark bruised tongue that seems most alive, drumming in her mouth as if it were a naked heart. Agata wonders what to say: perhaps that she is looking forward to spending more time with Renee when she is well again. After a while a nurse slips in pushing a trolley. 'I'm going to make your mouth feel better, all right my love?' she addresses the sleeping woman. Several bright pink swabs resembling miniature candyfloss make their appearance and are expertly swished around Renee's mouth. Renee's lips greedily open and close in an attempt to catch more moisture. After the ablutions are over the nurse comes round the bed to rub Agata's arm. 'It's all right to hold her hand, love.' Seeing Agata looking hesitant, the nurse grabs her hand and places it under the blanket.

Renee's hand is swollen and sweaty in hers, like a slab of meat; touching it strikes Agata as much too intimate; she half expects Renee to angrily push her away, but nothing happens, so she holds on. At the periphery of her hearing she catches sounds from the ward, words: *cuppa*, *fish-pie*, and *knickers*. How strange it must be for Renee, the pudgy girl from Berlin, to lie here captive, surrounded by these alien sounds. Agata tries to resurrect some bits of German. She can't think of any, so she begins to hum quietly a German children's song Mama taught her. Then quickly stops, in case it makes Renee homesick. Scrutinizing Renee's face she sees something she hasn't noticed before: Renee's nostrils, even in their waxy paleness, resemble Mama's. Also, she now sees something familiar in her chin. Slowly, she leaves Renee's hand in the fuggy warmth under the cover and, in a shockingly daring gesture, begins to stroke her face: first the forehead, then her fingers slide higher until they reach Renee's matted grey hair. 'You'll be all right,' she whispers, feeling vaguely fraudulent. 'I'm so happy that I met you. Doris sends her love.' Her mother's name makes Agata think of another day, hopefully far in the future when she might be sitting by Mama's bed. The thought is so unbearable that for a moment she shuts her eyes. When she opens them, she is confronted by Renee's startled, wide-open gaze.

'Renee?' Agata quickly draws back, as if caught in an indecent act.

Renee takes no notice of her. Her pupils remain fixed on the sugary blue curtain, her bruised tongue searching clumsily around her parched lips. 'Papi?' she moans in a little girl's voice. Before Agata has time to react, her eyes are closed again, the whole event over in a few seconds.

When Harry comes back carrying a cardboard tray with a cup of tea and a slice of lemon drizzle cake, Agata tells him that for a brief moment Renee opened her eyes and made a sound. 'Oh what marvellous news! God bless!' Harry is beside himself with joy. 'I knew that she'd wake up, I knew it! Well done, darling.' He pats his wife's once more unresponsive cheek. To Agata he says, 'Your visit has done the poor girl a world of good, you must come again.' Most of all Harry is keen to know if, by chance, Agata managed to make sense of the sound his wife made.

'I can't be totally sure,' she says, 'but it sounded a little like Harry.'

31

From the sofa, Agata watches the Eastern bloc tear itself apart, the events piling up with hurricane speed. It is mesmerising. And exhausting. Sometimes the TV breaks into an unintelligible flicker, as if the screen can't contain it all. Two million East Germans invade Berlin, the biggest celebration of the century. A few days later Agata watches the Prague Spring hero Alexander Dubček and the dissident playwright Václav Havel greet thousands from a Wenceslas Square balcony. How she longs to be there! In spite of freezing Arctic winds an even more massive crowd gathers on a hill above Prague ringing their keys, a death toll for the old regime. Mama proudly informs them that she was there to ring hers.

Harry phones to say that Renee has regained consciousness, can sit up and looks forward to seeing Agata soon. Now everything seems possible, Agata thinks again about Annetka's child, her cousin. And about that database in Israel. No reason why she couldn't try to register there; she has already asked in the local travel agent about the cost of an airline ticket, and though it isn't cheap, it isn't exorbitant, nothing she can't manage. Agata could go in a week or two, before Mama comes over for Christmas; she already has all the relevant notes, all the personal details, everything typed out. She goes to knock on Richard's door.

'What is it? I'm busy.'

'Please. There is something I want to discuss.'

When Richard finally opens the door, he isn't wearing his usual corduroy waistcoat but an old t-shirt. He listens to Agata's plan, then makes a face as if she is planning to undertake an interstellar trip. Is she out of her head?

'Why? Maybe we could all go,' she suggests, not caring where the money will come from. 'It'll be interesting for Lily to see the Wailing Wall and Bethlehem and...'

'Haven't you heard about the Intifada? About people being blown up on buses?' Of course she has, but what about the IRA bombs in London? 'I don't get you,' Richard says. 'You're ready to risk your child's life because of a crazy obsession with people who may not even exist. Or, if they do, frankly don't give a damn about you. You're making a fool of yourself.'

'I might be making a fool of myself,' she says. 'While you – you aren't even capable of being properly, I mean *truly* close to anyone. Just like your mum.'

'I guess we can't all be like you and your excellent Mama, joined at the hip.'

Agata puts her foot in the door. 'Shall I tell you what *your excellent* mother once told me?' she says, not bothering whether Richard declares an interest. 'She told me that she hated, absolutely hated giving gifts. And so her happiest time was in the war because, simply, there was nothing to give.'

'You've just made that up, haven't you?' Richard laughs, caught off-guard, nonetheless. 'And even if Mum did say something like that – she probably didn't mean it.'

'She did mean it, she did! I don't know why you defend her; she was horrible to you. Didn't she ask your dad to fix a lock on the fridge?' Hearing herself talking to Richard in this way gives Agata a sudden taste of triumph, inexplicable yet satisfying. However dubious, however ridiculous it seems, it feels that she is levelling her score with him.

For a moment Richard stares at her and then, seemingly short of air, tugs at the t-shirt's collar. 'Come on, Agu. Let's stop.'

She has boarded a roller-coaster. 'Don't you understand?' she hisses. 'Your mother actually had the nerve to tell me she had the best time of her life when my entire family went up in smoke. The irony of it never even crossed her mind!' Where is all this is coming from, what is she saying? It's not that Richard's mum didn't ever mention something of the sort, but Agata never cared about anything she said, and neither did Richard. 'You think I'm mad, don't you?' she carries on, regardless. 'Running around. Going out of my way to…'

'Agata!' Richard grabs her shoulders. 'Listen. Even if you dig out a whole town, a whole shit-load of relatives, it won't make any difference. Because that's how you were born: with a hole inside you, like people born with a club foot. So you'd better get used to it.'

'A club foot?' Agata laughs. 'I'm a cripple? Or maybe a monster. Whrroa! Whrroa!' She limps around dragging a leg behind her, beating her chest like King Kong. 'Is this why you phoned my relatives? To warn them that a monster is coming?'

'Shut the fuck up, will you!' Richard yells, his voice losing all its usual haziness. Instinctively Agata pulls back. He bends closer, carefully forming his words. 'You know what? I sent Dora all that stuff you've been doing behind her back.'

It takes Agata a beat before it sinks in. She darts to Mama's room and throws the cupboard open: all the typed pages she has patiently assembled and hidden there next to her journal, even Stuart Blakely's sketch of the family tree, are gone. She sprints back.

'What did you do that for? You idiot!' she shrieks, ignoring that Lily is asleep upstairs.

Richard raises his hand and rips his t-shirt right down his chest. 'Dora's worried sick about you!' He shouts, staring at the injury he has inflicted on the t-shirt. Agata has never seen him damage anything before, he sometimes take things apart, to figure out how they work, but this... 'What happened to her family isn't her fault,' Richard hisses. 'Get that through your thick head, you fucking victim junkie!'

Agata takes in his features: cleft chin, stubby nose, fidgety eyelashes. Chest glistening with sweat. So what if Richard and Mama are right and there is something wrong with her? *So what?* She aims straight at his mouth – a right-handed jab Klaus Tuttenhoffer called it. Under her knuckles she feels something crunch. She barely manages to regain balance before Richard's hand boomerangs back and a blow jolts her head. The next blow comes with a reduced conviction as if a quilt has been thrown over her, muffling everything.

'Here. Feel that?' Richard sobs. 'Now you've got something to bawl about!'

'Congratulations! You've done it!' Agata claps. 'You've done it!' Her top lip is tingling. She licks it. It is sticky. Leisurely, she wipes it with the back of her hand. Deliberately, almost jubilantly, she smudges the blood all over her face.

On the stairs she collides with Lily plummeting down in her pyjamas. 'Mummee! Daddee! Please! It's too much!'

Their daughter, their Lily, her little features shrunk with fear. Now not even dexterous Richard can piece them back together.

32

A drawn figure crawls on all fours under puffs of smoke; a man in sky-blue trousers is squeezing his head between his knees; a woman in a red dress hurtles down a yellow slide pretending she is not about to die. Agata slips the emergency flight instructions back in their pocket and looks out of the window at the sea of clouds. Two nights ago Evie phoned to announce, amidst salvoes of laughter, that she and Uli are getting married.

'The wedding is on Friday. You coming, Gatushka?'
'Which Friday?'
Another irresistible explosion. 'Why, this one of course.'
While she was packing, the phone rang again. Harry Stoloff calling to say that Renee is feeling much better and ate a serving of mash potatoes, bangers and green peas, bless her. Harry happened to be on business in London so how about if he popped in for a cup-a-tea to meet the family? He'd leave Teerabula in the car to spare the sofa.

'Munich? A funny place to go,' Harry cackled when she told him, ready with an anecdote: not long before, Harry had a client from Munich whom he overheard saying that all Jews are hairy as apes. So Harry said to him, 'Thomas, do you mean that Our Lord on the cross looked like a crucified monkey? *Cha, cha!* You should've seen that Kraut's face!'

Relatives!

*

Glass lifts, buffed steel escalators, noiseless conveyors transport her from the airport to the S-Bahn train which speeds through the sleet to a Munich suburb. Evie is waiting at the station. As always, after not seeing her for some time, Agata is surprised by her beautiful face, the light in her eyes. From the instant they embrace everything seems hilarious: the Siberian weather, the new Czechoslovak government, Evie's impending marriage. When Agata lets it slip that Richard and she might be parting company and who knows, with all these changes, she might move back to Prague, take Lily with her, teach her Czech, 'Life's weird isn't it?' Evie listens with professional calm. Then points to Agata's lip, the swelling so slight that no one else would ever notice.

'You want to talk about this now or later?'
'Later.'
The car plunges into the rain and Agata gladly sinks into the warm seat.

Watching Evie signal, she remembers teaching her friend left from right: *touch the parting in your hair, that's where left is, where it isn't is right.* Now Evie reports her current troubles: one minute her daughter Sarah appears happy about the wedding, and next Evie hears her crying in her room, and despite the years of psychology training she feels ill-equipped to help her own child. Furthermore, Uli is going through a bad patch, about life in general and the wedding in particular. A holistic doctor advised Evie to regularly feed him thickly buttered slices of rye bread. As soon as they get home, she promises some to Agata. Half an hour later they walk into the house, to find Uli and three tall, broad-shouldered men polishing off the last slices of Evie's thickly buttered bread, irrigating it with organic wine.

'Dietrich, Gunther, Lothar,' Uli introduces them. 'They're building the marquee in the garden for tomorrow.'

'A marquee in winter?'

The friends flash their molars. 'We have *Technologie.*'

Outside, the rain is falling in thick ropes, and the forecast isn't good. Gloomily, Uli tries on his new suit of natural Irish linen. 'When all this is over,' he warns, 'I'm never going to wear it again.' Printing a hundred and fifty party invitations also seems an extravagant mistake. Evie only laughs and gets more bread out of the freezer. The friends pull on their parkas and dive into the downpour, slapping each other for courage. *'Also, ja. Ach Mensch!'*

While Evie is converting her analyst's couch into a bed, chatting about her patients, Agata waits for the right moment to tell her news. Not about her and Richard, about Renee Stoloff and the miraculous return of Annette from the horror of the camps. And the possible existence of Annette's child. Except every time Evie pauses, Agata holds back.

Once she is alone, Agata opens her bag and pulls out Richard's corduroy waistcoat. It used to be green, but with time, its furrows have turned muddy and dotted with splotches where paint and glue have eaten into the cloth. She undresses, slips it on, and climbs onto the stiff, unyielding couch. Curled up in Richard's garment, she inhales his familiar scent. She listens to the rain beating on the marquee canvas, to Uli and his friends laughing and swearing at each other. She imagines their sturdy legs scaling the metal structure, the wet parkas sticking to their backs. Knights conquering the deluge to erect a temple to love.

She recalls Mama telling her that whenever she hits bad times, she talks to herself as if there were two of her. 'All right, Doris?' she says. 'We've been through worse, so let's buck up.'

Worse. When Agata asked Lily to come with her – she'd only miss one day of school – Lily said she preferred to stay home with Dad. And when Agata went to say goodbye, Lily went limp in her arms. Limp and mute, playing dead.

*

She wakes to a rainless, if not glorious, morning. The wedding ceremony is in the local town hall. Agata is hoping that Evie will ask her to be her witness, but Evie doesn't mention it. And it makes sense, you don't ask someone with whom you already have a childhood bond, you forge a new one by asking a newer, local, friend. She is introduced to Uli's parents and his sisters, all tall, blond, and strikingly handsome, though sharing the same strange rawness around their lips, as if the whole family had been involved in an accident.

Evie keeps interrupting the ceremony with bursts of giddy laughter. A string quartet plays some Dvořák and as the happy couple emerge into a raging blizzard, rose petals and rice are hurled quickly over their heads before everyone dashes for cover.

By early afternoon the weather takes another turn: a strong wind blows from the Alpine slopes. They call it *föhn*, the kind of wind that makes surgeons postpone their operations for fear of nerves. Inside the marquee it tears the paper tablecloths from their hands while they try to staple them to the long wooden trestles on loan from the local school. Someone brings in bouquets of wild flowers flown in from who knows where: daisies, wild roses, marigolds, poppies, cornflowers. An exchange of glances between Evie and Agata is all that is needed: cornflowers, supposedly Hitler's favourite bloom, were not allowed in their homes. Though here in Munich, no one seems to mind.

Close to a hundred men and women soon fill the marquee, kept a pleasant temperature by the heating *Technologie*. Uli's mother is the only one to wear the traditional Bavarian dirndl – another no-no in Evie's and Agata's families – an upmarket version in subdued beige, white and brown.

Agata doesn't know a single soul, but her friend is too busy to bother with introductions and Sarah runs around with her own mob. Nothing to do except dive into the mêlée, her lack of German not a problem, here everyone speaks better English than she does. What keeps her going is the comforting thought that when she becomes tired of merrymaking she can slip back into her room, but when she tries to put this into practice, she finds a litter of sleeping babies scattered around her couch, the air heavy and foul.

Meanwhile Uli's family have arranged themselves in a group for photos and a singsong about the newlyweds. They make an impressive sound that reverberates round the tent, shaking out the pollen from the wilting wild flowers. Including all the in-laws and children, they are a good fifty strong and judging by the frequent laughter their rhymes bristle with wit. Then there is a startling burst of an oriental tune as a troupe of maidens, eyes darkened by kohl, hair hidden inside colourful scarves, sweeps into the marquee, Evie at the helm; and how they jiggle their hips, how the silver coins rattle on their breasts and their bellies wobble! Soon the 'Sisters of the Desert' have them all clapping to the tap of their tambourines, to their tongues vibrating with piercing calls whose urgency no one here, perhaps not even the dancers themselves, understand, but who cares? Agata joins the twisting human snake, dancing and swaying until she too is out of breath. If Mama could see her prancing around, arms entwined with strangers whose fathers and grandfathers sang and swayed in the local beer halls before donning their uniforms... Well, she can't.

To Agata's sorrow, the parents of the twin babies are amongst the die-hards, still pecking at the leftovers at four in the morning. Their dad keeps fooling around with a baguette, sticking it into his crotch, making everyone crack up. Everyone but Uli, whose glazed eyes flit about until they home in on Agata. 'My father fought in the war aged sixteen,' he tosses in her direction.

'Uli, *ich bitte dich!*' Evie pleads with him.

Uli continues glaring at Agata. 'Can you imagine a boy of sixteen in a war?'

She indicates that she can't and suppresses a yawn; it costs her nothing to show politeness. Besides, what she presently cares for most is for her couch upstairs to be vacated. There is an uproar, the friend is now parading an amusingly limp baguette.

'When he was captured, he swallowed all the addresses.'

'What addresses?' Agata is drawn in against her will.

He shrugs and she longingly eyes the empty sofa she has spotted in the other room and thinks of going in search of a blanket. Uli loosens his crumpled linen jacket. 'Afterwards he put himself through business school, got married, had us six kids.'

'Well, aren't you lucky to have such a large family,' she remarks, though even she is getting tired of her own mantra.

'Lucky? Ha!' Uli howls. 'Don't you know that big families are hell?' Evie breaks off a chunk of the baguette from her friend's lap and stuffs it straight into her new husband's mouth. He swallows it in one go. 'The whole family was wounded,' he informs Agata.

She was right then, there was surgery, perhaps even stitches. 'Was it a car accident?'

'No, it was the war.'

'The war? None of you kids were alive then.'

Uli rolls his melancholic head. 'My mother and father, they try to be liberal, try to forget. Mother cries every time someone mentions Jews. More now that I married a half-Jewess, but they are still, how do you say? Of their time. Only now, they are philo-semites. You understand?'

That's when Agata spots the last of the parents edging towards the door. 'Hey, what about your babies?' she calls to them.

'Babies?' They look as if they have never heard of such a thing. 'Oh you mean *our* babies! They're asleep of course! We come back in the morning.'

Mercifully, nothing escapes Evie. She skips up the stairs and promptly reappears carrying the whining twins, and hurls them into their parents' arms. At last, Agata is free to stagger to her room and fall on the bed, still warm from the babies.

*

After a day of cleaning, Evie lends Agata a woollen coat. As they walk through the deserted suburban streets in the encroaching dusk, Agata notices that, essentially, Evie hasn't much changed; her neck still sits on her shoulders in that same disarming way as when she was a toddler, she still places her toes outwards, and there is still the delicate blue mark on her temple that Agata used to touch to feel her pulse. Now she manages to tell her friend about the discovery of Renee Stoloff. And about her aunt Annette coming back from the camps alive. About Annette's son she says nothing, after all it may turn out to be only a wishful fancy.

'What?' Evie halts and gapes at her in disbelief. 'You're telling me Doris kept this a secret? How could she be so – so selfish?'

Selfish? Does Evie realise how terrible it must have been for Mama returning after the war to find that her family was gone and how…?

Her friend cuts her short. 'I know all that, but Doris would never *ever* admit that you, her daughter, have also suffered, that it also impacted you. Because with Doris, everything's only ever about her.'

'That's *not* how it was!' Agata protests.

'Wasn't it? Then why wouldn't she talk to you about anything? It's because she had to be the silent hero and you were to be the same. And when you couldn't – because you were just a child – she'd stare you out with those frightening eyes of hers, letting you know how disappointed she was with you.'

Agata stuffs her hands in her pockets, marches ahead. The sickle moon is wedged between the dark roofs as if flung there in rage by a giant's hand, occasionally a bird swishes past, or perhaps at this hour it is a bat.

'You're not being fair,' she says when Evie catches up with her. 'You've studied psychology, had years of therapy, but my mother had no such luxury. She had no one to rely on, only herself. She would've broken down.'

Evie shakes her head. 'So she broke you instead.'

*

When they get back, Uli reports that Richard phoned and said it was urgent.

'I have bad news, Agu.' Richard says as soon as he picks up, and while he draws his breath, Agata holds hers: has something happened to Lily? 'That relative of yours, Renee Stoloff?' Richard says at last. 'I'm sorry. Her husband phoned to say that... well, that she passed away.'

Her initial impulse is to laugh with relief. And only then, is she struck by the significance of what Richard has just told her. 'When? I thought she was on the mend. When did it happen?'

'This morning, apparently. Her husband asked if you'd be willing to give a eulogy at her funeral.'

'Me? Why me? I hardly knew her.'

'Well, besides your mother, you seem to be her only family. He expects the funeral will be in two weeks or so.'

So that's how it is when someone related to you, albeit someone you've barely met, dies. In an instant you lose something vital, irretrievable. Gone is the chance to visit Renee in her cosy cottage; to get to know her, to hear her stories; no chance for Mama to ever meet her cousin again.

It's the first time Richard and Agata have spoken since she left, and after a pause, each waiting for the other to say something, Richard murmurs. 'Agu? When are you coming back?' Then, perhaps anxious about what Agata might say, he asks if she knows where his waistcoat has gone, he's been looking for it everywhere. And Agata is flooded with gratitude that he hasn't mentioned what happened between them before she left.

That night, perched on her uncomfortable couch, she stares at an empty page. So far, she has only scribbled the title: RENEE'S EULOGY. What is she to say? That she met Renee only once, twice precisely, although the second time Renee wasn't really there? Or maybe she was, she did call for her Papi after all. She thinks of the rasping sound of Renee's breath, the spongy feel of her hand, her bodily smells. Rarely has she felt such a physical closeness to anyone, and at the same time such a distance. Now all she is left with are questions: Where was Renee when she heard that her parents were murdered? Who told her? Mrs McNulty? A teacher at school? How did she carry on, where did she get the strength? There is no one to ask.

*

The following morning Evie brings out the box of old family photos and they sift through their joint Christmases, their summer holidays. 'Look!' they cry. 'Do you remember?' Here is a black and white snapshot of Evie with a teddy bear, aged about three, with a caption in a childish handwriting: *Gatushka's Evie*. And here is one of Agata, aged about seven, with a caption *Evie's Gatushka*.

'Tam-ta-da-daaa!' Evie waves around a sepia photo. 'I bet you've never seen this one.' Here is Agata's father, handsome as ever in his dark-rimmed glasses, arm around a young woman in a white blouse, both smiling. Except for the bulge of her stomach, hardly discernible under her folded hands, the woman looks painfully thin. 'Your dad Pavel with your Mama pregnant with you!'

Agata bends closer. It is her father all right, but the woman next to him isn't Mama, definitely not, even if those heavy eyelids look similar. The tip of her nose is different, and she looks sterner. Or perhaps not stern – tired. Is she the same woman Agata saw in her dad's wedding photograph that Lily found in Mama's drawer in Prague? – a type her father must have been drawn to.

'This isn't my mother,' she says.

'Don't be daft,' Evie laughs. 'This is Pavel and pregnant Doris, who else would it be? Only your Mama looked much skinnier, it was after the war.'

'No. This must be my dad's first wife. He was married before.'

'Your dad's who?' Evie gasps. 'Christ almighty, what else haven't they told you? Did he have another child then?'

Just then the doorbell rings and Uli calls from the hall, *'Mutti und Papa sind hier!'*

Evie rushes off to greet her new parents-in-law and Agata inspects the picture again, reversing it against the light. Something she does when she wants to check a drawing. Viewing it the other way round usually reveals some hidden irregularity you wouldn't normally notice. What she sees is a figure in a white blouse, her tilted head weighing her thin neck, her eyes, two large spheres gazing past Agata. Instinctively, as if to see who the woman is looking at, Agata glances back. And in the mirror on the wall behind her meets her own face. The time between taking in her reflection and grasping who that pregnant woman sitting next to her father is, couldn't have lasted more than a fragment of a second.

'Gatushka, look what Uli's parents gave me.' Evie reappears clutching a large box, making a face. 'A bread-maker. Please come and say hello.'

Agata wants to move her head, but it now weighs as heavy on her neck as that woman's in the photo. She tries to roll it from side to side, watches Evie float in and out, her laughter ricocheting around, tearing at her ears. To steady herself she holds the back of the chair. At home Agata has two photos of this woman: in one she is captured on a street with a friend, in the other she leans against a bench, squinting into the sun, blissfully unaware of what is to come.

33

The procedure at the German-Czech border used to take hours, but since the barbed wire has been cut, the train hardly stops. The guards march briskly through, glancing indifferently into passports, leaving behind a wet trail dripping from their coats. As soon as they are gone, Agata's fellow passengers, an elderly couple in identical Alpine hats, unpack their lunch: rolls wrapped in linen napkins, coffee in a Thermos flask. The wife glances at Agata and smiles. Agata clutches her stomach indicating that she is full. In truth she hasn't eaten since yesterday's lunch, since she understood who the woman carrying her father's child was.

The German couple are now dozing, their hats slipping down their foreheads. Agata climbs over their outstretched legs. Standing in the corridor she watches the train cut a track through the forest wrapped in snow, the trees so near she imagines she can hear the tingling of their icy branches. In the middle of nowhere the train slows down and she watches a group of joggers run across a field of frozen grass until they become no more than colourful daubs on white canvas, a Brueghel painting come alive. Closer by, a man is treading a path, followed by three dogs. One throws itself on the snow and rolls around, vapour steaming from its snout, its fur sending off rainbow showers.

Agata presses her forehead against the cool glass. What she has stumbled across is so unexpected, so unforeseen, that for a moment she wonders if she hasn't made it up. Why didn't her parents tell her? Was Mama ashamed to inherit her husband from her younger sister, is this why she said nothing all those years? And what about Annetka's child, no longer a mere cousin – her half-sibling.

*

The tram drops her off in front of Mama's apartment block. Agata takes the lift, then presses the bell. No answer. Knowing that in the afternoons Mama always works at home, she rings again and waits for the shuffle of her slippers, her eye in the spyglass. Nothing stirs. Disappointed, she trudges to the floor below where a neighbour keeps Mama's spare key.

'Ach. Gatushka! Welcome back! Doris must be thrilled to have you here.'

'I've just arrived,' Agata explains. 'But Mama must have gone out.'

The neighbour says she heard her mother this morning. 'Doris always has music on while banging her typewriter, both full blast. I keep telling her, you should slow down.' The neighbour who is three years younger than Mama has already had heart surgery and a hip replacement. She proudly hobbles around to demonstrate the outcome.

When Agata unlocks the door, she is met by the familiar mixture of moth balls and eau de cologne.

'Mama?' she calls, as if expecting her mother to play hide and seek with her. She fingers the small box of *Mozartkugeln* she brought from Munich. Mama's favourites, ready to hand over as peace offering or at least, a sweetener.

In the kitchen, next to the transistor radio, is a partly eaten cake. She flicks the switch and there is an explosion of sound; Mama must be getting hard of hearing. A speaker, addressing a large gathering, is saying that *truth and love must triumph over lies and hatred*. 'That was Václav Havel,' says the announcer.

Everything is in order in the sitting room. Carnations have their stems cut so short that the blooms barely reach the rim of their vase. Agata breaks off a bud that must have wilted since their last inspection; Mama is an unrivalled expert on stretching the lifespan of flowers: snip off the dead bits, change the water daily, drop in half an aspirin. The same goes for the potted plants stationed around the flat, many languishing on a critical list for years before Mama, with a heavy heart and usually only due to the shortage of space, pronounces them deceased. On the coffee table: a slim brochure with a title *Healing Springs of Teplice*. The handwritten dedication says, *To my dearest Doris with deepest respect, yours forever Petr Peterka*. My dearest Doris, yours forever. Agata salutes Mama's inexhaustible capacity for tying people to her for life.

In the bedroom, the first thing she sees scattered on Mama's desk are her typed notes. What did Mama make of them? She probably hasn't heard about Renee's death. Then the phone rings and it's her mother's friend Hanka. She and Doris were to meet in a café at three and now it's twenty to four and Doris isn't there. This, despite knowing what a palaver it is for Hanka to get on the tram these days. 'Now it makes sense,' she says. 'The minute you stick your nose through the door, Gatushka, everything else must wait. Including us, Doris's old friends.'

After she hangs up Agata remembers that she hasn't checked the bathroom yet. Seeing that the door is half open and the light is on, she pauses.

'Mama?' she calls. Silence. Cautiously, she peeps in. No one sprawled on the tiles, on the radiator the towel is still wet, a length of dental floss lies on a shelf like a single strand of hair. Mama always makes sure to turn all the lights off, so she must have been in a hurry to meet her friend, yet if she set out to meet Hanka, why hasn't she arrived?

Back to the bedroom. There is a sound of a police car from the street. Maybe Agata should call them – what is their number in Prague? Searching for the telephone directory she notices that one of her typed pages, the one on the top appears slightly smudged. Smudged and a little buckled, as if clear liquid has dripped on it, at the point in the notes where Agata described seeing the photo of Mama's parents, sitting in a meadow in Wild Šárka.

In her entire life Agata has seen Mama cry only once: all those years back when a family friend called to say that Agata's father had died.

*

The city bus trundles up the hill. The girl standing above Agata sucks teasingly on a stud jutting from her boyfriend's lower lip. The old man next to her keeps sending them disapproving looks, but they only have eyes for each other. Most passengers disembark by a vast estate, lugging bulging grocery bags. There may be a revolution in the making, but still, everyday life carries on. 'Next stop Wild Šárka!' The conductor announces.

The valley, named after a woman warrior who, according to legend, lured men to their deaths with her beauty, stretches below her as far as Agata can see. She starts downhill, keeps to the main path careful to avoid patches of slippery ice. There are only a few people about, hurrying in the opposite direction with their dogs. One or two turn after her, alone and dog-less; the sky is a thick grey blanket of cloud, it will be getting dark soon. Mama's family came here for Sunday outings and, as Renee told Agata, she and her parents also came while they were in Prague. While the Jews were still allowed to visit parks. Renee's father, who had his Leica always at hand, took pictures and made everyone laugh. After the war, one of his photos of children playing on a Theresienstadt street found its way into a book. *Artist anonymous*, the caption read, but someone who was there pointed out to Renee that it was taken by him, her Papi. Of course the daily life in Theresienstadt couldn't claim to be half as photogenic as the daily life in Auschwitz. By then Renee's Papi must have lost, along with his camera, his passion for looking at the world through a lens.

The road winds under the tall trees. To Agata's right, a dent in the undergrowth signals a path leading upwards. Agata checks that no one is watching, then plunges in and is instantly swallowed by the evening gloom. She begins to climb the gentle slope, the silence broken only by the faintest of sounds, while her breath seems to thunder. Around her the leaves are hidden in their winter skins, frozen puddles crack underfoot and occasionally a bough stretches out and pokes her. Here Mama taught her to crawl around and sniff out any mushrooms that were hiding under the trees. When she found one, Agata would first press her lips to its creamy rim asking it for forgiveness. Only then she pulled out the stem, speckled with bits of earth like a new-born with afterbirth. Agata has walked through here innumerable times, but always with Mama, and always in the daylight. Now the only way to see the path is to follow the blobs of snow sticking to the mud.

She stumbles into the clearing without knowing and it receives her with a sigh. She glances around and in the drizzly mist makes out a solitary tree. Judging by its size it must have been planted here only last spring. In years to come it will spread its branches and dominate the view. She starts moving towards it. It looks like a young birch, yet before she reaches it, it begins to glide in her direction. Not a birch then, a person.

She imagines seeing them from above – for now this seems the safest way – two tiny figures in the middle of a woodland glade, the bushes crouched animals around them.

'Mama!' she calls out.

Slowly, Mama continues up the hill. On reaching Agata she pauses, heaving. 'Ah, Gatushka,' she says as if they had prearranged a rendezvous. 'Your husband phoned to tell me that Renee died. Apparently, you're supposed to speak at her funeral. I have to say I don't envy you.'

'Mama, I need your help.'

'With your parting words?'

Agata firms up her feet, draws a breath, reins in her heart. 'Please tell me what happened to Annetka's child. He was my half-brother, wasn't he?' She is surprised to actually use those words.

'Your *half-brother?*' her mother repeats, searching around the trees, the bushes, even the sky above, as if calling them to witness Agata's folly. 'Where did you get *that* from, Gatushka?'

'Evie showed me a photo of Dad and Annetka. She was his first wife, wasn't she?'

'I already told you, didn't I? Dad's first wife was called Steffi. She disappeared during the war somewhere in Siberia.'

'But in that photo of him and Annette, Annetka is pregnant.'

'Yes, that's right. Annette came back pregnant.' Mama briefly closes her eyes. 'She never said who the father was, and we never asked. And she did manage… she managed to bring the child nearly to full term. Except then… To have her back and to lose her again? That's something I couldn't accept. Annetka had typhus, Gatushka.'

'I'm sorry,' Agata whispers.

'Sorry?' A glance in her direction makes Agata worried that she sounded flippant. 'My mother, your grandmother – I remember her blushing the same way as you, from the neck,' Mama remarks. 'Our Annetka inherited it from her. As a teenager it used to drive her crazy.'

'And her child?'

Mama smiles. Then slowly strokes Agata's cheek. Lets her hand linger... 'Her child was a *girl*, Gatushka. A little girl. That tiny little creature was all I had left after Annetka was gone.'

A little girl. Those three simple words open up something in Agata, something enormous that she can't even begin to comprehend. A scene plays out as vividly as if she saw it in a dream, and as real: Annette, her slim hands on her belly, her eyes serious under their heavy eyelids, asking her sister to promise that should she not be around, Doris would adopt her baby as her own.

'What are you saying, Annetka? Why are you being silly?' Doris pretending to laugh, running off to a concert or to some other event. Doris was always in the midst of things, and Annette used to wish she could be more like her, but that was before. Now Annette can't remember why she ever wished that, she is too tired to have wishes now.

And so, it is Doris who rocks the baby girl in her arms, while Pavel busies himself with feeding formula.

*

'And that girl?' Agata breathes out, hardly daring to ask; she tightens her every muscle, every filament, checks them for readiness. 'What happened to her?'

Mama has focused on something in the distance. Standing so close to her Agata can feel the touch of her coat, stiff with cold. A strand of hair whips the side of her face, hard as a shard, and a shiver runs down her back. Beside her, under her boyish haircut her mother's profile looks carved from ice. As long as they remain in this suspended, frozen state, no more words can be said, nothing more can be divulged.

The wind picks up, making everything around them whisper and creak. They step from foot to foot to keep the circulation going, swing their arms. Tipping her head back, Mama searches her pocket for a handkerchief to wipe a drop from her nose. 'Please, Gatushka, I don't know how to answer you,' she says. 'I simply had to find a way to go on. And there is nothing, nothing I can do about it now. So forgive me if...' She stuffs the handkerchief back in her pocket and looks at her feet where the dry leaves form a yet to be deciphered script.

Far on the horizon the sky lights up with fireworks and Agata remembers the *Mozartkugeln* still in her pocket. Mama's hands are too stiff with cold to pick up the round sweet, to unwrap it from its golden foil, so Agata does it for her. As she pops the smooth chocolate between her mother's lips, her fingertips meet the moistness of her mouth, the warm gust of her breath.

About the Author

Anna Fodorova is a Psychoanalytic Psychotherapist and Counsellor. Her background is in animation and script writing. She has made animated films for the BBC, Channel 4 and Munich TV. She has written feature length live action scripts (BBC Screen 2) and published a children's book.
Her novel *The Training Patient* was published in English in 2015 in Czech in 2019.
Anna's memoir about her mother, the well known Czech writer Lenka Reinerová, was published in Czech in 2020 and in German in 2022.
We have published Anna's short stories in anthologies on several occasions.

About Arachne Press

Arachne Press is a micro publisher of award-winning short story and poetry anthologies and collections and novels particularly for young adults, with a Saboteur Best Anthology(2014), Wales Book of the Year Poetry Category Winner (2022), Holyer An Gof YA class winner (2022) under our belts, and a Carnegie Medal nomination. We were a regional finalist for the Bookseller Small Publisher of the Year 2022.
We keep fiction and poetry live (when world events permit) through readings, festivals (in particular our Solstice Shorts Festival), workshops, exhibitions and all things to do with writing.

https://arachnepress.com/

Follow us on Twitter:
@ArachnePress
@SolShorts

Like us on Facebook:
ArachnePress
SolsticeShorts2014